Basic Aerc[illegible]
and Dy[illegible]
Flight for Pilots

Dr Ray Neve

FLYER BOOKS

First published in Great Britain in 2001 by

Seager Publishing Limited,
9 Riverside Court,
Lower Bristol Road,
Bath, Somerset BA2 3DZ

British Library Cataloguing Publication Data

ISBN 0 9532752 4 8

Editor: Ian Waller.

Design and illustrations: Stephen Dent.

Aircraft illustrations: Corel.

Cover photographs: Flyer collection

Printed and bound in Great Britain by Ashford Colour Press Ltd.

Contents

PREFACE 7

CHAPTER 1 DEFINITIONS, AXES AND FLIGHT CONTROLS 9
What's it all about?

CHAPTER 2 DIMENSIONS AND UNIT SYSTEMS 16
How shall we measure flight?

CHAPTER 3 CONFIGURATION 28
Why are some aircraft ugly and some beautiful?

CHAPTER 4 THE ATMOSPHERE 39
A lot of hot air about pressures and densities

CHAPTER 5 BASIC FLUID FLOWS 49
How do we generate forces in air?

CHAPTER 6 THE GENERATION OF LIFT 58
Has mankind finally equalled the birds?

CHAPTER 7 DRAG AND ITS EFFECTS 71
Something we'd prefer to be without

CHAPTER 8 PERFORMANCE 88
How do we get the best out of our aircraft?

CHAPTER 9 THE CONTROL OF FLIGHT 106
Putting it all into practice

CHAPTER 10 STABILITY 118
Will it fall out of the sky?

CHAPTER 11 HIGH SPEED FLIGHT 134
What happens if we go faster?

BIBLIOGRAPHY 146

ANSWERS TO PROBLEMS 148

INDEX 150

About the author

Dr Ray Neve runs the Aeronautical Engineering degree course at City University in London. Prior to this he worked with the British Aircraft Corporation (now BAE Systems) in the design office at Weybridge and the flight test centre at Wisley. In his spare time, he is an enthusiastic (but impoverished) member of Surrey and Kent Flying Club at Biggin Hill.

Preface

THIS BOOK has been written for pilots. The days when flying skills and knowledge could be acquired "on the job" without recourse to any formal education process are long gone and trainee pilots must now study some of the material covered by aeronautical engineering undergraduates, albeit at a less mathematical level. Pilots need to understand, for example, why the aerodynamics of an aircraft change markedly when flaps are deployed and why one does not immediately set the flaps to zero when recovering from a stall. Why is it so important not to position oneself too close behind a "heavy", even if one is piloting a moderately large aircraft? What makes some designs inherently more stable than others? Why does an aircraft designed expressly for use in aerobatic championships have quite different stability characteristics from a trainer? Why can some aircraft now fly at angles of attack which seem to contravene the normal rules about wings stalling at values greater than about 16°?

Some of these questions have been answered in the past by some excellent books such as Kermode's "Flight Without Formulae", but generally the treatment is qualitative, not quantitative; they do not "put any numbers in". The present book does just that and is designed to satisfy the early needs of students undertaking degree courses in the piloting of transport aircraft. These have now become established in the USA and are represented in the UK by the Air Transport Operations BSc and ATPL degree course at City University in London. This addresses the probable future stipulation that all commercial captains shall be graduates or of graduate standing. This is already the requirement in some countries and the developments inherent in the European Joint Aviation Authority (JAA), perhaps superseded by the European Aviation Safety Authority (with legal powers), will tend to reinforce the moves towards graduate pilots rather than away from them. Despite all that, however, I believe this book will also be of use to all those embarking on a PPL course and to current pilots.

Some chapters are quantitative in nature, the others qualitative. In the former case, worked examples are shown in the text and examples for the student to try are at the end of the chapter.

I am grateful to all those who have made comments (qualitative and quantitative) over the years about my own flying and teaching skills and I hope this book will help to induce in others a fascination for the subjects of its title.

R.S.N.
Dept. of Mechanical Engineering and Aeronautics,
City University, London.

1

Definitions, Axes and Flight Controls

What's it all about?

Introduction

MOTHER NATURE got there first of course, as usual, and mankind's earliest attempts at flying involved some very hazardous looking machines modelled on birds. Many brave people chalked up a large total of serious accidents trying to emulate bird flight in the days before science had proved quite conclusively that humans do not have chest muscles powerful enough to lift off the ground simply by a flapping action. Modern successes in man-powered flight involve the pilot pedalling as hard as possible to drive a propeller; lift is produced by forward motion, not by flapping. Even then, the same scientific laws have to be adhered to and it's interesting to note, for example, that a small bird and a modern jet airliner both use up about 3% of their body mass per hour in flight; fat is being burned up in the former case, Avtur in the latter. However, modern aircraft have many similarities with birds and much of the terminology is common. This chapter is concerned with setting down some definitions and names on which the rest of the book can be based.

The Important Parts

The fuselage

It is dangerous to refer to any part of an aircraft as being the most important part because there will always be some criterion against which it could be judged less important, however temporarily. But probably everyone would agree that, aerodynamically speaking, the fuselage is the most useless. Fig. 1.1 shows the major parts of a Boeing 737 and while the fuselage is certainly vital in containing the payload, some of the fuel, the crew and most of the electronics, it contributes very little to keeping the aircraft aloft in terms of generating lift. Some designers have even produced aircraft without a fuselage ("flying wings") but we'll have a look at those in Chapter 3. In any aircraft, the designer will nowadays make the fuselage as streamlined as possible to minimise drag. However, in a two-seat light aircraft there will also be a decision to be made whether to place the crew members in a tandem configuration, just to keep the fuselage as slim as possible, or side-by-side,

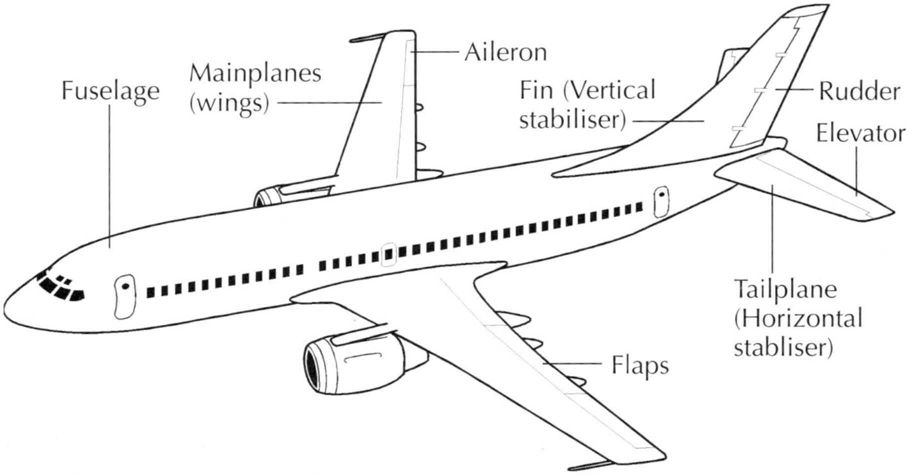

Figure 1.1 The main flying and control surfaces of a conventional aircraft

so that each occupant can see what the other is doing. In a conventional aircraft, the fuselage also provides a "lever arm" in the sense of producing a nose-up or nose-down pitching moment, or a nose-left or nose-right moment when the tail surfaces are moved; but more of that later.

In our comparison of birds and aircraft, the fuselage is obviously analagous to the bird's body, each containing all the essential organs to sense and control the flying machine involved.

The wings (mainplanes)

Undeniably important to birds and aircraft are the wings, or mainplanes; the latter title is sometimes used to distinguish these surfaces from the tailplane. The wings produce lift from forward motion and do so because of their curvature (camber) and the angle they make with the oncoming airstream. In the case of a bird, a flapping action is also required to produce forward propulsion, while an aircraft will obtain this from its engines. A glider uses a forward component of its wing lift to pull it forward and, unless it is in a region of rising air (a thermal), it will gradually lose height. Some birds, of course, are also very effective gliders and they will tend to be the larger ones who soar in thermals looking for their food, rather than small ones who simply make short flights between possible food sources.

The usefulness of the wings is by no means restricted to producing lift. They also often contain the majority of the fuel and the main part of the undercarriage, as well as commonly support the weight of the engines. These are useful in the sense that any weight distributed along a wing helps to even out the bending stresses, resulting in a lighter wing structure.

Two cases immediately spring to mind where wings are either redundant or simply missing: a hovering Harrier aircraft and a helicopter. In the former case, the weight of the aircraft is being borne entirely by directing the engine thrust downwards, although this cannot be sustained for very long without using up a major fraction of the fuel on board. In the latter case, the wings are replaced by a rotor which produces lift by rotation of several blades, each of which has a cross-section similar to a wing. This is not as efficient a method of producing lift as forward motion and it costs more to transport a given number of people over a given distance than in a conventional aircraft.

Flaps

Over the inboard sections of the wing are usually found hinged and movable surfaces called flaps. These are essential in providing more lift for the aircraft at lower speeds and are therefore valuable in minimising an aircraft's approach speed and concomitant dangers on landing. In the same sense that fleas have smaller fleas on their backs to bite them, flaps on modern aircraft can also have their own flaps, giving further extension of the lifting surface when required and further lowering the landing speed.

Ailerons

Over the outboard sections of a wing are to be found further hinged surfaces called ailerons. These rotate in opposite directions to produce more or less lift on opposing wings, thus creating a rolling action. Their position near the wing tips obviously give them the maximum possible lever arm for producing a rolling moment.

The ailerons are connected to the pilot's control column: in the case of a stick, a movement to the right produces a lifting of the right (starboard) aileron and depression of the left one; with a yoke, a right hand down motion produces the same effect. In both cases this leads to less lift from the right wing, more from the left one and a consequent rolling motion to starboard. A problem arises here, however, if the port and starboard ailerons are deflected by the same angle. The downgoing one produces a greater "drag" increase than an equal deflection on the upgoing one, so there is a tendency for the nose to turn ("yaw") towards the wing with the depressed aileron. Unfortunately, the depressed one was meant to produce a rolling and turning motion in the opposite direction so this is referred to as "adverse aileron yaw". For this reason, the ailerons on most aircraft are "differential" ones; that is, the deflection angle of the downgoing one is less than that of the upgoing one. The upgoing aileron can be deflected to an angle of about 15 to 20°. whereas the downgoing limit is about 10 to 15°.

Another possibility is to use "Frise ailerons". These are shaped so that the part of the aileron forward of its hinge will protrude into the oncoming airstream if that part is depressed (i.e. aileron trailing edge up) but not if elevated, so a greater drag is then produced on the wingtip in the chosen rolling and yawing direction. As most designers use either one of these methods or a combination of both, this adverse yawing phenomenon is nowadays not much of a problem, although this has not always been the case.

The fin (vertical stabiliser)

At the rear of the fuselage is the fin, or vertical stabiliser, which essentially has the job of keeping the aircraft flying straight. If anything happens to upset this balance and the nose moves to left or right, the fin then becomes a weathervane and generates a side force to return the nose to its original heading. The size of the fin is therefore critical and extra fin area is sometimes generated by adding a ventral one to the bottom of the fuselage. This can have a beneficial result in improving the spinning characteristics of the aircraft; we shall return to these points in a subsequent chapter.

At the fin's trailing edge is the **rudder**, which serves exactly the same purpose as that on a boat. Deflection of this hinged surface produces a side force in the same way that the flaps produce extra lift for the wings. The rudder is connected to the pilot's pedals, a leftwards push resulting in the nose moving to the left. The rudder usually has the greatest allowable deflection angle of any of the control surfaces, about 30°. This is because rudder authority is needed to be sustained longest of all with decreasing speed, especially for kicking off crab angle on landing with a crosswind or for spin recovery, of which more later.

The tailplane (horizontal stabiliser)

Close to the fin but extending horizontally is the tailplane, or horizontal stabiliser, which in stability terms acts like the fin, but in the vertical plane. A flight disturbance which caused the nose to rise would result in the tailplane being thrust downwards, thus producing a lift force to return it to its original position. Tailplane size is also vital, therefore, since rapid correction is needed. Some aircraft have this surface at or near the nose, which obviously results in different flying characteristics, but we'll deal with those in Chapter 3. The term tailplane is therefore a misnomer for these aircraft types and the word "canard" is used to describe them. This difficulty is probably also the reason why alternative names are sometimes used for the fin and tail: vertical and horizontal stabilisers respectively. These terms tend to be used more in the USA but even this does not really solve the problem; the reader is invited to decide which is the horizontal and which the vertical stabiliser on an aircraft in a 60° banked turn!

At the rear of the tailplane are hinged surfaces called **elevators**; they act like the rudder but produce vertical changes instead of horizontal ones. They are connected to the control column such that a backward movement by the pilot produces

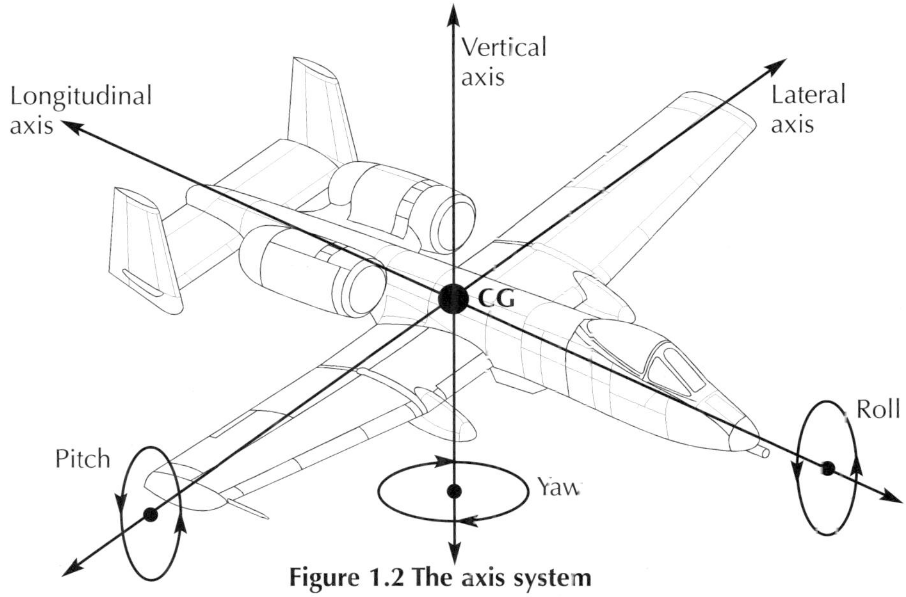

Figure 1.2 The axis system

upgoing elevators, a downgoing tailplane and an upgoing nose. Typical maximum elevator deflections would be about ± 25°.

The Axis System

The paragraphs above have referred to the various ways in which an aircraft can move, so it is now essential to set down the axis system about which all these movements take place. There are in fact six basic ways in which the position or orientation of an aircraft can change. The simplest mode of moving anything would be in a straight line, just as a marble would be constrained if rolling in a groove. If the marble is allowed instead to roll over the surface of a desk, it has two degrees of freedom since, if a straightforward x-y graph is pictured as superimposed on the desk, the marble can move to any value of x and y and get there by any means it likes. A car being driven around on flat ground has a similar freedom but if it is driven fast over a hump-backed bridge another (vertical) axis is introduced, in the mathematical sense. We now have an x-y-z system and three degrees of freedom, altitude being the third.

An aircraft has all three degrees of freedom just mentioned, but three more besides, since it is free also to **rotate** about any of the three axes just introduced. An aircraft therefore has six degrees of freedom (so does a badly driven car!) and any motion undertaken by it will be along or about any of the three axes, or a combination of several of these motions at once. When a body becomes a projectile above the Earth's surface, it will always move in such a way that its centre of gravity will trace

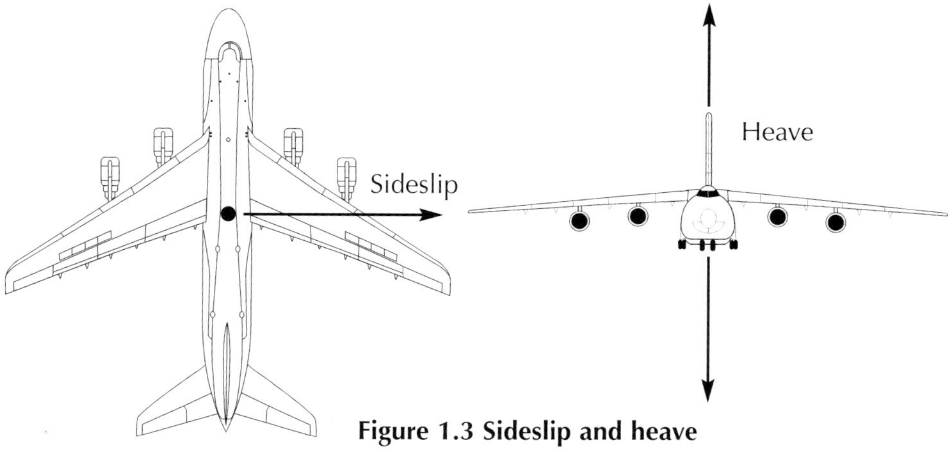

Figure 1.3 Sideslip and heave

out a path which is approximately a parabola, irrespective of whether it is rotating, asymmetric in shape or whatever. For this reason, it is usual to use the centre of gravity, or CG, as the point through which all three axes are assumed to pass (see Fig. 1.2). While the three axes must be at right-angles to each other, we now have a choice of directions in which they should point. It would obviously be logical to have one of them passing through the CG and the nose and tail, since the aircraft will spend most of its flying time travelling along this axis. This is therefore referred to as the longitudinal axis. It should be noted that, in plan view, most aircraft are symmetrical about this axis.

The next most obvious axis to define would be perpendicular to the longitudinal one and perpendicular to the line joining the wingtips. In straight level flight, this would correspond fairly accurately to the line of the weight of the aircraft, although the latter will of course always be perpendicular to the ground, irrespective of the flying state of the aircraft. This is known as the vertical (or normal) axis. Since the three axes must be perpendicular to each other, there is no choice about the third one; it must lie across the aircraft, wingtip to wingtip in the case of a wing with no sweep, and this is known as the lateral axis.

Motion along the lateral axis is called "sideslip" (Fig. 1.3), along the vertical axis is "heave" and along the longitudinal axis is simply "forward flight". Rotation about the longitudinal axis (Fig. 1.2) is called "roll", about the lateral axis is "pitch" and about the vertical axis is "yaw" (not to be confused with sideslip). It's important to remember that an aircraft might exhibit several of these motions and rotations at any one time, which is what makes the study of aircraft stability and control so fascinating. Just to confuse the issue, there is another set of axes called "wind axes" which are easier to use if the dynamic behaviour of an aircraft is being studied. In this system, the longitudinal axis is replaced by the line along which the aircraft is actually flying; that is, the line traced out by its CG. This is not the same as the longitudinal axis since the aircraft might be flying along with its nose above the horizon, especially at low speed. This axis system is more useful when studying the forces on an aircraft because lift is automatically defined as being perpendicular to the oncoming wind and drag as being parallel to it.

Summary

In terms of the flying and control surfaces described above, we can therefore now summarise the motions as follows:

Ailerons give control in **roll**. Stick movement by the pilot causes one aileron to rise and the other to fall, giving more lift on one wing and less on the other.

The **tailplane** gives stability in **pitch**. Anything which causes the aircraft to pitch nose-up (for example) will result in the tailplane being lowered into the airstream and a consequent increase in tail lift, restoring the aircraft to its initial state.

Elevators give control in **pitch**. A stick-back movement by the pilot will raise the trailing edge of the elevators to cause a downforce on the tailplane and consequent nose-up result. The aircraft then starts to climb.

The **fin** gives stability in **yaw** ("weathercock"). This acts exactly like the tailplane but about the vertical axis of the aircraft.

The **rudder** gives control in **yaw**. This acts like the elevators but about the vertical axis.

Conclusion

Obviously, the complicated process which constitutes the flight of an aircraft cannot be summarised in a mere five statements, nor would knowledge of the above five statements be even remotely sufficient to equip anyone to fly as a pilot. But they do represent the basis of what this book is about and subsequent chapters will build on this information. Aircraft which are "unconventional" and do not resemble the 737 of Fig. 1.1 will be discussed in Chapter 3. However, the underlying principles of flight still follow the logical rules mentioned above.

2

Dimensions and Unit Systems

How shall we measure flight?

BEFORE CONSIDERING the physics of aircraft flight, we need to address the subject of units and dimensions, not least because aeronautics in particular is riddled with different systems, largely for historical reasons and because of the international way in which it has evolved over many decades.

If you are standing in the middle of nowhere and ask anyone the distance to the nearest town, they will probably give you an answer in either miles or kilometres (km), depending on which country you are standing in. Conversion between these two unit systems is not very difficult (1 mile is about 1.6 km) but aviation is a particular minefield in this respect, with a pilot being quoted runway lengths in metres (m), distances in nautical miles (n.mile) or km, aircraft weight in pounds force (lbf) or metric tonnes (t), speed in knots (kn)(= nautical miles per hour) and rate of climb in thousands of feet per minute (ft/min)! For engineers, it's sometimes even worse, with engine specific fuel consumption sometimes being quoted in terms of "per decanewton of thrust" (daN). This chapter will deal with the nature of the measures themselves and indicate how to flit accurately and speedily between two systems.

The S.I. and Imperial Systems of Units

As soon as people started to trade, they needed comparative measures so that, for example, a trader in one country ordering a specified weight of grain could be sure that the grain provider knew how much was needed. When the science of accurate measurement took hold, agreed conversion factors became available between the unit systems of various countries and, although some archaic measures are still in use, the vast majority of nations use either the so-called Imperial system of units (evolved largely from the UK) or the Système International d'Unités (SI) based on the metric system. As customers come from all over the world, aircraft manufacturers and operators need to be proficient in specifying performance and handling qualities in both unit systems.

The fundamental units of any system are based on mass, length and time (or force, length and time), with other measures deriving from these. For example, area depends on the square of length, volume on its cube, and so on. On that basis, the Imperial system uses a pound mass (lbm), a foot (ft) and a second (s); SI uses a kilogramme (kg), a metre (m) and a second. The units of force are slightly more complicated and are dealt with later. Even with these basic quantities specified, we need to incorporate some additions in the form of prefixes to the units. An aircraft's range specified in metres is a large number so a unit one thousand times larger is used and given the prefix "kilo", meaning 1000. Going in the opposite direction, the specification of the diameter of a small aircraft component needs a unit much smaller than a metre and a millimetre (mm) is the obvious candidate ("milli" = 1/1000). The various prefixes which might be encountered in aviation are listed below.

Prefix	**Symbol**	**Multiplier**
giga	G	10^9
mega	M	10^6
kilo	k	10^3
hecto	h	10^2
deca	da	10
milli	m	10^{-3}
micro	μ (Greek "mu")	10^{-6}

In general, the prefixes are used in multiples of 1000, but "deca" is included above because of its use in specifying engine thrust and "hecto" because of its use in pressure measurement. Let's now look at the fundamental units and some derived ones.

Mass

Mass is a measure of the amount of basic material present in a body and is normally measured in kg or lbm. It is essentially a measure of inertia, the ability not to be moved very easily, and a large mass needs a greater effort to set it in motion than a smaller one. This must **not** be confused with force or weight; the weight of an object depends on where you are in the universe and 1 lbm of sprouts on the Moon's surface **weighs** only about one sixth of 1 lbm of sprouts on the Earth's surface (so where would **you** buy sprouts?). Aircraft weights are regularly quoted in both lbm and kg, although the actual numbers involved become fairly unmanageable for large aircraft and the more satisfactory metric tonne (1 t = 1000 kg) is used.

The official conversion factor is

1 kg = 2.20462 lbm or **1 lbm = 0.4536 kg**

but the approximation 2.205 would normally be accurate enough. A tonne is therefore about 2205 lbm, compared to the Imperial ton of 2240 lbm, so 1 ton = (2240/2205) = 1.016 t.

Length and Distance

The conversion factor for length is

$$1 \text{ m} = 3.2808 \text{ ft} \quad \text{or} \quad 1 \text{ ft} = 0.3048 \text{ m}$$

but for distances we sometimes need to go into deeper waters and use a system derived from maritime navigation. Historically, a nautical mile was taken to be one minute of longitude at the equator, so the distance around the equator is (60 x 360) = 21600 n mile. A nautical mile would also be the length of a minute of latitude if the Earth were a perfect sphere, however, there is some flattening at the poles so this equivalence is slightly inaccurate. In SI terms, the conversion is now agreed at

$$1 \text{ n mile} = 1852 \text{ m} = 1.852 \text{ km}$$

which means that it is also equal to 1.1508 statute miles so

$$\text{speed in mile/h} = 1.15 \times \text{speed in knots}$$

Angle

Although there is no difference between the SI and Imperial systems in the definition of angles, we do need to introduce the idea of a "radian" rather than degrees for measuring them. A radian is defined as the angle subtended at the centre of a circle by an arc one radius long. Fig. 2.1 shows that as the arc AB increases in length, the angle θ subtended at the centre also increases. When AB (measured around the arc, not as a straight line) exactly equals the radius r of the circle, θ is one radian. Since the periphery of a circle is $2\pi r$ long, the angle θ will be $360/2\pi°$, or about 57.3°. The advantage of using radians is that, for small angles, the tangent or sine of an angle is approximately equal to the angle **in radians**. We shall make use of this later in the book, but it's interesting to note here that this is the origin of the well known 1:60 rule in navigation which says that if you are one mile wrong (sideways) in 60 miles of travel, then you are 1° wrong in your heading. We can now see that this should really be called the 1:57.3 rule, but 1:60 is much easier on the tongue and the memory!

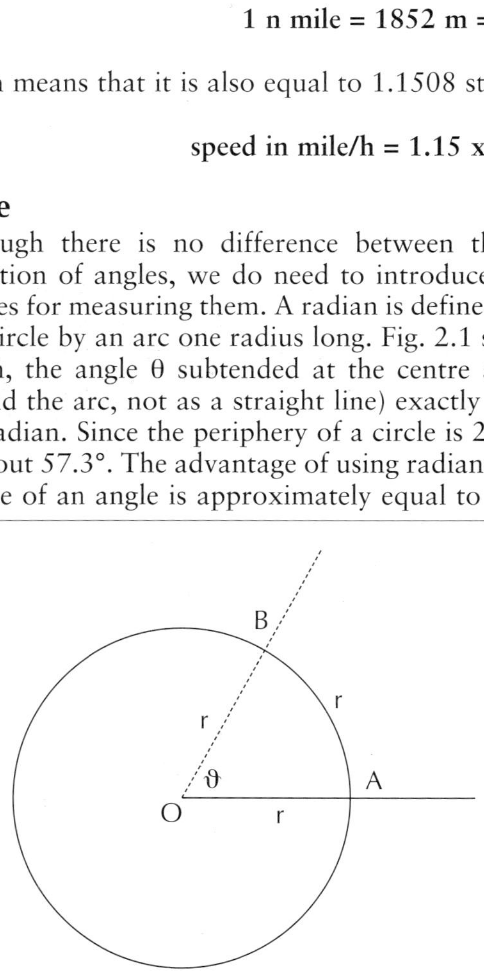

Figure 2.1 Definition of a radian

Time

No conversion factors are needed here since both major unit systems use the second for time.

However, the second is a relatively short time period for pilots, who encounter rates of climb in ft/min and endurance in hours. On the other hand, response times when an aircraft is hit by a gust would be measured in seconds and rates of roll in degrees per second.

Area

As areas are measured in terms of a length multiplied by a breadth, we must expect the units to be m^2 or ft^2, so the conversion here will be 3.2808^2 or

$$1\ m^2 = 10.764\ ft^2 \quad \text{or} \quad 1\ ft^2 = 0.092903\ m^2$$

These conversion factors are essential in dealing with wing areas.

Volume

Just as area involves the product of two lengths, volume involves three (length x breadth x height) so the units will be m^3 or ft^3. The conversion factor, accurate enough for our purposes, would be

$$1\ m^3 = 35.313\ ft^3 \quad \text{or} \quad 1\ ft^3 = 0.02832\ m^3$$

However, pilots are most of all concerned with volume when dealing with fuel and that tends to be measured in gallons or litres. A litre is a thousandth of a cubic metre so from the numbers above it is 0.03531 ft^3; 1 ft^3 is near enough 6.23 gal, so a litre is about 0.22 gal (= 6.23 x 0.03531). As if this weren't bad enough, there are two types of gallon: an Imperial one and a US one, the latter being about 83% of the former. We can therefore draw together all the above to quote some conversion factors rather more useful to pilots.

1 gal = 1.201 USgal or **1 USgal = 0.833 gal**
1 litre = 0.21997 gal or **1 gal = 4.546 litres**
1 litre = 0.26417 USgal or **1 USgal = 3.785 litres**

Velocity or Speed

Speed is the rate at which a given distance can be traversed, so it must have the units of m/s or ft/s. The denominator (time) is the same here so the conversion factor is the same as for metres to feet, although these units are not the ones that any pilot would see on the airspeed indicator; those would be knots (n mile/h). A nautical mile is 1852 m and an hour is 3600 s so the conversion factor would be 1852/3600 = 0.5144.

1 knot (n mile/h) = 0.5144 m/s = 1.69 ft/s = 1.15 mile/h

At high speeds and/or high altitudes, the flow around an aircraft is more likely to depend on its speed relative to the local speed of sound, the ratio being called the Mach number M. This has no units because it is the ratio of one velocity to another, so it doesn't really fit into this section, but it's worth pointing out that the speeds of sound involved are about 340 m/s at sea level (or 660 kn or 759 mile/h), although the value falls off with altitude.

Acceleration

Just as speed is the rate at which distance is changing, so acceleration is the rate at which speed is changing. An aircraft which is accelerating at 3 m/s^2 is increasing its speed by 3 m/s every second. The conversion factor will be the same as for metres to feet, but an interesting point here is that accelerations are often related to the gravitational value of 9.81 m/s^2 or 32.2 ft/s^2. This is the rate at which any body would accelerate downwards (in a vacuum) in free-fall. An acceleration of 19.62 m/s^2 is therefore said to be at the rate of "2g", a figure usually exceeded fairly easily by an aerobatic pilot in a loop.

Acceleration rates also figure prominently in calculations made by designers in estimating take-off runs, although here the figure would relate to the longitudinal axis motion, not the vertical.

Density

The density of a substance is the mass of a unit volume of it so units would be kg/m^3 or lbm/ft^3. A cubic metre is a fairly large volume unit so "point values" are usually implied; that is, the mass in a cubic millimetre is just as valid, provided it is multiplied by 10^9 (the cube of ten cubed!) to give a figure per cubic metre. The density of water is 1000 kg/m^3, a nice round figure because this is where the concept of a kilogramme comes from, so the density of other substances is sometimes related to that figure and referred to as relative density or specific gravity. This has no units because it is a ratio, but on that basis many metals would have a value of about 4 to 5, light alloys such as aluminium about 2.7, Avtur would be 0.785 and Avgas about 0.72. The advantage of using relative density is that the number involved is independent of the amount of material being measured and of the units being used to do the measuring. However, one must finally return to units when specifying, for example, the weight of fuel being carried in an aircraft. The following are accurate enough for our purposes.

Substance	*Density (Imp)*	*Density (SI)*	*Relative density*
Avgas	44.9 lbm/ft^3	720 kg/m^3	0.720
Avtur	49.0	785	0.785
Water	62.4	1000	1.000
Air at sea level	0.0766	1.225	0.001225

$$1\ lbm/ft^3 = 16.0185\ kg/m^3 \quad \text{or} \quad 1\ kg/m^3 = 0.062428\ lbm/ft^3$$

Force

Force is one of the most important concepts dealt with here, especially when it is remembered that the lift force is what keeps an aircraft in the air. And yet it used to provide endless problems for schoolkids in the days when Imperial units were used, although the concept is mercifully trouble-free in the SI system. The trouble arose from the use of the same unit, the pound, for mass and force, whereas the SI unit for mass is the kg and for force is the newton (N). A newton is defined as the force that will accelerate a mass of 1 kg at 1 m/s^2, whereas 1 lb force (lbf) will, by definition, accelerate a mass of 1 lbm at g ft/s^2 (32.2). This means that, in the Imperial system, to obtain an acceleration of 1 ft/s^2 one must either use a unit of force of 1/g lbf (called a poundal) or use a mass of g lbm (called a slug!). The air density quoted in the above table would then have been 0.002378 slug/ft^3 and it is true to say that the aircraft industry, faced with the above choice, has always chosen to keep the lbf in tact and use a "slug density".

Calculations involving force later in this book will tend to use SI units, but it is as well to be aware of the complications with the Imperial ones. One area where aviation seems to have incorporated the worst of both worlds is in quoting engine specific fuel consumptions. This is a measure of how much fuel is being burned per hour for every unit of thrust produced, so in the Imperial system it would be quoted in lbm of fuel per pound of thrust per hour (lbm/lbf.h). The strict SI equivalent would be kg/N.h, but in an effort to approach the same level of number the newton is replaced by a decanewton (1 daN = 10 N) as this is approximately 1 kgf (which, strictly speaking, is 9.81 N). Under the SI system, therefore, specific fuel consumption is expressed as kg/daN.h which is only 2% different from kg/kgf.h or lbm/lbf.h. As a matter of interest, a modern passenger aircraft like an Airbus A320 in cruising condition is using about 0.6 kg/daN.h for a thrust of about 1900 daN (4270 lbf) per engine. It is then travelling about 0.2 n.mile (0.37 km) for every kg of fuel burned.

1 lbf = 4.44822 N or **1 N = 0.22481 lbf**

Pressure

Pressure is defined as force per unit area and is one of the most important concepts in aerodynamics. This is essentially a localised concept since a large force over a very large area might produce a smaller pressure than a smaller force over a smaller area. This can be seen at its most vivid if one considers a pair of shoes with stiletto heels. The weight of a human body spread over the main area of the sole is tolerable so far as a lawn is concerned, but putting the same weight on only the heel area causes excruciating pain to the grass! 1 lbf spread over a square foot is not a very high pressure compared to the atmospheric value (about 2116 lbf/ft^2) and 1 N spread over a square metre (also called a pascal, Pa) is even smaller (about 1/100000 of an atmosphere). So physicists and meteorologists long ago resorted to a much bigger unit called a bar, which is 100000 Pa. This subject is dealt with in more detail in Chapter 4, which is concerned with the atmosphere.

Here, we merely quote the conversion factors.

$$1 \text{ lbf/ft}^2 = 47.8803 \text{ Pa} \quad \text{or} \quad 1 \text{ Pa} = 0.020885 \text{ lbf/ft}^2$$

Temperature

As with pressure, temperature will be dealt with again in Chapter 4, but here we need to set down the units involved. Temperature is simply a comparison of thermal energy levels. If two masses are brought together and one conducts heat energy to the other, the one giving away energy is said to be hotter. Since temperatures are only comparisons, we need some benchmarks against which to set up scales for measurement. The freezing and boiling points of water offer two very useful markers and the Celsius (formerly Centigrade) scale has the value zero for the first and 100 for the second. The equally used Fahrenheit scale has values of 32 and 212 for these markers, so the divisions °F are obviously smaller than those of °C. In fact, since the difference between freezing and boiling water represents 100°C and 180°F, the former must be 1.8 times bigger. It is therefore relatively easy to set down a conversion rule:

To convert °F to °C, subtract 32 and divide by 1.8 (or multiply by 5/9)
To convert °C to °F, multiply by 1.8 (or by 9/5) and add 32

When dealing with temperature **ratios**, as we shall do in Chapter 4, we need an absolute scale, not one of the two just mentioned, since they were arbitrarily dependent on the properties of water. If one goes on removing thermal energy from an object, there will eventually be reached a point where no more can be extracted: that is called "absolute zero" temperature. On the above two scales its value is -273.15°C and -459.67°F (-273 and -460 are good enough for our purposes). This system, starting at absolute zero, is known as the Kelvin scale when its divisions are equal to those of Celsius and the Rankine scale when equal to those of Fahrenheit. The symbols are K and °R and it should be noted that the former does **not** carry the small ° marking.

We can therefore summarise:

Freezing point of water = 32°F = 0°C = 273 K = 492°R
Boiling point of water = 212°F = 100°C = 373 K = 672°R

Moment or Torque

The concept of a force acting on the end of an arm or radius gives us a "moment" or torque. This gives us the means to remove the wheel nuts when changing the wheel on a car and the means of removing or inserting screws in a piece of wood. In the former case the radius is the length of the brace involved and in the latter is the radius of the screwdriver handle. The numerical value of this parameter is given simply by the product of the force and the radius, so the units must be Nm or ft.lbf. The aeronautical application is obvious when one considers the action of causing a pitching moment by deflecting an elevator, causing greater or less lift on the tailplane. The radius in question is then the so-called tail arm, the distance from the CG to the lift centre of the tailplane.

1 Nm = 0.73756 lbf.ft or **1 lbf.ft = 1.3558 Nm**

Work done

To do work, a force has to be moved through a distance. If a wing and a set of engines lift an aircraft weighing W newtons to an altitude h metres, they have done Wh newton-metres of work in lifting. There will also have been some work done by the engines in overcoming drag forces, but that is a separate calculation. In both cases, a force (weight or drag) must have been moved through a distance and the absence of either would give a zero result. This concept of no work being done might be hard to swallow for a person carrying a very heavy weight on their shoulders (and they would not thank you for trying to explain it) although the fact remains that they are doing no work (in the vertical sense) unless they raise the heavy weight through some distance.

The units are obviously the same as for torque so the above correction factors still apply. However, in the case of work done, 1 Nm is sometimes called a joule (J), so one could equally well write

1 J = 1 Nm = 0.73756 lbf.ft

Momentum

In everyday speech, the word momentum is normally used in the context of something having built up this impetus by virtue of motion and, by implication, needing some stopping thereafter. The scientific definition is also along these lines but more specific; momentum is the product of mass and velocity for a moving body, so the units will be kg.m/s or lbm.ft/s. The concept of "stopability" is valid here because the momentum is also a measure of force times time; that is, if the same force is applied to a mass for double the time, then it will acquire twice the momentum and will need either twice the restraining force to stop it in the same time or twice the time to stop it with the same force.

1 lbm.ft/s = 0.138255 kg.m/s or **1 kg.m/s = 7.233 lbm.ft/s**

Energy

An often misused term but essentially the same as work done; that is, force times distance. This can be manifested as "potential" energy if a mass has been raised to a certain height or "kinetic" energy if it has been accelerated to a known speed. However, once again, the two are interchangeable. If a glider pilot pushes the nose below the horizon, potential energy of altitude will be exchanged for the increased kinetic energy of a higher airspeed. In fact, energy, work and heat transfer are all interchangeable. At the point of touching down on the runway and applying its brakes, an aircraft's kinetic energy is dissipated in heating up the brake pads, and the loss of newton-metres of one is showing up as joules of the other.

For an aircraft of mass m flying at a velocity V at height h above the ground,

$$\textbf{potential energy} = mgh \qquad \textbf{kinetic energy} = \tfrac{1}{2}mV^2$$

but consistent units must be used (kg,N,m,s or slug,lbf,ft,s).

The conversion factors are as for work done.

Power

The last concept to look at is that of power, which is by definition the **rate** of doing work, so its units are Nm/s or ft.lbf/s. The former is known as a watt (W), a fairly small unit so prefixes usually come into play: heating elements in kettles would be rated in kW and aircraft engine power in MW. The ft.lbf/s is also a fairly small unit and when engines were introduced into industry the factory and mine owners wanted to know how many horses they could pension off for each engine they bought. The concept of "brake horsepower" was therefore introduced and 1 bhp was considered equivalent to 550 ft.lbf/s. By analogy with horses and engines, a Boeing 747 on initial climbout is probably needing about 50 MW from its engines, or about the combined output of 20 locomotives!

Since 1 ft.lbf has already been established as 1.3558 Nm (see Torque) we therefore have conversion factors for power:

1 ft.lbf/s = 1.3558 Nm/s = 1.3558 J/s = 1.3558 W

1 bhp = 745.7 J/s = 745.7 W = 0.7457 kW

1 kW = 1.341 bhp or 1000 bhp = 745.7 kW

So How Do We Do a Conversion?

The ease of converting from one system to another obviously depends on how many units there are to be converted and how "close" they are to the basic units. For example, converting from m^3 to ft^3 involves cubing only the conversion factor, whereas the change from m^3/s to USgal/h is nothing like as straightforward. The most difficult cases are almost certainly dealt with using the following equation, where "new" and "old" refer to the unit systems we wish to convert to and from:

$$\text{New no.} = \text{Old no.}\left[\frac{\text{Old mass}}{\text{New mass}}\right]^{n1} \bullet \left[\frac{\text{Old length}}{\text{New length}}\right]^{n2} \bullet \left[\frac{\text{Old time}}{\text{New time}}\right]^{n3} \qquad \text{Eqn. 2.1}$$

or, if it is necessary to work in force, length and time units:

$$New\ no. = Old\ no. \left[\frac{Old\ force}{New\ force}\right]^{n1} \bullet \left[\frac{Old\ length}{New\ length}\right]^{n2} \bullet \left[\frac{Old\ time}{New\ time}\right]^{n3} \qquad Eqn.\ 2.2$$

where n1, n2 and n3 are the power to which each unit is raised in the original definition. A straightforward case to use for demonstration would be converting atmospheric pressure in lbf/in^2 to N/m^2 (or pascals). At sea level, the average pressure is about 14.7 lbf/in^2, so we could use Eqn. 2.2 above (since force is involved rather than mass) and we should note that, in the expression "lbf/in^2", force appears in the numerator as lbf to power 1, length in the demoninator as inches to power 2 and time does not appear at all. We therefore have n1 = 1, n2 = -2 and n3 = 0, so:

$$New\ no. = 14.7 \left[\frac{lbf}{newton}\right]^{1} \bullet \left[\frac{inch}{metre}\right]^{-2}$$

$$= 14.7 \left[\frac{4.448}{1}\right]^{1} \bullet \left[\frac{1}{12 \times 3.281}\right]^{-2}$$

$$= 101358$$

Therefore it would seem that 14.7 lbf/in^2 is the same pressure as 101358 N/m^2 (or Pa). Because of various rounding errors, we have arrived at not quite the correct answer which is 101325 Pa or 1.01325 bar or 1013.25 mbar.

The above method always works, no matter how grim the conversion process looks, but we could probably have performed this fairly easy conversion using the following logic.

A lbf is 4.448 times bigger than a newton. A metre is 12 x 3.281 (=39.37) times longer than an inch, so 1 m^2 must cover the same area as $(39.37)^2$ in^2 (=1550). Therefore a load of 1 lbf spread over a square inch would need to be repeated 1550 times over a square metre to get the same pressure, or 4.448 times that number if the load were in newtons. The product of 1550 and 4.448 is about 6894, so 1 lbf/in^2 is about 6894 Pa and, in turn, 14.7 lbf/in^2 would be 6894 x 14.7 = 101347 Pa. Allowing once again for rounding errors, we have arrived at the same answer.

Conclusion

We have seen in this chapter that aviation uses a variety of different units, drawn not only from the Imperial and SI systems, but also involving one or two remnants from the seafaring world. It will not be satisfactory in the future, nor is it now, to claim that one was brought up under a different system and is therefore not prepared to deal in different units; it will be necessary to be able to convert between the various unit systems with not too much difficulty. Examples of such conversions have been given in the chapter.

Exercises - Chapter 2

1. A Tupolev Tu204 carries a payload of 21000 kg. Convert this to lbm.

2. A Piper Aztec has a mass of 5200 lbm but landing fees are charged per tonne. Determine its mass in tonnes.

3. A gas turbine engine consumes 1.2 t/s of air in cruising condition. How many lbm/min is it gulping?

4. The standard lengths of R.A.F. runways used to be 6000 and 9000 ft. Convert these to metres.

5. The wingspan of an Airbus A340 is 197 ft 10 in. Convert this to metres.

6. Convert a speed of 430 kn to (a) mile/h (b) m/s (c) ft/s (d) km/h.

7. The wing area of a Boeing 737-200 is 102.0 m^2. Convert this to ft^2.

8. A photographic intelligence aircraft can survey 10000 $mile^2$ in one flight. How many flights will it need to survey an area measuring 420 km by 530 km, assuming suitable airfields are available as starting points?

9. An airliner has a fuel tank total capacity of 15.3 m^3. Convert this figure to (a) ft^3 (b) in^3 (c) cm^3 (d) USgal (e) gal.

10. At a certain place on the Earth's surface, the value of the gravitational acceleration is measured as 9.8072 m/s^2. Convert this to ft/s^2.

11. Calculate the weight of 4040 USgal of Avtur (relative density 0.785) in (a) N (b) lbf and its mass in (c) t (d) ton.

12. An object measures 645 x 645 x 450 mm and weighs 2600 N. Calculate (a) its mass density in kg/m^3 (b) its relative density (c) its density in lbm/ft^3.

13. An engine has a specific fuel consumption of 0.52 kg/daN.h when producing 1600 daN of thrust. How many lbm of fuel is it using every second?

14. Convert 985 mbar into lbf/in^2.

3

Configuration

Why are some aircraft ugly and others beautiful?

IF YOU ASK a person of reasonable artistic ability but no special aviation knowledge to draw an aircraft, the chances are that you'll end up with a drawing resembling anything from a Spitfire to a 747. However, it is likely that all such drawings would be of what would normally be called a conventional layout. A main lifting wing would sit each side of a single fuselage at about the mid-length point and a tailplane and fin would sit at the rear end of the fuselage. A cursory rummage through a standard reference book such as Jane's, however, would show a very considerable variation from this standard pattern, especially if one includes sporting or experimental light aircraft. Even the first powered aircraft to lift off the ground, the Wright brothers' biplane (Fig. 3.1), was not of this ilk; aside from being a biplane, it had its "tailplane" at the front. Clearly, therefore, there are good reasons why aircraft look as they do and this chapter will not only look at the reasons for this, but also take the chance to define a few terms which we shall need to use subsequently.

Biplanes versus Monoplanes

In the earliest development of aircraft, biplanes were distinctly in the majority. This was largely to gain maximum lift from the crude aerofoil sections of those days, but also because experiments with potentially faster monoplanes often resulted in disasters. The structural engineering aspects of single wings were poorly understood and Bleriot's version was a rarity. Even with the First World War requirement that aircraft become machines of war, with the need for higher speeds and great manoeuvrability, designers still largely stayed with the trusty biplane whereas in the Second World War the monoplane was distinctly in the majority.

Nowadays, aircraft structures is a fine art and a designer can produce a monoplane to withstand appalling demands in military action or to lift gigantic loads in civil use. Biplanes are therefore restricted almost entirely to the sporting and aerobatic fraternity. There are advantages: a greater wing area means a lower wing loading (weight divided by wing area), and we shall see later in the book that this means lower stalling speeds and potentially better performance from small airfields. Also, having two sets of wings means that each one can have a shorter wing span; this

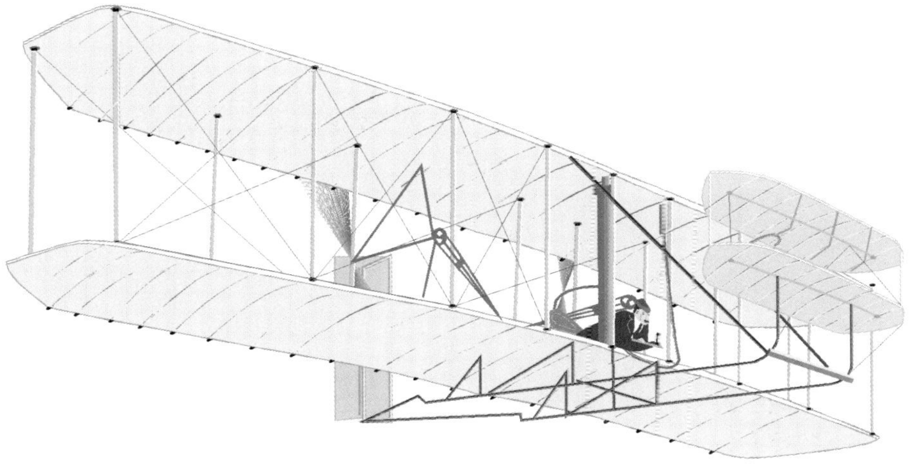

Figure 3.1 The Wright biplane

gives greater manoeuvrability in roll because the inertia of the aircraft about its longitudinal (fore-and-aft) axis is much lower. We shall see, once again later in the book, that there is an aerodynamic reason why the shorter span would give better rolling response, something any pilot of a modern high performance glider knows about if they try to carry out a flick roll!

The advantages of the monoplane, however, have generally won. The increased wing area of the biplane means greater drag (the force opposing forward motion), not simply because there is more metal or canvas stuck out in the airstream but also because there are twice as many wingtips, each one producing a vortex which represents shed energy (which can never be recovered). The monoplane's range for any given fuel load is therefore longer and this is what counts with high fuel prices. The drag of a biplane can be minimised by suitable choice of vertical gap and horizontal stagger between the wings, but the resulting aircraft can have some very pilot-hostile stalling characteristics.

Canards

The Wright biplane's tail-first configuration has already been mentioned and it's interesting to look at why this also seems to have become relatively rarer amongst modern aircraft. Configurations having a second lifting surface forward of the mainplanes are usually called "canards" and their advantages are becoming evident again with the advent of high speed, fly-by-wire interceptors such as the X29 (Fig. 3.2). In these aircraft, manoeuvrability is paramount, usually at the expense of stability, but then an interceptor pilot would not welcome too much of that anyway. The flying response of these aircraft to pilot stick input is computer controlled because of the poorer stability and a computer crash would result in the pilot leaving the aircraft with some urgency!

Figure 3.2 The X-29

The clear advantage of a canard is that a nose-up change of attitude, flaring on take off or landing, for example, is achieved with an **upwards** force on the canard but with a **down** force on a conventional tail. The total lift from mainplane and secondary surface combined is therefore greater in the former case, being thus further from a stalling condition. A further advantage is also connected to the approach to a stall; the need for the nose always to pitch down for quicker stall recovery. A canard would therefore need to stall **before** a mainplane and must be set at a greater angle of incidence (the setting angle relative to some fuselage datum). A conventional tailplane would need to be set at a lower angle to ensure that it always stalled **after** the mainplane. Indeed, there are many conventional aircraft flying around with a slight download on the tail in cruising flight so the main wing needs to produce even more lift to offset the weight of the aircraft.

The disadvantages of canards essentially stem from the fact that as mini-wings they also produce wingtip vortices and, whereas a conventional rear tail is generally well inside the axes of the vortices from the mainplanes, the reverse is true for canards - their shed vortices pass well inside the main span. In the approach condition, when angle of attack (the angle between the oncoming airstream and the line joining leading and trailing edges of the aerofoil) is high for both surfaces, the effect of the canard's vortices can be a marked one. As these problems are always at a maximum at low speeds, it is obvious that faster aircraft requiring high manoeuvrability are able to capitalise on the advantages of canards, whereas slower ones would regard the disadvantages stated above to be unacceptable and very careful design would be needed for low-speed handling. Canards are therefore likely to become increasingly common on future fly-by-wire fighters but remain in the minority for light aircraft.

In theory, a conventional tail can always be mounted sufficiently high or low to be out of any serious wing flow problems, although even then care is needed. It must not be in a position where it shields the fin from sideflow in a spin and it must not be exactly in the wing wash at stall, otherwise it may be unable to generate enough lift to pitch the aircraft nose-down for recovery from the stall. This nasty condition is called deep stall or superstall and can contribute to some very interesting behaviour in an aircraft with a tailplane mounted on top of its fin. In some cases, nothing short of a deployed tailchute would extricate the aircraft from this dangerous condition and these chutes are now fitted as standard when test pilots are taking a new high-tail design through stalling tests.

Figure 3.3 B2 stealth bomber

Tailless Aircraft

It's tempting to ask what would happen if we dispensed with a tailplane or canard surface to avoid the various complications listed above and it's certainly true that aircraft have been designed without either. Delta winged aircraft obviously come to mind, but these are better discussed under the heading of wing sweep. However, "flying wings" have taken to the skies although, up to a few years ago, hardly any progressed beyond the testing stage. Initially conceived as a low drag configuration because of the lower surface area being wetted, they are nowadays likely to be just as attractive for their low radar signature, as in the case of the B2 bomber (Fig. 3.3).

The underlying problem with a wing-only configuration is that it has an inherent nose-down pitching moment about its centre of gravity (at zero lift) because of the pressures around it. On a wing with no sweep, this tendency could be countered by reflexing the trailing edge upwards, producing a slight nose-up moment. However, on a swept wing the same effect can be produced by using "decalage". The root sections, which have more of their area ahead of the CG, have a greater angle of attack than the tip sections, which are essentially aft of the CG, thus producing a nose-up tendency. The latter method has much better CG tolerance than the former; that is, it will retain much better stability as the CG moves during flight. CG positions are hardly ever constant; military aircraft redistribute their mass as they drop weapons and even civilian ones do so as they use up fuel, or passengers move about.

While the absence of a tailplane gives rise to the pitching considerations above, the removal of a fin and rudder can also lead to problems of directional control and stability. To some extent, a swept wing gives a restoring moment in the directional sense because the forward-going side causes more drag, thus righting itself, although increased drag by any method would be suitable. The hinged control surfaces at the wing's trailing edge, usually called elevons as a conglomeration of the more conventional elevators (tail) and ailerons (wings), can be used in the same direction to change pitch but in opposite directions to produce either or both of a rolling or a yawing motion.

By and large, tailless aircraft haven't caught on, certainly not for passenger transportation, not least because a commercial version would have to be very large indeed to accommodate within itself all the items which are normally housed in a tubular fuselage, hung below the wings or contained within them. Any future giant passenger-carrying flying wings will need either to conform to airport handling limits of an 80 m wingspan or have wingtips which can be raised to a vertical position to give an effective 80 m span.

Swept Wings and Deltas

Swept wings are essentially a requirement for flight at high subsonic Mach numbers. The Mach number is the ratio of the aircraft's true airspeed to the local speed of sound and pilots during the Second World War began to encounter some inexplicable control problems when trying to pull out of involuntary dives at well above 450 kn, a considerable fraction of the speed of sound at high altitude. In many cases, they found (if they hadn't already tried to jump out!) that as they reached lower altitudes they were able to regain control. At 36000 ft, the speed of sound is about 570 kn, whereas at sea level it's about 660 kn. A dive speed of 500 kn therefore corresponds to a Mach number of 0.88 in the former case and only 0.76 in the latter. During the War, both sides started experimenting with the idea of wing sweep, but obviously did not exchange their ideas, and although the first wave of jet fighters after the War such as Meteors, Vampires and F84s had unswept wings, their successors, Hunters, F86s and MiG15s had some measure of sweep.

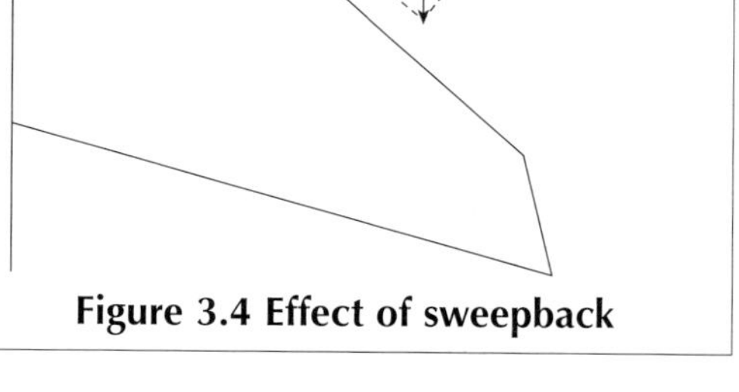

Figure 3.4 Effect of sweepback

The basic idea is that the velocity of air approaching the wing's leading edge can be split into two components, one parallel and the other perpendicular to it. The theory is that the wing section essentially responds to the normal (perpendicular) component and this is lower than the true airspeed by the cosine of the wing's sweep angle Λ (Fig. 3.4). The air is therefore cheated into thinking that the wing is travelling slower than it really is (at a Mach no. $M.\cos\Lambda$ instead of M) and problems caused by approaching the speed of sound are avoided, until one tries to go even faster. Another way of looking at this is to realise that with a swept wing the aerofoil section chord parallel to the air flow (as opposed to normal to the leading edge) is longer, so the thickness/chord ratio of the wing is lower giving potentially less drag. There are also some stability benefits to be had from sweep but these will be dealt with in more detail later. The majority of modern airliners have a moderate degree of sweep in their wings (around 25°), enabling them to cruise economically at about M = 0.82 at 36000 ft. Even more advanced methods of wing design enable some aircraft, like the Citation X, to cruise at about M = 0.9, but there is a limit to how much one can cheat the onset of shock waves and the only civil aircraft to have flown faster than that (Concorde, M = 2.2) does so under the vastly different flow conditions well beyond the speed of sound.

Unfortunately, one can't have something for nothing and swept wings also have their demerits. The principal one concerns the destination of the low energy air which sits next to the wing surface; the so-called "boundary layer". We shall look at this topic in more detail in Chapter 7, dealing with drag, but here we need to note that the air in contact with the surface will be at a standstill relative to the surface because of friction and air suffers from frictional effects just like any other fluid or solid. This layer, in turn, slows down the one above it and so on, so that the full speed of the outside airstream is not reached until one has travelled away from the surface by a noticeable distance. At the rear end of a large aircraft, this boundary layer could be 30 cm (1 ft) thick, having developed from nothing at the nose. Because of the pressure distribution on a swept wing, there is a tendency for the wing's boundary layer to be pushed to the wing tips. While this in itself may not be dangerous, when the aircraft is at high angle of attack, for example on approach, the accumulation of low energy air at the tips will result in their stalling before the roots. We have therefore lost lift aft of the CG and maintained lift forward of it, a dangerous nose-up pitching tendency when we really need a nose-down one. For that reason, all manner of tricks have been developed to minimise the progress of the boundary layer to the tips and the resulting dangers, including fences at about 2/3 span, saw-tooth leading edges to reduce thickness/chord ratio and vortex generators to mix the low energy air with free stream air just above it.

Sweeping the wings forward, as with the X29 (Fig. 3.2), would reverse that problem and the benefits of lower thickness/chord ratio would be retained. Unfortunately some of the benefits for lateral stability are also reversed and forward sweep is likely to be useful only for fly-by-wire aircraft because of this stability degradation.

In purely evolutionary terms, it would seem a logical next step to fill in the area between a highly swept wing and the fuselage to make a triangular plan-view shape, or Greek letter delta (Δ). The plan view of the British Aerospace Lightning makes this point very clearly; its wing looks exactly like a triangle with a much smaller triangular chunk removed. Admittedly, the Lightning had a tailplane and fin, so this is perhaps a red herring, but there is no doubt that delta wings satisfy an important requirement in aviation.

With a straight (i.e. unswept) wing, the bulk of wingtip vorticity is shed at the tips, whereas in the case of a delta, vortices are being shed more gradually all the way down the leading edge. At high angles of attack, two gigantic vortices roll up over the top of the wing and enable it to survive to much higher angles of attack before stalling, although the amount of lift produced is no greater than a conventional wing. This is why deltas always exhibit a very high attack angle on approach to landing and why one of them (Concorde) needs a nose drooping mechanism to enable the pilot to see anything ahead. This is, however, exactly the same property which makes a delta useful in another respect. The inability to generate a lot more lift from a sudden angle of attack change means that it will also give the pilot and any weapons-aiming system a much smoother ride in bumpy conditions. It's interesting to note that the Vulcan and the Victor bombers were basically designed to the same specification but the former's designer opted for a delta configuration whereas the latter's went for a combination of high sweep angle at the wing roots and low sweep at the tips, the so-called crescent wing. In later years, when the need arose (for radar evasion reasons) for these bombers to approach their targets at a very low level and lob their bombs at the enemy, the Vulcan was modified to do so whereas the Victors were generally modified to be tankers.

In a sense, the crescent wing gave some of the advantages of both low and high sweep angles; the former for lower approach and landing speeds (and therefore less rubber on the runway), the latter for high cruise efficiency. However, an even better solution is to make the wing sweep angle a variable, as with the Panavia Tornado, the Rockwell B-1 and the General Dynamics F111 (Fig. 3.5). This also, of course, involves the drawback of increased airframe weight because of the sturdy mechanism needed to support and rotate the wings but the Tornado has been an undeniably successful aircraft.

Where shall we put the engines?

If an aircraft needs only one engine, the question of where to put it is a relatively simple one: whether it pulls or pushes the aircraft forwards, it must be on the fuselage centreline for obvious reasons of symmetry. If two are needed, the matter becomes more interesting and involved, especially if one considers what is going to happen if one of them fails during take off. If they are not on the same vertical plane as the fuselage centreline, a moment will develop causing the aircraft to yaw away from the still active engine. Instant rudder action will be needed, but we shall see in a subsequent chapter that all aerodynamic forces on an aircraft are proportional to the square of speed (i.e. twice the speed, four times the force) and it may well be that the aircraft is not yet travelling fast enough for the rudder effect to equal the engine yawing moment. A classic case of this was the Mosquito in WW2, where the engines were so powerful that single engine failure on takeoff resulted in an alarming yawing and rolling motion. One solution is to place both engines side by side near the centreline (Jaguar, Phantom) or one on top of the other (Lightning). The advantage in the latter case is that no yawing moment can develop with a single engine failure, although a pitching one can.

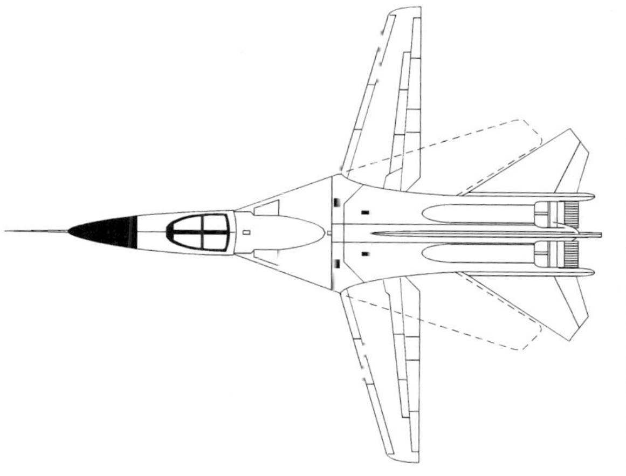

Figure 3.5 General Dynamics F111

In some cases, designers have resorted to placing both engines in pods at the rear end (BAC 111, DC9, Challenger (Fig. 3.6)) but this obviously moves the CG rearwards and the wings must be set further back to maintain balance. The DC9 has a particularly long snout. The setting of the engines high also introduces changes about one of the other axes; there is going to be a nose-up pitching moment when power is markedly reduced, as opposed to the nose-down moment one tends to expect.

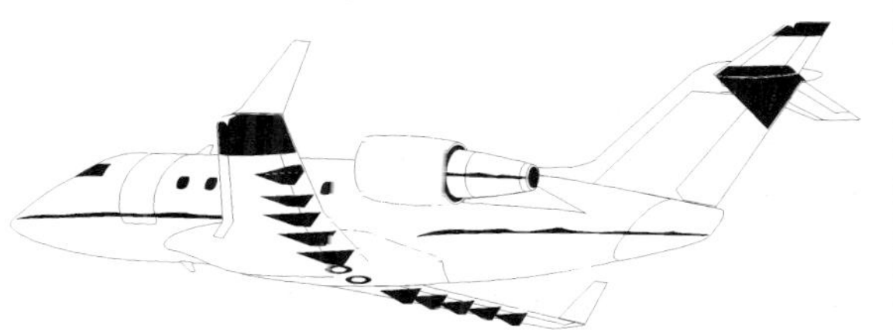

Figure 3.6 Canadair Challenger

The mounting of jet engines inside or very close to a fuselage also introduces the problem of how to guard against the possible damage from hot jet effluxes. The need for protection of the rear end is avoided if the engines are mounted inside, but then a long jet pipe will be needed, involving some extra loss of power.

The mounting of three engines is not easy either. In most modern aircraft, the designers have gone for an arrangement of two being slung under the wings and the central one mounted either in the fin (MD-11, Fig. 3.7) or in the rear end of the fuselage (Tristar, 727, Trident). In the latter case, some careful design is needed of the intake ducting to ensure that the engine receives a uniform

Figure 3.7 McDonnell Douglas MD-11

Figure 3.8 Antonov 124

airflow distribution after what is essentially two right-angle bends from the front base of the fin area. Poor design here could lead to markedly reduced engine power.

When four engines are involved, the trend seems to have been to mount them all under the wings, as in the Airbus A340, the Galaxy C5 and the Boeings 707 and 747. Earlier efforts to mount all four in pods at the rear (VC10, Ilyushin 62) do not seem to have caught on. The advantages of underwing placing are very real ones and these apply whether two or four engines are involved: the airflow over the wing is less disturbed, a lower thickness/chord ratio can be used and the engines need almost no jet pipes. The disadvantages centre on the need to prevent ingress of rubbish from the ground during take-off and landing and this can lead to some longer undercarriages than might otherwise be needed. One palliative is to flatten the lower part of the circular cross-section of the intake (Boeing 737-400) but in some cases designers have avoided any problems by mounting the wing itself on top of the fuselage, as in the case of many military freighters, where a low fuselage is obligatory for loading purposes (Antonov 124, Fig. 3.8). Another disadvantage of slinging four engines under the wing is that the two outboard ones are a considerable distance from the aircraft centreline and not only introduce a marked yawing moment on failure, as with the two engines case, but also represent enormous masses at considerable radial distances if any wing vibration (flapping) problems develop. Even worse, if the wing is flapping, it doesn't take much imagination to see that if the engine pod is below the plane of the wing it will be subjected to vibration parallel to the lateral axis, becoming an enormous pendulum in the process!

High or Low Wings?

We have just considered why the designer of a large freighter would need high-slung wings, but this mounting position is not unique to freighters and many designers have come up with high-, mid- or low-mounted wings for different aircraft, even within the same general category. In trainers, one finds high-wing examples (Cessnas) and low (Tomahawk, Bulldog, Chipmunk). In military circles there are high (Harrier), mid (F16) and low (Phantom) cases (Fig. 3.9, top, centre and bottom) and, interestingly, this leads us into a discussion about the angle at which the wing is mounted on the fuselage, as seen from the front. If the wing tip is higher than the root, the angle is called dihedral; the reverse is called anhedral. We shall see in a subsequent chapter that dihedral and a high wing setting both tend to make an aircraft more stable laterally whereas anhedral and a low wing mounting have the opposite effect. The wings of the Harrier are set high because the engine directs hot gases vertically downwards when in the hover position and

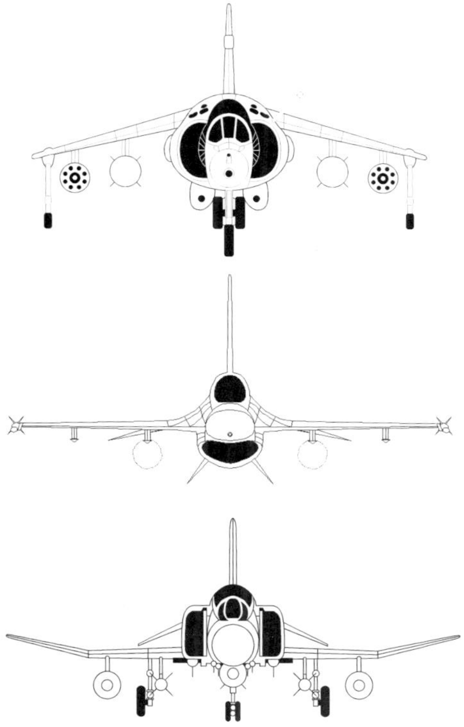

Figure 3.9 Dihedral (bottom), anhedral (top), none (centre)

clearly there must be no solid surface except the ground below them. The designer therefore gave the Harrier a marked anhedral to maintain the high manoeuvrability of the aircraft. The Phantom, on the other hand, has a low wing and the designer has increased its stability slightly by giving the outboard sections of the wings some dihedral. The specification of these angles is closely controlled and much wind tunnel testing is needed to determine the ideal values for any particular aircraft. The application of too much dihedral, for example, can lead to an aircraft developing an unacceptable "Dutch roll", an uncomfortable combination of roll and yaw which we shall look at in more detail in the chapter on stability.

Conclusion - Ugly or Beautiful?

So we come back to the question set at the head of this chapter: why are some aircraft ugly and others beautiful? It should be obvious by now that any aircraft looks like it does for perfectly good engineering reasons. Early aircraft were designed before the glories of aerodynamics, structures and stability had been properly researched and, although surviving examples may have a great following amongst aviation historians, they cannot generally be described as beautiful. Advances in engineering led to sleek, streamlined and powerful successors, culminating in some designs which even an art critic would have to agree were beautiful. Many aviators consider the Hawker Hunter to have been at the pinnacle of that bunch, but everyone has his or her own favourite, including some modern

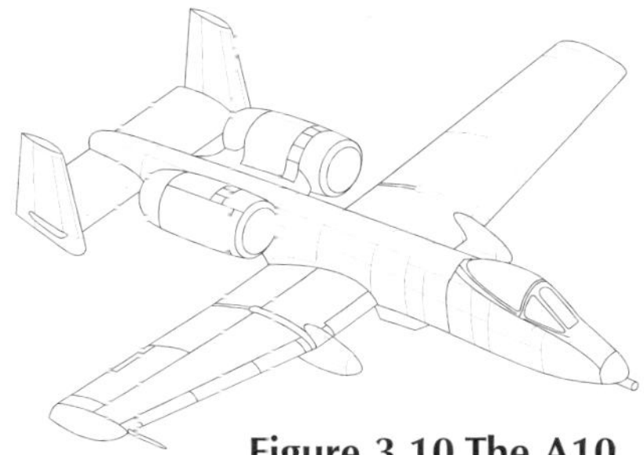

Figure 3.10 The A10

transport aircraft. These examples operated at just below the speed of sound but the need, particularly by the military, to operate in and beyond the transonic region (Mach no. greater than about 0.8) led to shapes which were predetermined by aerodynamic considerations rather than artistic ones and generally had a more angular appearance with jagged edges. Even some of the subsonic cases have obviously been designed for effectiveness rather than to please the eye. The A-10 (Fig. 3.10) is lethally efficient for close air support but not a great crowd-puller in appearance. The two enormous engine pods are mounted well above the plane of the wings to give a minimum infrared signature from the ground. The F117 "stealth" fighter (Fig. 3.11) also presents a minimal radar signature to an enemy and the complicated geometry needed to achieve that has resulted in a shape which looks as if it ought to be of interest to a lepidopterist.

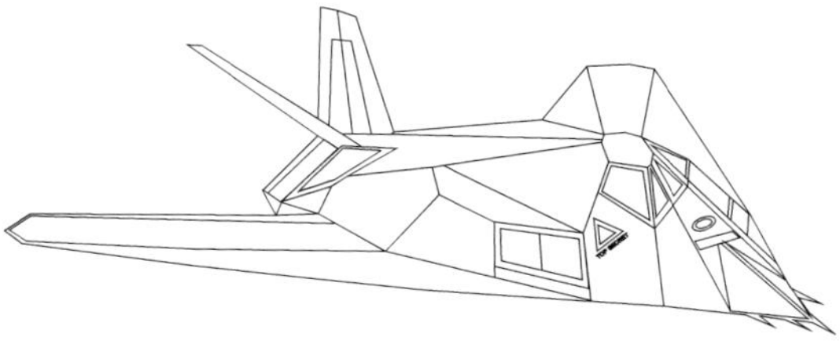

Figure 3.11 The F117

4

The Atmosphere

A lot of hot air about pressures and densities

THE ATMOSPHERE can act as friend and foe. In the former guise, it is the medium in which all aircraft have to fly and without its molecules of nitrogen and oxygen there could be no lift force. Of equal importance, the far smaller constituent of the atmosphere, water, can act as a terrible adversity if in its liquid form (rain or clouds), causing severely reduced visibility, or in its solid form (ice), causing not only a weight increase but even changing the shape of an aircraft, usually not for the better. Even its temperature has a direct influence on performance because as air gets hotter, its density (mass per unit volume) decreases and take-off and landing runs become longer, disastrously so in extreme cases. It's therefore worth having a closer look at the atmosphere and this chapter will also enable us to define some of the terms involved.

Temperature

In atmospheric terms, temperature is simply a measure of the internal energy level of the air; in other words, the violence with which molecules are jumping about. This can be increased by adding heat energy which, in the case of the atmosphere, would normally be either by contact with, or convection from, the ground (thermals) or by direct heating from the sun. However, air is a poor thermal conductor so it's not surprising that temperature decreases as we climb away from the ground. The rate at which it drops is called the lapse rate and this varies somewhat with position on the Earth's surface so, for calculation and comparison purposes, we need a standard and this is called the International Standard Atmosphere (ISA). Under this system, the lapse rate λ (Greek letter lambda) is taken to be -0.00651 K/m (degrees Kelvin per metre). The Kelvin is a temperature scale starting at absolute zero (that is, no thermal energy at all) but has the same graduations as the more familiar Celsius one and on that basis absolute zero corresponds to about -273°C. Even Siberian Airways captains wouldn't experience temperatures like that so it is better to stay with the Celsius scale, although we shall need to return to the Kelvin scale when dealing with temperature **ratios**. Also, pilots are familiar with altitudes quoted in feet so the lapse rate is better expressed as -1.98°C/1000 ft, or more conveniently -2°C/1000 ft.

This lapse rate is taken to be independent of the temperature at sea level so that if, on a given day, the temperatures in London and Edinburgh are respectively 15°C and 10°C, then at 5000 ft above those cities the temperatures will have dropped to about 5°C and zero; that is, each has dropped by the same 10°. In practice, the ISA assumes a temperature of 15°C at sea level so that a hot day at 30°C would be referred to as an "ISA+15 day".

If the lapse rate did not vary at all, atmospheric temperature would reach zero K at about 144000 ft, but at altitudes greater than about 11 km (36080 ft) the value becomes more or less constant at -56.5°C until at about 21 km it starts to rise again to about -2.5°C at 50 km. The protection which the atmosphere gives us at ground level no longer applies in its upper reaches.

Fig. 4.1 shows the temperature profile as a graph; the plot for lower altitudes is a straight line because the lapse rate has been taken as constant. The region below 36000 ft is known as the troposphere and that above as the stratosphere. The junction is called the tropopause and this is exactly where most gas turbine-powered aircraft on flights of more than a few hundred miles would cruise. Air conditioning systems must therefore be able to keep passengers and crew comfortable under these appalling external conditions; we shall see in the following sections that the pressure and density are very low too.

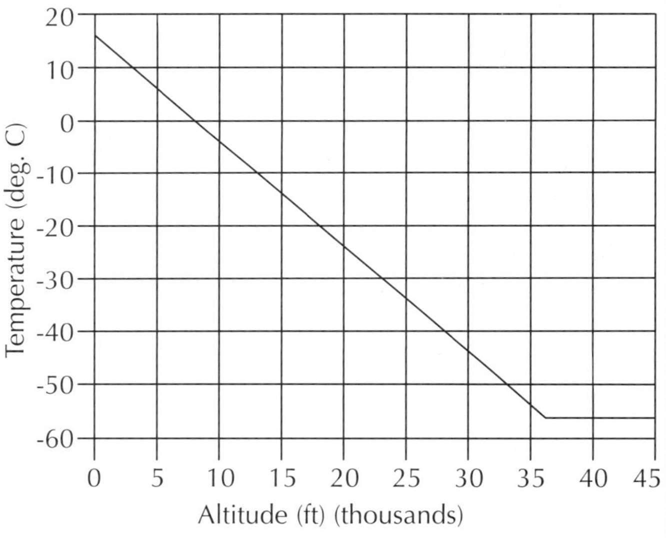

Figure 4.1 ISA temperatures

Pressure

The pressure of a gas is also a measure of its energy level, although here we are concerned with the force that it can exert on an object placed in it. Following on from the definitions in Chapter 2, if we consider the air contained within a closed box, it is easy to imagine the force produced on a side of that box by all the air molecules bashing against it. The total of all those collisions would vary from moment to moment but, under normal conditions, there would be so many molecules in the box that we would experience a time-averaged value. If the total force on one side is divided by the area of that side, we have the concept of pressure, measured in newtons per square metre (N/m^2) or, more commonly, pascals (Pa). If the box is assumed to be very small, then we approach the concept of pressure at a point. If the box is replaced by a piston and cylinder, and the piston is gradually pushed into the cylinder, the pressure will obviously increase because the same number of molecules is now bashing against a reduced surface area and there is a concomitant increase in gas temperature.

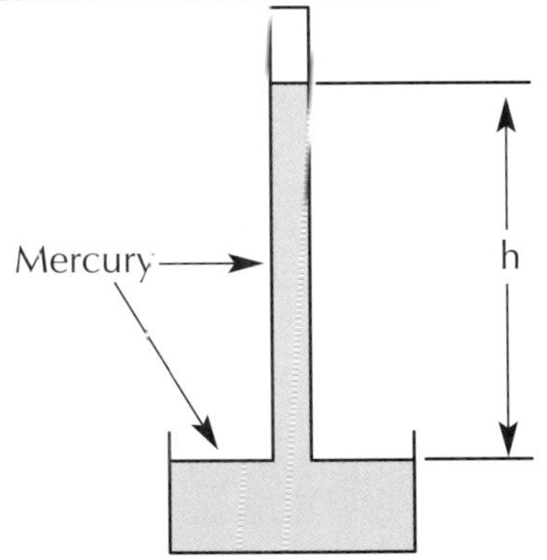

Figure 4.2 The Mercury barometer

Atmospheric pressure at sea level is caused by the weight of air above and therefore we must expect this value to decrease as we climb, because there is proportionately less air above us. The best way to measure the pressure in the atmosphere is to invert a glass tube, sealed at one end and full of mercury, in a bowl of the same fluid (see Fig. 4.2). The mercury in the tube will fall until the atmospheric pressure on the bowl fluid just supports the weight of the mercury column inside. The region in the tube just above the mercury will contain only mercury vapour molecules and will be at a pressure very close to zero (vacuum). The height h of the column will vary from day to day, but an average taken over a year would be 760 mm (29.92 in.). It can easily be shown that the pressure p at a point in a fluid is equal to the height h of the column above it times the density of the fluid ρ (Greek letter rho) times the gravitational acceleration g ($9.81\ m/s^2$):

$$p = h\rho g \qquad \textbf{Eqn. 4.1}$$

The density of mercury is about 13590 kg/m^3, so at sea level the pressure is about 101300 Pa (0.76 x 13590 x 9.81). A pascal is a very small unit of pressure so engineers and scientists find it more convenient to work in terms of something 100000 times bigger and this is called a bar. Meteorologists and aviators prefer to get rid of any decimal places and deal with four-figure numbers, so they use a unit of only 100 Pa called a millibar, because it is then one thousandth of a bar. Sometimes, especially in the USA, the millibar is also called a hectopascal (hPa).

1 atm = 1.013 bar = 1013 mbar = 1013 hPa

In an aircraft it is clearly inconvenient (and dangerous) to carry an inverted tube of mercury so pressures are measured in an altimeter using the expansion of a hollow metal capsule, sealed at ground level during manufacture, but that is more relevant to a book on instruments. However, even this must be calibrated against a standard mercury column before use.

With increasing altitude, pressure decreases, not just because there is less air above but also because the temperature and density are both decreasing. This means that we can't expect a convenient straight line graph for pressure against altitude, as we had with temperature, and Fig. 4.3 shows the curve involved. At sea level, the slope of this graph is such that

pressure falls at about 1 mbar for every 30 ft of altitude

and this convenient rule of thumb is generally accurate enough up to 10000 ft. For higher altitudes, most pilots would resort to tables or the rather more approximate method involved in using the circular slide rule on the back of the Dalton-type navigation computer ("whizz wheel"). Tabulated values for the ISA are given in Appendix 1 at the end of this chapter, from which it can be seen that at 4000 ft atmospheric pressure has already dropped to 86% of its sea level value and to only 74% at 8000 ft. This latter figure is the value to which most air conditioning systems set the "cabin altitude" when cruising at 36000 ft, for example, so the implications for passengers with breathing difficulties are obvious.

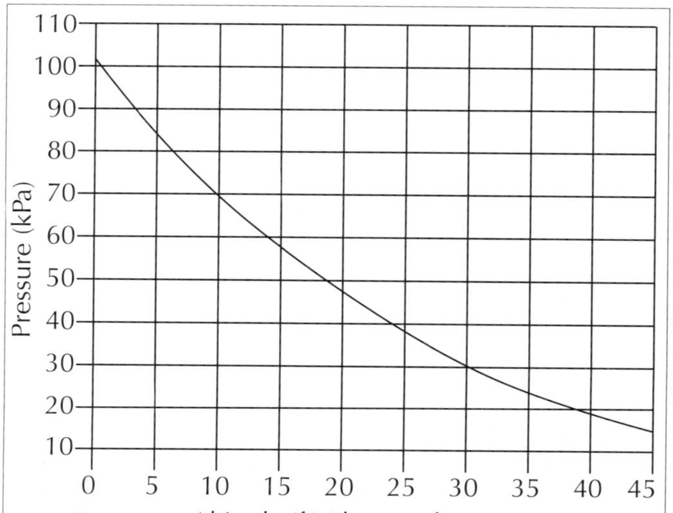

Figure 4.3 ISA pressures

It is often better to work in terms of non-dimensional ratios, such as the pressure p divided by its value at sea level p_{SL}, and some of the columns in Appendix 1 have been shown in this format. The pressure ratio p/p_{SL} can fairly easily be shown to be equal to the temperature ratio T/T_{SL} raised to the power 5.256:

$$\frac{p}{p_{SL}} = \left[\frac{T}{T_{SL}}\right]^{5.256} \qquad \textit{Eqn. 4.2}$$

This equation has been used to produce the pressure ratio column and is easy to use with a scientific calculator, provided it has an x^y key. A spreadsheet is even better! It should be noted that we are dealing with ratios here so the temperatures must be in Kelvin (i.e. absolute) units since the Celsius scale is simply a convenient arbitrary scale based on the freezing and boiling points of water. To avoid working out the temperatures first, the following equations in terms of altitude h might be found more useful:

$$p/p_{SL} = (1 - 0.02256h)^{5.256}$$ **where h is in km**

$$p/p_{SL} = (1 - 0.006878h)^{5.256}$$ **where h is in thousands of feet.**

The pressure ratio p/p_{SL} is usually denoted by δ (Greek letter delta).

Density

The mass of a fluid divided by the volume of its container is its density (see Chapter 2), usually denoted by ρ (Greek letter rho). If the fluid is a gas and heat is applied to the container, the latter will expand (assuming that it can) against its surroundings and the gas density will decrease (same mass, larger volume). If the container cannot expand, the pressure will rise (same mass but more internal energy) but the density will be unchanged (same mass, same volume). There is therefore a link between pressure, temperature and density, usually called Boyle's Law or Charles' Law in school Physics, but also known as the Equation of State:

$$p = \rho RT \qquad \textbf{Eqn. 4.3}$$

Use of this equation relies on all the quantities being expressed in the same unit system, so p must be in pascals, T in degrees Kelvin and ρ in kg/m^3. The term R, known as the gas constant, will then be in J/kg.K and its value will depend on the gas in question. For air, it has a value of 287 so we now have the means of calculating air density for any given temperature and pressure.

Example: What is the density of air at airfield level if the temperature is 15°C and the pressure is 1013 mbar?

Solution: T = 15 + 273 = 288 K
p = 1013 mbar = 101300 Pa
R = 287 J/kg.K

so, from eqn. (4.3), $\rho = p/RT = 101300/(287 \times 288) = 1.2256\ kg/m^3$

For those who think that air is a very light or thin substance, it may come as a surprise that a cubic metre of it contains as much as 1.22 kg or 2.7 lb. However, we rely on this property to gain lift and many pilots know that, at high altitude where the density is much lower, an aircraft's stalling speed can approach its cruise speed, especially in tight turns!

Since the equation for ρ contains p (which varies as T to the power 5.256 [Eqn. 4.2]) divided by T (to the power 1), we must expect density to fall with altitude as T to the power 4.256; values are once again shown in Appendix 1. The density ratio ρ/ρ_{SL} is a very useful term in performance calculations and is usually denoted by σ (Greek sigma). The square root of σ is often even more useful, so that also is shown in the table.

QFE and QNH

Now that we have seen how temperature, pressure and density vary in the atmosphere, it's important to look at some of the consequences. Perhaps most important of all is the setting of the altimeter. Atmospheric pressure at an airfield varies from day to day because of meteorological changes, so it would be pointless to have an altimeter in an aircraft calibrated only for a given pressure. If a depression passes over and the pressure falls, the instrument might indicate to the pilot that he is at a height of a few hundred feet when the pilot can see perfectly well that he is sitting on the apron. He therefore needs an adjusting knob to reset the instrument needle to zero. The tiny subscale attached to the adjustment knob will then show the local atmospheric pressure in mbar and this is always called **QFE**. Contrariwise, of course, on the ground you can always use an altimeter to show you the local atmospheric pressure by simply setting the needle to zero.

When flying away from an airfield, it is essential to know the sea level pressure so that local high ground can be cleared and so that all aircraft in the same region and at the same altitude have the same value shown on their instruments. This pressure setting is called **QNH** and is advised regionally by air traffic controllers. Above a specified altitude, which varies locally to some extent, even the regional QNH value is superseded by an international setting of 1013 mbar so that aircraft on international flights are all using the same reference value. The extreme importance of using the correct QNH for the current altimeter setting region (ASR) is evident when considering an aircraft flying from one region to another, where the regional QNH is much lower; that is, the pilot is heading for the centre of an atmospheric depression. **If the local sea level pressure is much lower than the value set on the altimeter, that instrument will be indicating an artificially high altitude** and this already dangerous situation could be made worse if the pilot is, in addition, heading towards rising ground!

A pilot approaching another airfield with QNH set on his altimeter will need the local controller to give him a QFE value so that, when in sight of the new airfield, he can set the instrument to show height above the ground, not altitude above sea level. Unless the airfield is below sea level, **the QFE will always be lower than the QNH** and the pilot will need to **"wind off" millibars to show a lower altimeter reading.** In the case of an airfield at 600 ft, for example, this reduction would be as much as 20 mbar.

Pressure Altitude

If an aircraft has 1013 mbar set on its altimeter subscale then the altitude shown by that instrument is called the **pressure altitude.** This introduces the interesting concept of negative pressure altitudes since, on a day when atmospheric pressure is high, an aircraft sitting on the ground at sea level with 1013 set on its altimeter instead of the (higher) correct value will show a negative height above the ground. If atmospheric pressure at sea level drops to only 1003 mbar, an altimeter with 1013 set on it would show about 300 ft, the ISA altitude at which the pressure would be 1003 mbar.

Example: An aircraft sits on the ground at an airfield 120 ft above mean sea level (AMSL). What is its pressure altitude if regional QNH is (a) 983 mbar?
(b) 1033 mbar?

Solution: (a) QNH is sea level value so at sea level the pressure altitude will be (1013-983) x 30 = 900 ft. The airfield is therefore at (900+120) = 1020 ft pressure alt.

(b) Pressure alt. = (1013-1033) x 30 = (-20) x 30 = -600 ft so the airfield will be at (-600+120) = -480 ft pressure alt.

Density Altitude

Altimeters work on pressures so that commonality of pressure settings is particularly important in avoiding collisions with obstacles or other aircraft. But when it comes to aircraft **performance** we need another relative term - the **density altitude.** Engine performance depends on the mass of air being ingested, so pistons or compressors drawing in less dense air will be handling a lower mass flow for the same speed of entry, since

Mass flow = (velocity) x (density) x (cross-sectional area of flow)

If the temperature at a given altitude is higher than it would be under ISA conditions, then atmospheric density will be lower, so an aircraft flying there would be drawing in air less dense than the pilot might have expected. In other words, the aircraft's performance in terms of lift, drag, thrust, fuel consumption, etc. will be as if it were at higher altitude. A good rule of thumb is:

A 1° (C or K) rise in temperature is equivalent to being at 120 ft higher altitude

so that, on an ISA+10 day, an aircraft on an airfield at 600 ft AMSL will perform as if at 600 + (10 x 120) or 1800 ft and is said to have a density altitude of 1800 ft. On very hot days at high altitude airfields, this can make a very big difference to take-off performance; that is, much longer take-off runs.

Example: Check the validity of this rule of thumb with the equations we now have for variations with altitude.

Solution: As stated previously, the ratio of density to that at sea level will fall as temperature to the power 4.256.

$$(\rho/\rho_{SL}) = (T/T_{SL})^{4.256}$$

But the temperature ratio is falling as [1 - 0.006878h] where h is in thousands of feet or [1 - (6.878 x 10^{-6})h] when h is in feet. A one degree rise in temperature from 288 K (15°C) to 289 is an increase of 1/288 or 0.00347, about 0.35%. We therefore need to find the value of h in the equation

$$[1 - (6.878 \times 10^{-6})h]^{4.256} = 1 - 0.00347$$

and this is 118.6 or about 120 ft. [Mathematical note for readers (!): the above equation can be solved using the so-called binomial theorem that, for small x, $(1 - x)^n$ is approximately equal to (1 - nx)].

The effects of density on indicated airspeed

It will be shown later that all the aerodynamic forces on an aircraft in flight are proportional to air density, so increasing altitudes also imply decreasing lift and drag and therefore increasing stalling speeds. This has the knock-on effect that instruments relying on pressure differences, such as the ASI, will also show a reduction. Once again, there is a good rule of thumb, up to at least 10000 ft:

True airspeed > Rectified airspeed by about 2% for every 1000 ft climbed

The difference between rectified and indicated airspeeds will be dealt with in a subsequent chapter but the pilot or navigator should note that they are always travelling faster than their ASI shows by an amount determined by the above rule.

At least as important is the result that the aircraft will have to travel faster to build up the same force differences as at sea level. However, since the ASI is subject to the same pressure differences as the aircraft itself, it is not difficult to see that it will always stall at the same **indicated** airspeed. As mentioned earlier, the other side of this coin is that, as altitude increases, the **true** airspeed at stall is approaching the cruise speed and in aircraft designed for very high altitudes, such as the U2, the two can differ (at altitude) by as little as 10 kn!

Conclusions

This chapter has been rather peppered with numerical data and equations but it's worth extracting a few basic rules from it to remember:

1. The change in altimeter setting **from QNH to QFE** will always involve **"winding off millibars" to a lower setting,** unless the airfield in question is below sea level.

2. When flying **towards a low pressure zone**, an unadjusted altimeter will always

indicate **an artificially high altitude.**

3. **Hot days** and **high airfields** will individually lead to **lowered air density**, resulting in noticeably **poorer aircraft performance.** Taken together, they can lead to surprisingly **lengthened take-off runs.**

4. True airspeed will always be **greater** than indicated airspeed by an amount dependent on altitude. One result of this is that at extreme altitude, **indicated stalling and cruise speeds can approach each other rather closely.** On the other hand, an aircraft will **always stall at the same indicated airspeed,** irrespective of altitude.

APPENDIX
International Standard Atmosphere
(Approximate values)

Altitude (ft)	(m)	Temp. (dec.C)	Temp. (K)	Temp. ratio (theta)	Pressure (kPa)	Pressure ratio (delta)	Density (kg/m^3)	Density ratio (sigma)	Root sigma
0	0	15	288.16	1.0000	101.33	1.0000	1.2256	1.0000	1.0000
1000	305	13.0	286.18	0.9931	97.72	0.9644	1.1901	0.9711	0.9854
2000	610	11.0	284.20	0.9862	94.21	0.9298	1.1554	0.9428	0.9710
3000	915	9.0	282.21	0.9794	90.81	0.8962	1.1215	0.9151	0.9566
4000	1220	7.1	280.23	0.9725	87.51	0.8636	1.0884	0.8881	0.9424
5000	1524	5.1	278.25	0.9656	84.30	0.8320	1.0560	0.8616	0.9282
6000	1829	3.1	276.27	0.9587	81.20	0.8013	1.0244	0.8358	0.9142
7000	2134	1.1	274.29	0.9519	87.18	0.7716	0.9935	0.8106	0.9003
8000	2439	-0.9	272.31	0.9450	75.26	0.7427	0.9633	0.7860	0.8865
9000	2744	-2.9	270.32	0.9381	72.42	0.7148	0.9338	0.7619	0.8729
10000	3049	-4.8	268.34	0.9312	69.68	0.6876	0.9050	0.7384	0.8593
15000	4573	-14.8	258.43	0.8968	57.17	0.5643	0.7711	0.6292	0.7932
20000	6098	-24.7	248.53	0.8625	46.55	0.4595	0.6529	0.5327	0.7299
25000	7622	-34.6	238.62	0.8281	37.59	0.3710	0.5491	0.4480	0.6693
30000	9146	-44.5	228.71	0.7937	30.08	0.2969	0.4584	0.3740	0.6116
35000	10671	-54.5	218.80	0.7593	23.83	0.2352	0.3797	0.3098	0.5566
36080	11000	-56.5	216.15	0.7501	22.35	0.2206	0.3605	0.2941	0.5423
40000	12195	-56.5	216.15	0.7501	18.83	0.1858	0.3028	0.2471	0.4971
45000	13720	-56.5	216.15	0.7501	14.81	0.1462	0.2384	0.1945	0.4410

Exercises - Chapter 4

In these questions, use may be made of any available equations or rules of thumb. If required, a check can be made afterwards against the calculator side of a Dalton computer.

For air, R = 287 J/kg.K

1. On an "ISA + 10" day, what will the temperature be at 6000 ft?
2. On a day when temperature is ISA + 15 and pressure at sea level is 1030 mbar, what will the air density be at (a) sea level (b) 3000 ft?
3. If the pressure at sea level is 1020 mbar, at what altitude is it likely to have dropped to 995 mbar?
4. A pilot has regional QNH of 1024 mbar set on his altimeter and is approaching an airfield where the air traffic controller has advised him that QFE is 1009 mbar. What is the airfield's altitude AMSL?
5. An aircraft is on the ground at an airfield 420 ft AMSL. Regional QNH is advised as 995 mbar. What is the aircraft's pressure altitude?
6. On a day when regional QNH is 986 mbar, a jet aircraft is directed to fly at FL60 (6000 ft with 1013 mbar altimeter setting). A nearby Cessna 150 has an altimeter reading of 5200 ft at the correct QNH setting. What is the vertical separation between these two aircraft?
7. An aircraft is flying at a pressure altitude of 5000 ft with an outside air temperature of 20°C. Calculate its density altitude.

5

Basic Fluid Flows

How do we generate forces in air?

THE IDEA THAT an object moving in a fluid has forces exerted upon it is not difficult to grasp. Even at low wind speeds, a cyclist is very aware of the extra effort needed to cycle against the wind rather than with it, while at the opposite end of the danger scale the driver of a high-sided vehicle knows only too well the risks involved in crossing the Severn Bridge in severe crosswinds. The maximising of forces beneficial to flight (lift) and the minimising of those restraining it (drag) are amongst the subjects dealt with in the next few chapters and we can approach this topic best by using the concept of a streamline.

Flow Between Streamlines

The word "streamlined" is in common use to describe a shape which would easily cut through a fluid to cause minimum drag force due to motion. It's easy to see how the art of streamlining aircraft has developed by looking at the difference between the aircraft used in the First World War and those transporting passengers around today. However, it does have a scientific definition, based on the idea that a streamline is everywhere parallel to the local fluid velocities. One obvious result of that definition is that there can never be any flow across a streamline so that two adjacent ones always have a fixed amount of flow between them; that is, a fixed "volumetric flow rate" in m^3/s or ft^3/s. This means that if the streamlines converge, the fluid must accelerate because the product of speed and area must remain constant. If there is also a density change, then this must also be accounted for and it would be more correct to say that the mass flow rate between two streamlines should be constant; that is, the product of density ρ, area A and speed V. The units are then kg/s or lbm/s.

$$\dot{m} = \rho AV \qquad \textit{Eqn. 5.1}$$

The dot over the m indicates that this is a **rate** of mass flow. If the mass flow rate and density stay constant in the above equation, velocity will therefore be inversely proportional to area so, referring to Fig. 5.1, if a flow of velocity V_1 at Station 1 passes through a restriction at station 2, its velocity will increase to V_1A_1/A_2. These

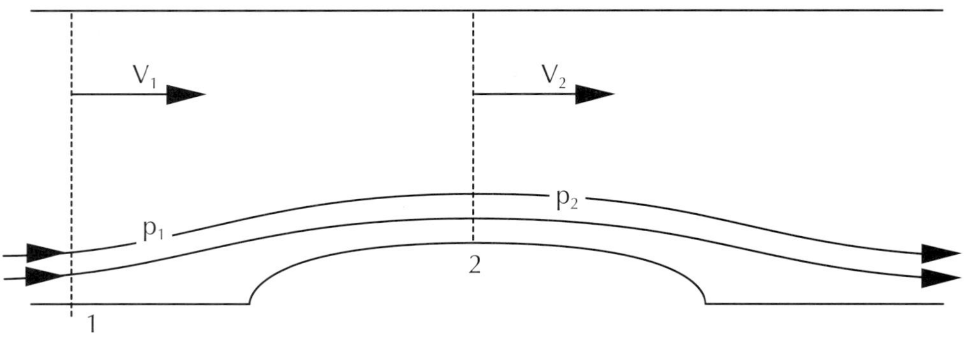

Figure 5.1 Effect of a constriction on a flow

are, in practice, average values over the flow cross-section; the speeds close to the curved surface will be higher than that.

Bernoulli's Equation

There is a tendency to think that if the fluid is being squeezed into a smaller area, its pressure might increase as well as its speed but, in fact, the opposite happens and the pressure falls, not in proportion to speed but to $(\text{speed})^2$. The relationship between the two was first set down by the Swiss mathematician Daniel Bernoulli and one of the most famous equations in aerodynamics bears his name:

$$p_1 + \tfrac{1}{2}\rho\, V_1^2 = p_2 + \tfrac{1}{2}\rho\, V_2^2 = constant \qquad Eqn.\ 5.2$$

In this equation, p is the so-called static pressure, V the speed of the fluid and ρ the fluid density. The suffices 1 and 2 refer to any identifiable points in the flow so 1, for example, could represent the area well ahead of an aircraft and then p_1 would be atmospheric pressure at that altitude and V would be the true airspeed. Position 2 could be any other point around the aircraft and the pressure and velocity there would then be given by the above equation. "Constant" means exactly what it says so if V increases in eqn. 5.2 then p must decrease to maintain the constant. This really expresses the idea that an increase in speed (i.e. kinetic energy) can be achieved only with the loss of pressure energy so that their sum remains constant. The shape in Fig. 5.1 causing the restriction can be seen to resemble the top surface of a wing so, replacing the upper wall by the Earth's atmosphere, it's obvious that a fast-moving aircraft could generate a suction above its wings simply due to this curvature. We saw in a previous chapter that at sea level the density of air is about 1.2 kg/m^3 so an air speed of 100 m/s (about 194 kn) would produce a value of $\tfrac{1}{2}\rho V^2$ of 6000 Pa (= 0.5 x 1.2 x 100 x 100) or about 0.9 lb/in^2. If this pressure is multiplied by the wing area of (for example) a Boeing 747 (511 m^2, 5500 ft^2) a lift force of 312 tonnes (713000 lb) is generated, a major fraction of the take-off weight of a 747!

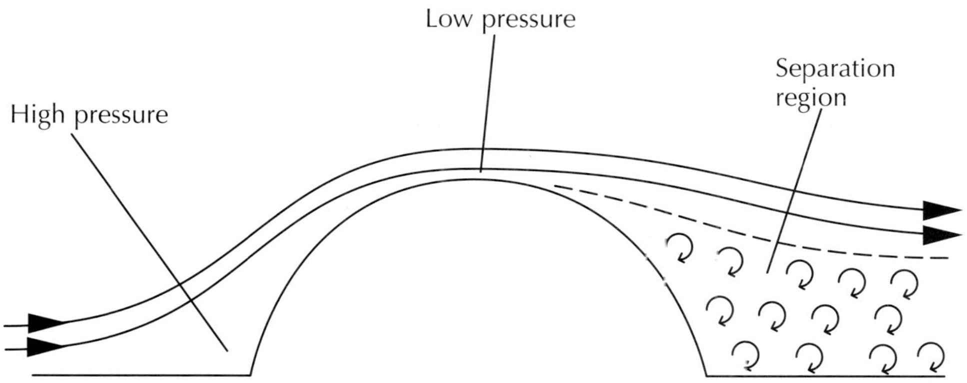

Figure 5.2 Bluff body produces separation

If the curvature of the raised area becomes too great (see Fig. 5.2), the difference between the high and low pressures becomes even greater and some serious changes to the flow develop. Bernoulli's equation says that an increase of pressure will result in a slowing down of the fluid so the air will decelerate after leaving the low pressure zone on the top. In most cases, it will slow down to a standstill and then leave the surface altogether, giving a large area of low energy air downstream of the object. This is like the area behind a large, blunt bus which used to be so beloved by small boys on bikes. The bus drags along a large volume of stagnant air behind it, enabling anyone in that region to benefit from almost zero relative wind speed. However, the benefit to the cyclist also appears as a deficit for the bus, since its engine is having to work harder to drag along the air.

We must therefore differentiate between shapes which are blunt (in aerodynamics terms), with a large volume of separated flow behind them, and those which produce a minimum of disturbance to the air, so-called streamlined shapes. The difference between the two in terms of engine power needed to achieve a given speed is very marked and the gradual development of aircraft shapes from bluff to very slippery is quite clear from Figs. 3.1 and 3.2, the Wright biplane and the X-29. We shall return to this subject in the chapter on drag, including some calculations to show how much worse some shapes are than others.

Different Types of Pressure

The term $\frac{1}{2}\rho V^2$ is therefore not to be sniffed at and will crop up time and again in this subject. Because it is so important, it is given its own name "dynamic pressure", the first word arising from the fact that it obviously has zero value at zero airspeed. By the same token, the term p is called the "static pressure" because it is the value which would be registered at a tiny hole in the surface, pointing sideways to the flow and receiving none of the ram effect of the moving fluid. The sum of static and dynamic pressures is called the total (or stagnation) pressure and is the value which would be registered by a tube pointing straight into the oncoming flow ("ram pressure").

Total pressure = static pressure + dynamic pressure

Clearly, the numerical difference between total and static pressures can be used to gain an idea of how fast an aircraft is moving and Fig. 5.3 shows a device familiar to all pilots (the Pitot-static tube) which consists of two concentric tubes, the outer one closed at the upstream end. The central tube brings the oncoming airflow to rest and therefore registers the total pressure p_0, whereas the outer tube has small holes bored in its surface, about six diameters back from the nose. These register the static pressure p and both p_0 and p can be fed to an airspeed indicator (ASI). This essentially employs an aneroid capsule (bellows: total pressure to the inside, static to the outside surface) to deflect a needle around a dial, giving us the basic idea behind an airspeed indicator. The static pressure line could also of course be tapped to provide a signal for another aneroid capsule in the cockpit, that in the altimeter, because the static pressure will fall with altitude. However, this static pressure is usually sensed at a point on the side of the fuselage where the local airspeed has returned to the aircraft's true airspeed after being accelerated around the nose earlier in its travels. We shall return later to the point that increasing altitude involves decreasing air pressure and density since the term $\frac{1}{2}\rho V^2$ will obviously fall too as ρ decreases.

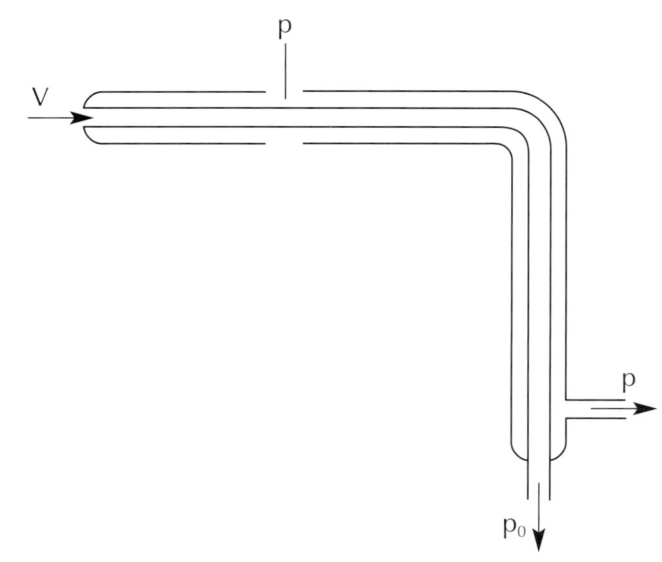

Figure 5.3 The Pitot-static tube

The term $\frac{1}{2}\rho V^2$ is also known as "q" in aerodynamicists' shorthand and, because it clearly depends on air density and $(TAS)^2$, q will determine how much force the pilot must use in executing a given manoeuvre at any given altitude and TAS. A pilot using powered controls has no "feedback" of what forces he in subjecting the airframe to, since changes are effected hydraulically or electrically, so "q-feel" has to be incorporated in these systems so that some measure of the aerodynamic forces involved is fed back to the control column.

The greatest pressure anywhere on an aircraft is going to be on its nose, or on any other surface pointing directly upstream. It makes no difference mathematically whether we consider an aircraft moving through air at a given speed or the air moving past the aircraft at the same speed; everything is relative, as Einstein pointed out. Using the second approach, we can see that total pressure is obtained at the stagnation point on the nose because the air is brought to rest there, relative to the aircraft. At every other point round the surface, the air velocity will result in a pressure lower than on the nose and if the air is accelerated sufficiently above the nominal speed of the aircraft, a suction will appear, relative to atmospheric pressure. All forward facing areas should therefore be rounded, to minimise the surface area over which the peak pressure applies and fuselages, nacelles and flying surfaces in general should be as slim and streamlined as possible.

A modern aircraft in cruise represents a very streamlined shape, but transition to a "dirty" configuration, with flaps, slats, lift dumpers and landing gear all deployed, is quite the opposite. Fortunately, this normally applies only during the approach and landing phase of a flight, when plenty of excess power is available so it is not worth, for example, streamlining the undercarriage if it is retractable. A fixed undercarriage is a different matter and the designer must decide whether streamlining would be worth the extra weight and cost. Apart from necessary fuel, every excess kilogramme has to be carried to the destination.

Wings, tailplanes and fins are normally slim and streamlined in cross-section but fuselages are not necessarily so and can contribute up to a third of the total drag of an aircraft. Simply making objects longer is not the answer because, as we shall see in the chapter on drag, a longer shape may gain from being less blunt but will at the same time have more "skin drag" because of its greater surface area. Also, in the case particularly of fuselages, a long rear end would cause severe scraping problems when flaring (rotating in pitch) on take-off or landing. The final shape of a fuselage is therefore always a compromise; the designer has to maximise the volume whilst minimising the bluntness and surface area - not an easy job!

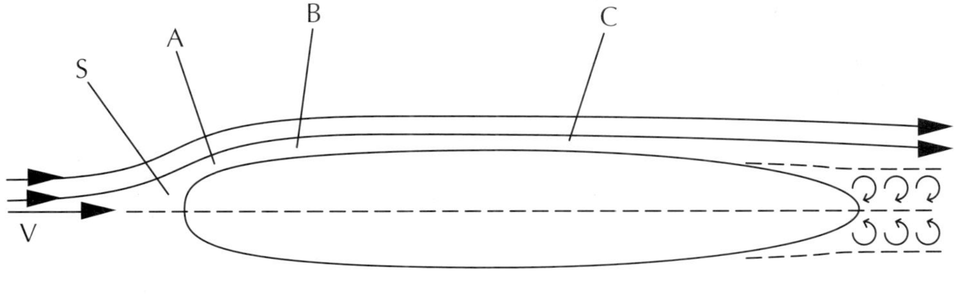

Figure 5.4 Flow about a streamlined object

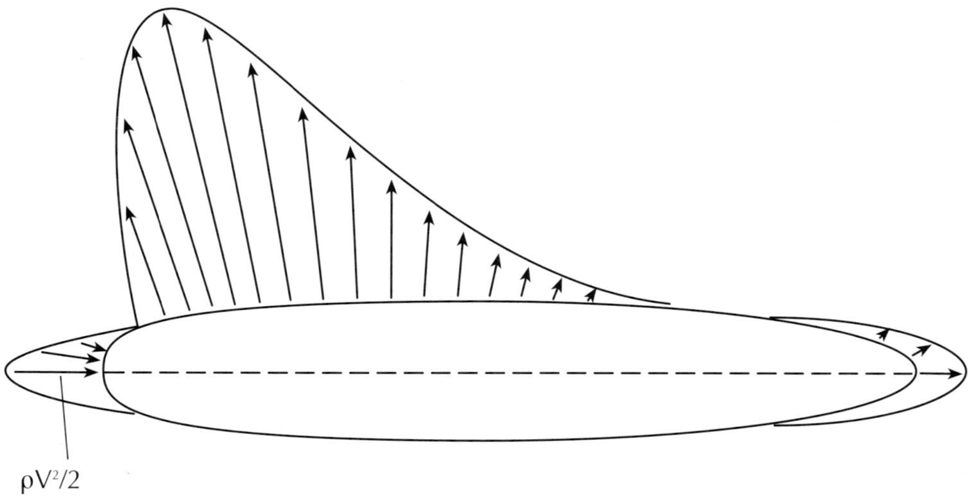

Figure 5.5 Pressures about a streamlined object

From all the above considerations, we can make some general comments about flow round a typical streamlined shape, such as a modern fuselage (see Fig. 5.4). Relative to the object, the air is brought to rest on the nose, producing a stagnation point S and the highest pressure anywhere on the object. In theory, this pressure will be $\frac{1}{2}\rho V^2$ above the surrounding atmospheric value and this is also achieved in practice. The air then accelerates around the curved nose, reaching "free-stream" speed at about point A. Since it now has a speed equal to the stream, it must be at the same pressure as the surroundings (Bernoulli). It continues to accelerate to its maximum speed at about point B so the pressure here must be below the atmospheric value. In fact, it could be two or three times the magnitude of $\frac{1}{2}\rho V^2$ below atmospheric pressure - quite a severe suction. Because the air is now encountering the parallel side of the fuselage, its speed begins to return to the free-stream value and probably does so by about point C, so the pressure here must have returned to atmospheric again. Downstream of point C, a complicated process takes place whereby the air has to negotiate the curved rear end of the fuselage and return to free-stream conditions aft of the aircraft. Fig. 5.5 shows a typical pressure plot around one side of the object, with the length of the arrows indicating the pressure level, positive or suction.

An obvious place to mount a Pitot-static tube would be at A since the local airspeed there is the same as the aircraft's speed and many aircraft adopt this position. Some care is needed, however, because point A may well move as the fuselage pitches nose up or down, or yaws, so a compromise position is often needed, using wind tunnel or flight tests to find the best one. Light aircraft very often have the Pitot tube under the left wing, at a point where the airspeed is equal to the free-stream value. Once again, flight testing against a standard is needed and since both possible positions are compromises, a calibration chart is required to relate the speed indicated on the ASI to the rectified value. During flight testing of a prototype, a Pitot-static tube would be mounted on a sting, way out ahead of the aircraft's nose, to give a value unaffected by the presence of wings or fuselage. However, such a long addition to the fuselage would be inconvenient in normal operation.

The obvious place to sense local static (as opposed to dynamic) pressure would be at point C, where the hole bored in the side of the fuselage is essentially sensing the local free-stream value and this is the position adopted in many aircraft. The hole concerned is very often only about 2 mm in diameter so it is important to check these holes are unblocked when carrying out a pre-flight inspection.

Pressure Coefficients

Whenever they can, engineers like to express the value of anything in terms of a pure number, as opposed to a number with units after it. This is known as "non-dimensionalising" and the pressure distribution around an aircraft is a prime candidate for being treated in this way. If we look again at Figs. 5.4 and 5.5 and make point 2 in Bernoulli's equation the stagnation point on the nose and point 1 the approaching air at speed V, we can see that V_2 is going to be zero (stagnation point) so $(p_1 - p_2)$ is simply going to be equal to $½\rho V^2$, and $(p_1 - p_2)/½\rho V^2$ is therefore going to be 1. At point A, where the local air speed is equal to the atmospheric value, the pressure must also have returned to atmospheric value so $(p_1 - p_2)$ must be zero. No units are involved in the values of this ratio because both $(p_1 - p_2)$ and $½\rho V^2$ have the units of pressure and the units therefore cancel, so this means that we could go all the way round an object like a fuselage representing the local pressure levels as pure numbers. These numbers are called pressure coefficients:

Pressure coefficient C_p = (local pressure - atmospheric pressure)/$½\rho V^2$ Eqn. 5.3

On this basis, a stagnation point will always come out as 1, points A and C as zero and the value at B will be below zero. Values as low as -3 or -4 are not uncommon and the minus sign indicates a partial vacuum, since the air has been accelerated from a stagnation point to beyond the true airspeed of the aircraft.

Example: An aircraft is cruising at 250 kn at an altitude of 15000 ft, where the pressure and density are 57.17 kPa and 0.7711 kg/m^3 respectively. On the outside skin of the fuselage, just above the captain's head, a pressure coefficient of -1.4 is registered. Calculate the local static pressure there.

Solution: $V = 250$ kn $= 250 \times 0.5144 = 128.6$ m/s. $\rho = 0.7711$ kg/m^3

so $\frac{1}{2}\rho V^2 = 0.5 \times 0.7711 \times (128.6)^2 = 6376$ Pa $= 6.376$ kPa

therefore $p_{LOCAL} = p_{ATMOS} - (1.4 \times 6.376) = 57.17 - 8.93 =$ **48.24 kPa**

Conclusion

We have seen that the variation of pressure around an aircraft can be quite considerable, from a few thousand pascals above atmospheric to several times that in the suction direction and the sum of all these pressure forces and the various frictional (shearing) forces give an overall aerodynamic force on the aircraft. The sum of all the components parallel to the free-stream is the so-called profile drag and the sum of all those perpendicular to it is the lift; we shall look at these in more detail in the next two chapters.

Exercises - Chapter 5

Where temperatures, pressures or densities are not quoted, use the ISA values given in the Appendix to Chapter 4

1. An air conditioning duct in an aircraft carries air at a speed of 2.5 m/s. The duct is of 104 mm diam. cross-section. What is the volumetric flow rate?

2. If the same duct as in Q1 carries air of density 1.1 kg/m^3 at 1.2 m/s, what is the mass flow rate?

3. If the duct of Q2 subsequently reduces in diameter to 50 mm to pass through a bulkhead, what will be the new air speed in the duct, assuming no density changes?

4. A container has three pipes connected to it, all of diameter 12 mm. Pipe A contains a liquid of density 1030 kg/m^3 flowing towards the container at 2.4 m/s whereas Pipe B carries a liquid of density 850 kg/m^3 at 2 m/s away from the container. Calculate the mass flow rate in Pipe C and state whether it is moving towards or away from the container.
[Hint: total mass flow for the whole system must be zero]

5. An aircraft has a true airspeed of 180 kn in air of density 1.205 kg/m^3. Use Bernoulli's equation (Eqn. 5.2) to calculate the pressure difference between the two tubes from its Pitot-static head in (a) Pa (b) mmH_2O.

6. Repeat Q5 for an aircraft with TAS = 150 kn at 20000 ft.

7. An aircraft flying at sea level registers a pressure difference on its Pitot-static head of 6430 Pa. Calculate its TAS in knots.

8. An aircraft flying at 10000 ft registers a pressure difference on its Pitot-static head of 180 mmH_2O. Calculate its TAS in knots.

9. If an aircraft is flying at 240 kn TAS at 15000 ft, what excess (ram) pressure in mbar will it experience on its nose?

10. Wings create lift by accelerating air over their upper surfaces. At one point on the upper surface of the wing of an aircraft flying at 180 kn TAS at sea level the air is accelerated to 1.3 times the speed of the aircraft. Calculate the local static pressure at that point in mbar.

6

The Generation of Lift

Has mankind finally equalled the birds?

IF WE TAKE the curved surface of Fig. 5.1 and add a flat lower surface, we are beginning to obtain the shape of a wing section and an idea of how streamline flow might pass over such a shape is shown in Fig. 6.1. Even if the flat lower surface were parallel to the oncoming airstream, this shape would produce some lift because of the upper surface curvature. However, if the section is inclined nose upwards, it will produce even more lift because the streamline curvature over the top becomes even more intense. The narrowing of streamlines over the upper surface produces even more suction and the deflection of air on the lower surface, close to the stagnation point (where we have total pressure), produces an upthrust. The angle between the wing chord (the line joining the leading and trailing edges) and the oncoming air flow is called the angle of attack and usually carries the Greek letter alpha α. This should not be confused with the angle of incidence, which is the angle at which the wing is set on the fuselage. In cruising flight an aircraft's angle of attack might be 3 or 4°, to generate enough lift, but everyone on board would obviously be grateful if the fuselage floor were at zero angle relative to the horizon (especially cabin staff, who need to stagger along aisles with trolleys) so the wing is normally set at the cruise **angle of incidence** to the fuselage axis.

This shape, however, is not very useful for an aircraft wing because the pointed leading edge produces a flow separation there and much better results are obtained

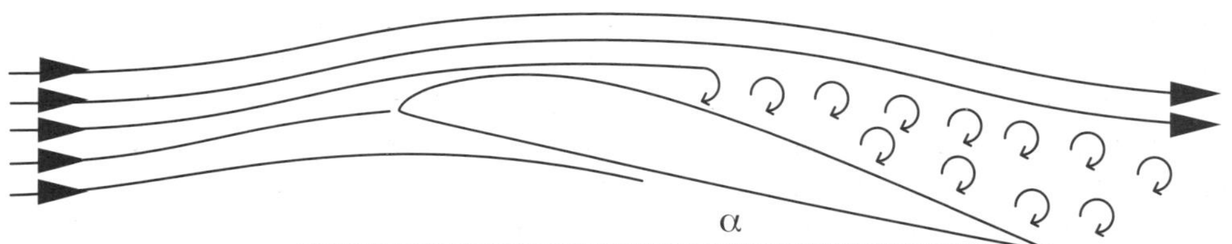

Figure 6.1 Flow over a curved surface at angle of attack α

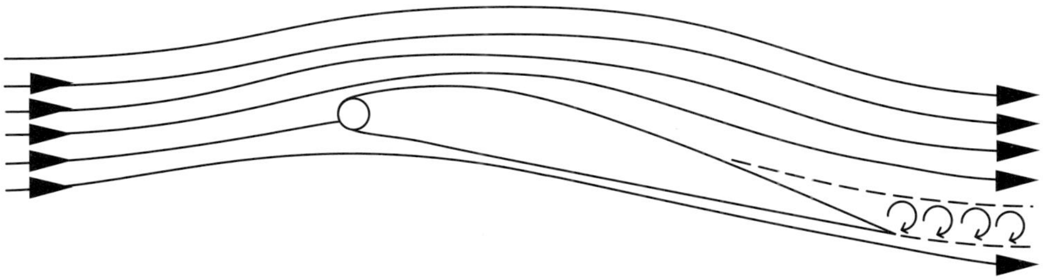

Figure 6.2 Flow over aerofoil section with circular leading edge

(certainly at air speeds well below the speed of sound) by having a leading edge which is basically a circular arc (Fig. 6.2). The stagnation point now moves to the lower side of the leading edge, leaving a very considerable suction over the upper side, because of the curvature, but now the flow over the upper surface adheres to the wing, probably most of the way to the trailing edge. Flow over the lower surface is deflected slightly downwards, producing a small positive pressure there, and emerges from the trailing edge with a small "downwash" component. The downwash has been produced by the wing and shows up (in the aerodynamic sense) as a lift force on the wing, giving a zero net force on the whole system of atmosphere plus wing.

Representing the pressure forces as arrows in the appropriate directions (and always perpendicular to the surface), we obtain the picture shown in Fig. 6.3[a] and the sum of all of them would be the resultant force R in Fig. 6.3[b]. This force can be split into two components, one perpendicular to the oncoming airstream (lift) and the other parallel to it (pressure drag). The *total* drag will also include some contributions from elsewhere; this will be dealt with in the chapter on drag.

The lift component will increase as α increases because the suction on the upper surface will become even more intense and it is a fact that until α reaches at least about 12°, a graph of lift against α is a straight line, while at higher angles something very disturbing happens to the flow over the wing's upper surface. Fig. 6.3[a] shows that although a severe suction applies over the forward upper surface, the pressure must increase again downstream of this so that it returns to atmospheric value near the trailing edge. We shall see in the chapter on drag that air close to the surface is slowed down by viscosity so that a "boundary layer" of slower moving air always surrounds a moving object. The slower air is decelerated even more by the increasing pressures (remember Bernoulli?) over the upper surface and eventually the flow separates from the surface, resulting in a massive area of disturbed flow and a concomitant massive reduction in lift force. This is of course the well-known "stall" and recovery will always require a nose-down motion to pick up speed and return the angle of attack to much lower values. Not all of the

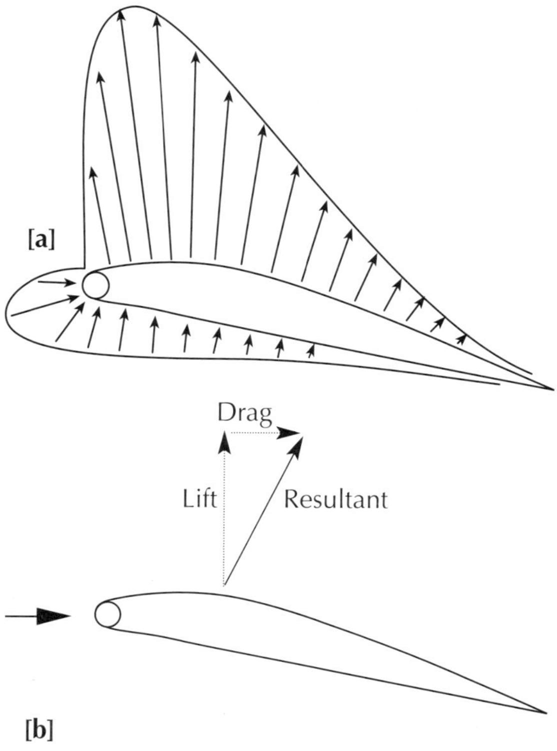

Figure 6.3 [a] Pressure distribution and [b] forces on an aerofoil section

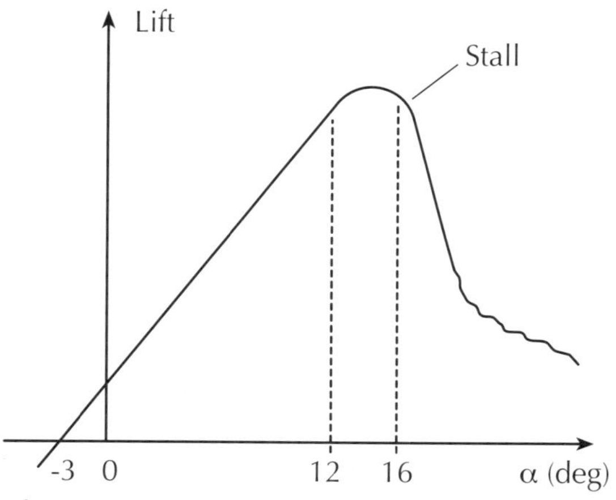

Figure 6.4 The effect of angle of attack on lift

lift is lost because there are still areas of the wing giving positive contributions to lift, even after a stall, and some stalls are in any case more forgiving than others, because of the way the wing has been designed. A graph of lift against α will therefore resemble that of Fig. 6.4 with the stall angle being at around 16 to 18°. The lift at $\alpha = 0$ is not zero (except on a symmetrical aerofoil) because, even at that angle, the upper surface curvature is generating some lift. Zero lift would be obtained at perhaps $\alpha = -2$ or -3°.

Nowadays, the thrust developed by some engines has become so huge that, particularly with smaller military aircraft, total thrust is a major fraction of the aircraft weight. In these circumstances, level flight can be maintained at angles of attack well above the stalling angle of the wings because the deficit in lift can be made up by the vertical component of engine thrust at such a high pitch angle above the horizon. This is known as "high alpha" flight and is being seriously studied because of its potential value in combat-style dog-fighting.

Camber and Thickness/Chord Ratio

In general, the lower surface of a wing will not be the flat surface shown in Fig. 6.2 and the addition of curvature to it will improve the lift. The total force on the wing will also be affected by the thickness of its cross-section,

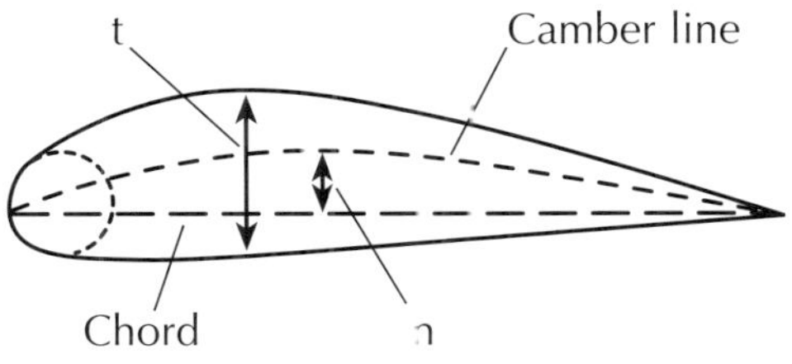

Figure 6.5 A high-lift wing section

although this effect will show up more as a drag change. These two geometrical variables can be defined from Fig. 6.5. The vertical distance from lower to upper surface is the thickness and its maximum value is usually at about 30 to 40% of the chord (0.3c – 0.4c) from the leading edge. The maximum value t divided by the wing chord c is called the thickness/chord ratio (t/c) and this can vary from about 5% in the case of the X-15 to 18% for heavy-lift or STOL aircraft, such as the DHC Dash 7.

If the locus of the mid-points of all these thickness verticals is drawn, we have a so-called camber line and the "camber" of the aerofoil is defined as the maximum distance h from this line to the chord divided by the chord c (h/c). Once again, this is a ratio and can vary from zero for a symmetrical aerofoil to about 4% for a high-lift one.

Wing sections can therefore be defined mainly by t/c and h/c. High-speed aircraft would tend to have low or zero camber and the minimum value of t/c ratio commensurate with structural strength. At high speeds, increased lift can be obtained simply by small increases in angle of attack; camber is unnecessary. Low-speed aircraft, on the other hand, are more likely to need some camber and this is where the 4% figure is more likely to apply.

In all cases, the point at which the lift appears to act (the "centre of lift") is around 0.25c from the leading edge (the so-called "quarter-chord point") and the value of α (in degrees) at which zero lift is obtained is very roughly equal to -(h/c) %; that is, a wing with 3% camber has a zero-lift angle of attack of about -3°.

Lift Coefficient C_L

This is a convenient point to introduce the dimensionless (i.e. pure number) version of lift called lift coefficient C_L, just as we did in the previous chapter for pressure. This approach can be used for most of the parameters involved in aircraft flight and has the advantage that performance can be assessed irrespective of which unit system (Imperial, S.I., etc.) is being used and independent of the size of the aircraft involved. The central idea is that if an aircraft had a wing which was suddenly doubled in area, we would expect it to produce twice the lift, assuming the pressures are unchanged. Equally, if it travelled twice as fast we would expect **four** times the lift (remember Bernoulli contains V^2, not V), and if it takes off from a very high airfield where air density is only 80% of sea level value, it can be expected to generate only 80% of the lift (Bernoulli again: $\frac{1}{2}\rho V^2$). This implies that if we divide lift by the product of wing area (S), the square of true airspeed and local air density, we ought to obtain a number ("lift coefficient") for that aircraft which varies only with α, since the pressures around the wing then change. In deference to Bernoulli, it is customary to insert the ½ too, so lift coefficient is defined as:

$$\text{Lift coefficient } C_L = \text{Lift}/\tfrac{1}{2}\rho\, V^2 S \qquad \text{Eqn.6.1}$$

The major advantage of this approach is that the performance of various wings can be compared, irrespective of their size or where they are being used and, in particular, a lift coefficient obtained by testing a model in a wind tunnel will apply to the (geometrically similar) full-scale version also, at the same angle of attack. This enables an accurate idea of stalling speed to be obtained before a prototype even makes its first flight, a very valuable piece of information for the test pilot! At the end of this chapter is a section dealing more generally with the question of "dynamic similarity" and the relationship of size, areas and weight.

It's worth a short diversion here to define wing area. An obvious value to use is the plan area of that part of the wing that's actually exposed to the air and this is called the net area. Alternatively, we could include the imagined part of the wing *inside the fuselage*; that is, the extra part obtained by producing the leading and trailing edge lines back to the fuselage centreline. This larger area is known as gross area and is the one normally used in aircraft calculations. It doesn't matter which we use so long as we stick to the same one and the S in Eqn. 6.1 is normally the gross wing area. The gross value will be used in the rest of this book, unless otherwise stated.

A plot of lift coefficient C_L against α for a typical wing section is shown in Fig. 6.6. This is obviously going to have the same shape as the curve in Fig. 6.4 but the vertical axis values now have no units; they are simply pure numbers. Before lift is lost, the value of C_L has climbed to about 1.5, so this represents the best that we can hope for from this particular wing section, in its "clean" state. It's worth pointing out how much better this is than simply using a flat plate at the same α; the latter would have produced a C_L value of only

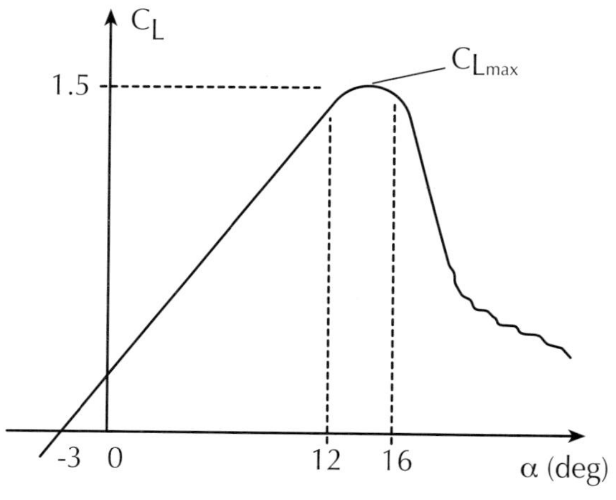

Figure 6.6 The effect of angle of attack on lift coefficient

about 0.7 and would have stalled at about 5°! Since, in cruising flight, weight must equal lift, we can modify Eqn. 6.1 to:

$$\text{Lift coefficient } C_L = Weight/\tfrac{1}{2}\rho\ V^2S \qquad \text{Eqn.6.2}$$

This means that if we can determine the maximum value of C_L (e.g. 1.5) from wind tunnel tests, then for any given weight W of the aircraft, we can calculate stalling speed from:

$$V_{stall} = \sqrt{(W/\tfrac{1}{2}\rho SC_{Lmax})} \qquad \text{Eqn.6.3}$$

This shows some very interesting relationships. Holding everything else constant, the stalling speed is proportional to the square root of weight, so an apparent doubling of weight (as in a 2g turn, for example) will increase the stalling speed by √2 or 1.414 (41.4%). Density, wing area and C_{Lmax} appear in the denominator so a **reduction** in stalling speed would result from an increase in those parameters. However, a **reduced** air density would equally result in an **increase** in stalling speed.

Lift Augmentation

Following the above reasoning, aircraft with small wings or those flying more slowly or at high airfields will therefore need to be flown at a higher angle of attack to maintain lift equal to weight. Conversely, since there is a maximum value to which α can be raised before a stall occurs, aircraft with small wing areas for their weight (e.g. the F104) will have very high stalling and approach speeds. The need has therefore developed over many decades for increasing the maximum value of C_L which can be obtained from a given wing and this has resulted in a considerable number of cunning devices, some of which can be found on almost any aircraft.

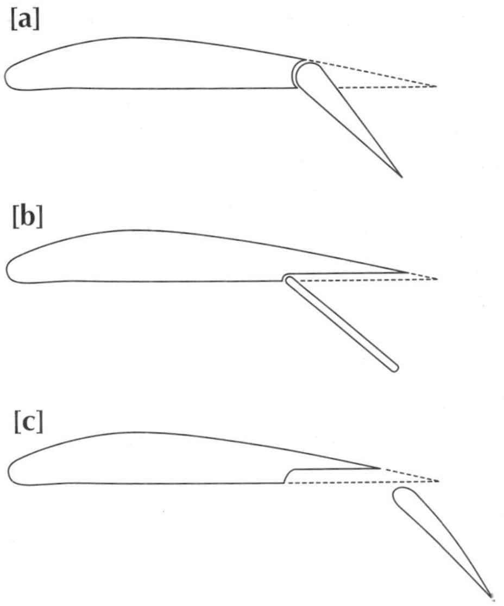

Figure 6.7 Types of flap: [a] Plain [b] Split [c] Fowler

Flaps

The simplest method of increasing C_{Lmax} is to use a hinged flap at the trailing edge of the wing (see Fig. 6.7). When deployed downwards, this effectively increases the value of α since the chord line, still joining leading to trailing edge, has been raised to a steeper inclination. There is a price to be paid, however, because the knee bend shape causes the flow over the upper surface to separate at the hinge position (Fig. 6.7[a]) so drag is increased. However, this is relatively unimportant during the approach phase, unless you are trying to glide into a field after an engine failure, in which case one should never deploy flaps until one is sure of reaching the field! A refinement is to make only the lower half inclinable (Fig. 6.7[b]) so that the upper surface flow remains undisturbed. Yet further improvement is obtainable by moving the flap backwards and downwards (Fig. 6.7[c]). These are known respectively as plain (or simple), split and Fowler flaps. The last example can, of course, be repeated to several levels, with the flap effectively having its own miniflap and so on. This type is almost universally used on modern airliners and has the very considerable additional advantage of increasing the wing's plan area so that S is increased, not just α and C_L. The effect on the C_L vs. α graph is marked (Fig. 6.8) and gives a usefully higher value of C_{Lmax} before stall. Flap deflection angle is controlled by the pilot; in a large aircraft, five or six different settings might be available while in a light aircraft there are normally only two, known as "lift flap" and "drag flap", or first and second stage.

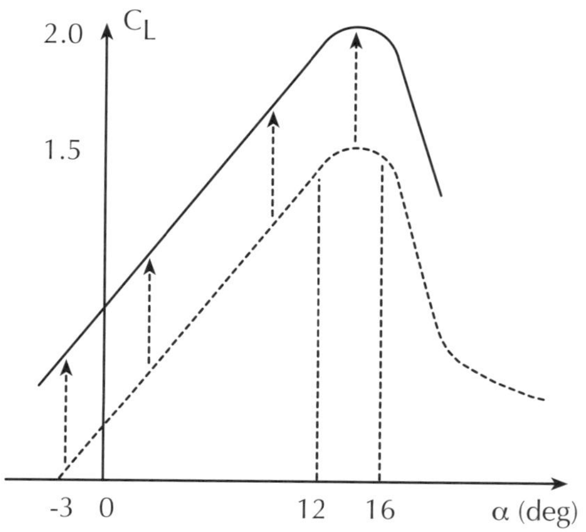

Figure 6.8 The effect of flap deflection on lift coefficient

Flap deployment therefore gives lower stalling speeds but with a sting in the tail: the increase in drag for a flap deployment of 60° is enormous. In fact, following a stall, the flaps (if deployed) should be retracted as soon as full power has been selected, but only as far as "lift flap", since the sudden retraction will reduce C_L, giving a higher stalling speed. Leaving drag flap in place will seriously delay acceleration back to a speed greater than V_{stall}. Fortunately, such flap deployment is normally in the latter stages of an approach, when drag is not an important issue. One advantage from such flap deployment (other than the lift increase) is that a more nose-down flight attitude results, giving much improved visibility on approach.

Slats and slots

Improvements are also available from modifications to the leading edge. When an aircraft is at high α and approaching a stall, the flow over the wing's upper surface can be improved considerably by an injection of higher speed air, at the surface and parallel to it, to rejuvenate the slack boundary layer fluid. Such a beneficial flow is

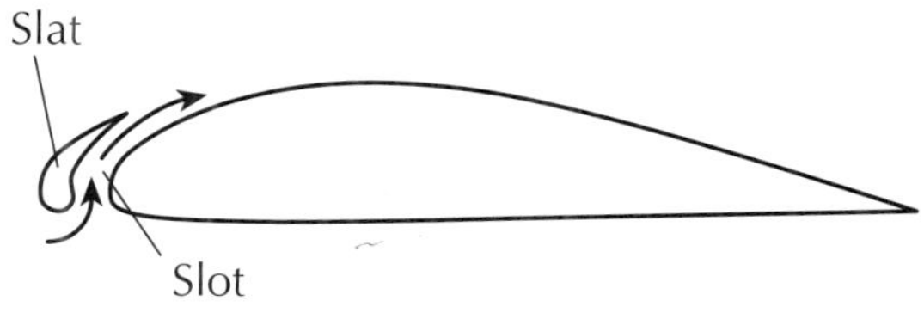

Figure 6.9 Leading edge devices - slats

available free of charge by opening up a canal between the high pressure air on the underside of the leading edge and the low pressure region on top (Fig. 6.9). The movable leading edge is called a slat and the gap is inevitably called a slot, and such devices are now common on most medium and large aircraft. Under normal flying conditions, the slat is retracted and becomes the leading edge once again. Their effect is additional to any C_{Lmax} improvement due to flaps and the combination of all these devices leads to useful reductions in landing speeds with the concomitant benefits of improved safety and lower undercarriage stresses and tyre wear. The extreme is reached with STOL (short take-off and landing) or carrier-based aircraft where even the flaps are "blown" to a high degree to obtain the maximum possible values of C_L.

The slope of the line on the C_L versus α graph (Fig. 6.8) is about 0.1 for every degree increase so at α = 12°, one would expect a C_L of about 1.5 (= 0.1[12-(-3)]). The improvements to be gained from using flaps and slats can be seen from some of the published C_{Lmax} figures. The SAAB 340 has a C_{Lmax} of 1.64 when the wing is "clean", 2.05 for take-off (i.e. partial extension) and 2.53 for landing (i.e. everything hanging out). The DC9, a long thin aircraft with relatively small wings, has flaps and slats good enough to give it a C_{Lmax} of 2.98 on landing, while the Boeing 737 manages a very impressive 3.10. Eqn. 6.3 shows that, if everything else is held constant, V_{Stall} is proportional to $1/\sqrt{C_{Lmax}}$. A doubling of C_{Lmax} from 1.5 to 3.0 would therefore bring down the stalling speed to $1/\sqrt{2}$ (= 71%) of its "clean" value. C_{Lmax} improvements have obviously been related to research advances. In 1903, the Wright brothers had available a C_{Lmax} of only about 1.3. Split flaps were developed in the mid-1930s and increased the figure to about 2.0. Fowler flaps emerged in the early 1940s giving about 2.3 and leading edge devices were added in the late 1950s, increasing the figure to about 3.0.

Angle of Attack at the Stall

Another very important point to make when considering the maximum lift available from a wing is that the stalling phenomenon is essentially a result of the wing shape being unable to hold on to the flow over the upper surface when the angle of attack becomes too high and the picture that one obtains with smoke traces in a wind tunnel at this moment is not dependent on how fast the air is travelling or the weight of the aircraft model being tested. A given **shape of wing** therefore always stalls at the **same angle of attack.** This useful result is used in the provision of small angle of attack vanes, sometimes just below the leading edge of the wing, sometimes on the side of the fuselage, but always useful in giving the pilot a warning of impending doom by sounding an audible alarm or, in more exotic aircraft, shaking or pushing the control column as the stalling angle is approached. Under the wing, they normally hang downwards under their own weight or are pushed into this orientation by the airstream hitting them. But when the angle of attack becomes high enough, the stagnation point moves across them and they are suddenly pushed in a forward or upward direction, thus activating an electrical signal.

Indicated and Equivalent Airspeeds

Yet another useful result from the aerodynamics of flight is that not only do aircraft always stall at the same angle of attack, they also always stall at the same **indicated airspeed** (**IAS**) appropriate to their weight at the time. This is yet another result from Bernoulli's equation (Eqn. 5.2). The dynamic pressure term $\frac{1}{2}\rho V^2$ is the driving force for the ASI's needle and, ignoring the ½ (because it's a constant) we can see that the instrument will respond to the term ρV^2, however it is generated. For example, if the density fell to ¼ of its value because of altitude, the same dynamic pressure could be generated by flying twice as fast, since V^2 is then four times its previous value. This affects not only the Pitot-static tube but the pressures over the whole aircraft so (for a given weight, etc.) it will always stall at the same value of ρV^2, irrespective of altitude. Looked at the other way round, it will always stall at the same **indicated airspeed.** The speed at which the aircraft is actually flying, the true airspeed (TAS), is of course higher than this since at altitude the ASI is registering an artificially low speed because the local air density is lower.

The difference between indicated and true airspeeds will be encountered again in Chapter 8, dealing with performance.

Geometrical and Dynamic Similarity

We have now used the same reasoning to reduce pressures and lift forces to dimensionless numbers (pressure and lift coefficients, respectively). But this approach can be used for a great many parameters in engineering and is based on the idea that scale model values for anything can be scaled up to full-scale ones, provided the model and the full-scale item are exactly the same **shape**, irrespective of size. This is known as "geometric similarity" and from this stems the idea that if you double the linear size of something, its surface area becomes four times (= 2^2) greater and its mass eight times (= 2^3) greater (assuming the same density for model and full-scale). "Dynamic similarity" is based on the idea that **forces** can also be scaled in this way and we have already seen this approach in action when using the lift coefficient of a model to estimate the lift force of a geometrically similar full-scale aircraft.

If most conventional aircraft are generally of the same shape, there ought to be a close relationship between their wing areas, weights and spans. Data for modern passenger aircraft are plotted in the final three figures of this chapter and are taken from published information for the Airbus family (A320 to A3XX), the Boeings (737 to 777) and some considerably lighter aircraft right down to the Beech King Air. Fig. 6.10 shows wing area plotted versus span and a clear relationship is evident from the mighty Antonov 225 at about 88 m span down to the King Air at 15.3 m. The graph is plotted on "log-log" scales because the ranges are considerable, but one of the advantages of so doing is that relationships of the form $y = x^n$ appear as straight lines of slope n. A line of slope two has been superimposed to show that wing area and $(\text{span})^2$ are indeed linked since the line passes close to many of the points.

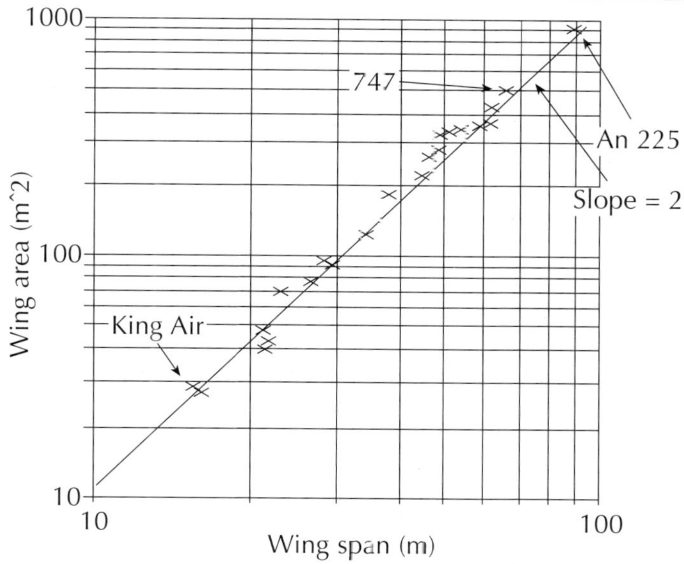

Figure 6.10 Correlation of wing area with span

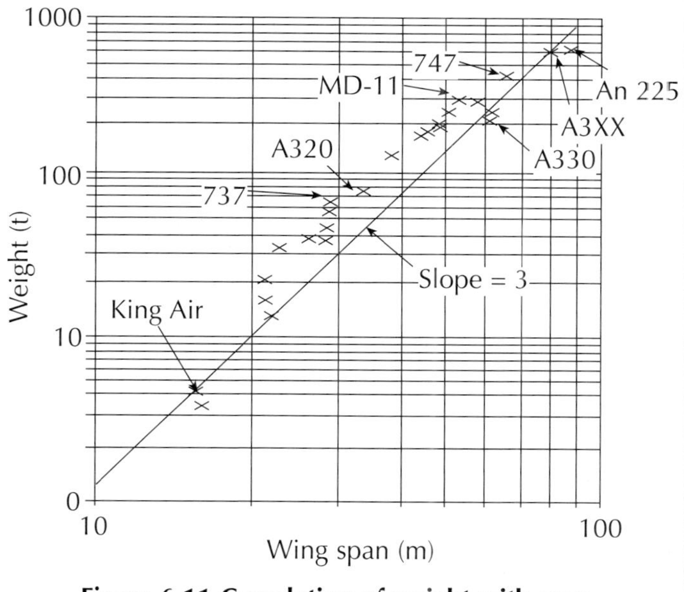

Figure 6.11 Correlation of weight with span

If the same procedure is used for weight, it can be seen from Fig. 6.11 that this is broadly proportional to $(\text{span})^3$. The way in which graph points deviate from the line is a measure of the fact that all aircraft are **not** the same shape; for example, the A340 fuselage is much more slender than that of the A320, in terms of diameter/length ratio. However, there is good agreement and if even smaller aircraft were added to the plot, they would probably not be too far off the trend line. At 9.14 m span, for example, the Piper Cherokee ought, according to the trend line, to have a weight of 0.99 t whereas its actual max take-off weight is nearer 1.1 t.

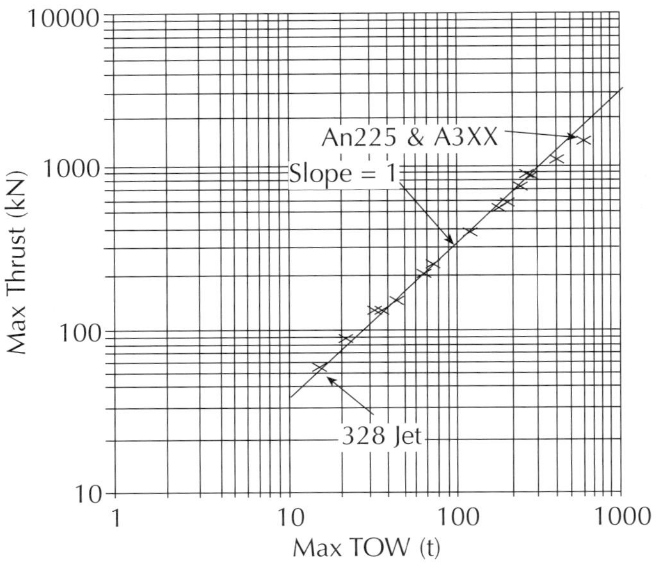

Figure 6.12 Correlation of total thrust with max takeoff weight

Looking now at imposed forces, Fig. 6.12 shows that **dynamic** similarity is also satisfied. A plot of maximum thrust for gas turbine-powered aircraft against max take-off weight is also a straight line, in this case with a slope of approximately one. A slightly better "best fit" would probably have been achieved with a slope of slightly less than one, since the very large aircraft are beginning to fall below the line, but the general trend is evident.

Since there is obviously a relationship between these variables, we could carry out a crude analysis to estimate the figures for, say, a future giant aircraft with a span of 100 m. Taking the largest one flying at the time of writing (an Antonov 225), having a span of 88.4 m, we calculate that the new span is going to be 100/88.4 (= 1.13) times as big, so the wing area is going to be about 1.13^2 (= 1.28) times that of the An 225 and the weight about 1.13^3 (= 1.45) heavier. This gives a likely wing area of about 1160 m^2 and a weight of about 870 t! As maximum thrust required has been shown to be in line with weight, it will need a total thrust of about 2000 kN (450 000 lbf). This is more than four times the thrust of the largest engines currently tested so five or six will be needed. In addition, the designer will need to deal with the problem of the current maximum wingspan of 80 m allowed by international airports for ground handling.

The data points of Fig. 6.12 generally conform to a straight line fairly well and there are good reasons why this should be so. Any aircraft seriously below the line would have an unacceptably long take-off run whereas one seriously above it would be uneconomic in the sense of being overpowered. Only a fraction of maximum thrust is used in the cruise condition and each engine would not only be heavier than it need be, but also operating at well off its ideal design condition.

Conclusion

The subtitle of this chapter asked whether mankind has yet equalled the birds and one would have to congratulate all those involved in getting somewhere near them. Wing design is a highly developed science and a suitable version can normally be produced for any given specification; the wings of birds have evolved over millions of years by Darwinian processes to give optimum performance for their own particular needs.

The most important conclusions from this chapter are that lift generally depends on angle of attack, air density, severity of camber, wing plan area and the square of true airspeed. Any given wing will generally stall at the same angle of attack (or maximum lift coefficient) but the actual stalling speed will depend on aircraft weight. Maximum C_L can be improved using flaps and slats to give a lower stalling speed.

Exercises - Chapter 6

Assume ISA conditions, unless otherwise stated, and use the atmosphere data in the appendix to Chapter 4

Reminder: 1 knot = 0.5144 m/s

1. Which type of aircraft is likely to have (a) greatest wing camber (b) lowest thickness/chord ratio? (i) Lockheed F104 (ii) A training glider (iii) Short Skyvan.

2. An aircraft in cruising condition at 250 kn.TAS increases its speed to 270 kn.TAS without changing its angle of attack. What percentage change in lift force will there be?

3. How fast must an aircraft fly at 25000 ft to generate the same lift at the same angle of attack as it could at 260 kn.TAS at sea level?

4. A Boeing 757 has a gross wing area of 185.25 m^2 and weighs 88 t. Calculate its lift coefficient if it is flying at a TAS of 310 kn (a) at sea level (b) at 10000 ft.

5. A commuter aircraft has a wing area of 41.8 m^2 and weighs 12 t. If wind tunnel tests have shown its maximum C_L values to be 1.6 (clean), 2.0 (take-off flap) and 2.6 (full flap), calculate its stalling speed at sea level for each of the three flap settings.

6. A twin-jet airliner has a weight of 48 t and wing area of 93 m^2. If wind tunnel tests have shown it to have a C_{Lmax} value of 2.9 at full flaps, calculate its approach speed (TAS) in landing condition ($V = 1.3V_{stall}$) (a) at sea level (b) at an airfield at 5000 ft AMSL.

7. A military aircraft has a weight of 51 t, wing area of 105 m^2 and C_{Lmax} in clean condition of 1.6. Calculate its stalling speed in a 1.6g banked turn at sea level.

8. A small commuter aircraft weighs 4 t, has a wing area of 27 m^2 and cruises at 240 kn.TAS at 10000 ft. If its lift coefficient is zero at $\alpha = -2°$ and 1.6 at $\alpha = 14°$, calculate its angle of attack in the cruise condition.

9. If the aircraft in Question 8 reduces its speed to 140 kn.TAS, by how much must the pilot change the angle of attack to maintain it in level flight?

10. A large airliner is being designed to have a maximum landing weight of 179 t and a C_{Lmax} at full flap of 2.5. Calculate what wing area is needed if it is to have a stalling speed at sea level of no higher than 120 kn.

7

Drag and its Effects

Something we'd prefer to be without

IN THE PREVIOUS CHAPTER, we looked at one of the four main forces acting on an aircraft (lift) and considered ways of maximising it. Here we look at another (drag) and consider how to minimise it. Drag is the force opposing the motion of an aircraft and in straight level flight at constant speed it exactly equates to the engine thrust. The force arises essentially because of the "viscosity" of air, its ability to resist a shearing action in adjacent layers. Even without quoting any numbers, it would be quite obvious to anyone that the viscosity of air is far less than that of water or sump oil. In fact, at 20°C, its viscosity is about 1/50th that of water and 1/12500th that of SAE30 oil. However, it is *not* zero and we have to live with the consequences. Ironically, we couldn't live without it anyway because it is impossible for a wing to generate lift in a fluid without viscosity, a so-called "inviscid fluid". By the same token, an axial flow jet engine could not operate in an inviscid fluid because it could not draw air into itself and compress it. Viscosity is therefore something we have to learn to love.

The drag force can be split essentially into three parts and we shall look at each separately. **Pressure drag** is caused by the fact that in any real fluid, the pressures do not cancel each other out all the way round the shape. In an inviscid fluid they would, but in a real fluid separations occur, leading to asymmetries of pressure. **Skin drag** is caused directly by viscosity and is the sum of all the frictional shearing forces on the skin of a body. **Induced drag** is caused by lift generation and is sometimes referred to as lift-dependent drag. It would be zero if an aircraft were generating no lift, but this does not happen very often.

Pressure Drag

Pressure or form drag is related to shape and is the one which would come to mind most readily when thinking of wind resistance. Logic suggests that blunt shapes ("bluff bodies") would be the worst offenders and that a flat plate held perpendicular to an airstream would be worst of all. This is very nearly true, although an even worse case is a cup shape with its open end facing the wind; that is, of course, why parachutes are so shaped. The open hemisphere produces about 20% more drag than a flat plate of the same frontal area and speed. If the hollow hemisphere is turned round the other way, a rather more streamlined shape is produced and drag drops to only about 35% of the flat plate value. The drag difference between these two extremes is very useful in producing the wind vane or anemometer which can be seen rotating on the roof of any A.T.C. building, with indicated wind speed dependent on the spin rate. The cups on each end of the instrument arm point in opposite directions (Fig. 7.1).

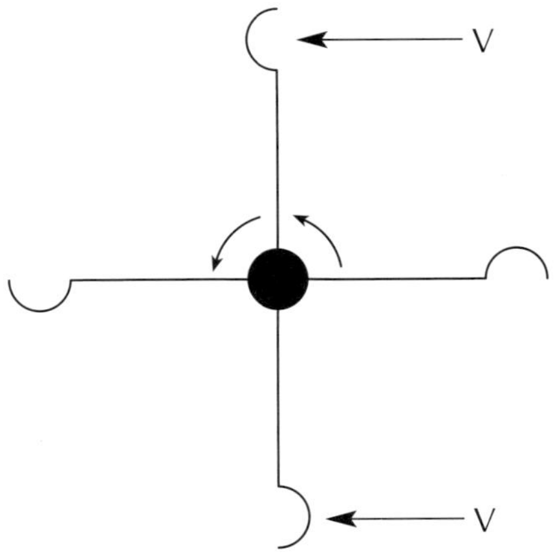

Figure 7.1 Wind anemometer

If two cups are combined to produce a sphere, the drag drops even further to only about 17% of the flat plate value, and if the sphere is elongated to produce a truly streamlined shape, like a dolphin or a drop tank, the drag falls to only about 7 or 8%. It would be tempting to elongate the shape even more, but then the drag will start to increase again because the surface area is increasing and a different form of drag (skin friction) is making its presence felt.

As with lift, it is equally easy to look at this problem in dimensionless terms so that we would have a drag coefficient (analogous to C_L), independent of size and speed, but dependent only on shape. If we consider the flat plate case (perpendicular to the airstream) again, the excess pressure on the front face will be very closely related to the dynamic pressure $\frac{1}{2}\rho V^2$ because the air has been brought to rest there, relatively speaking. Since force = (pressure) x (area), the drag would seem therefore to be proportional to $\frac{1}{2}\rho V^2 S$, where S is the frontal area of the plate. The drag coefficient for a bluff body is therefore defined in much the same way as lift coefficient, but using frontal area instead of wing area:

$$\textit{Drag coefficient } C_D = \frac{Drag}{\frac{1}{2}\rho V^2 S} \qquad \textit{Eqn. } 7.1$$

From the above reasoning, one might expect the value of C_D for a flat plate to be about 1; in fact, it's slightly greater at about 1.17 and the shapes mentioned above have values given in the table below.

Shape	C_D
Hemispherical cup ➔ ⊃	1.4
Hemispherical cup ➔ ⊂	0.4
Sphere	0.2
Elongated streamlined shape	0.09

As usual, the advantage of using C_D figures is that drag can then be evaluated for any size, speed and air density, provided C_D for that shape is known.

Example: Calculate the drag on a drop tank of diameter 400 mm (1.312 ft), mounted on an aircraft flying at 200 kn (103 m/s, 338 ft/s) at sea level if C_D for the drop tank is known to 0.09. Sea level air density is 1.225 kg/m^3 (0.00238 slug/ft^3).

(i) SI units: $\frac{1}{2}\rho V^2 = (103)^2 \times 1.225/2 = 6498$ Pa $S = \pi D^2/4 = 0.1257$ m^2
so drag = $0.09 \times 6498 \times 0.1257 = 73.5$ N

(ii) Imperial units: $\frac{1}{2}\rho V^2 = (338)^2 \times 0.00238/2 = 136$ lbf/ft^2 $S = 1.353$ ft^2
so drag = $0.09 \times 136 \times 1.353 = 16.5$ lbf = 73.5 N

There is a small amount of "rounding off" error in the above, but the answers are effectively the same and C_D is, in any case, independent of the units system used.

The designer must therefore attempt to use streamlined shapes in the construction of the aircraft, especially those parts which are permanently exposed to the airstream. In pressure drag terms, items like undercarriages and extended flaps are major drag producers but they are normally deployed only on approach, not in cruising flight.

Skin Drag

Just as the pressure forces around an aircraft have components at 180° to the line of flight, giving us form drag, so too do all the shearing forces caused by the viscous action of the air against the solid surfaces. The total of all these contributions is referred to as skin drag and to understand the nature of this, we need to look at a phenomenon called the boundary layer.

Boundary layers

No surface in engineering is perfectly smooth, although its smoothness can obviously be improved by vigorous polishing, so air molecules passing a solid surface and parallel to it will "stick" because they will be trapped in the minute surface imperfections. These molecules will, in turn, slow down the layers next to them, causing a layer of slower air next to the surface. This is called the boundary layer and if a plot is made of the speed of the air at each increment of height above the surface, a graph like Fig.

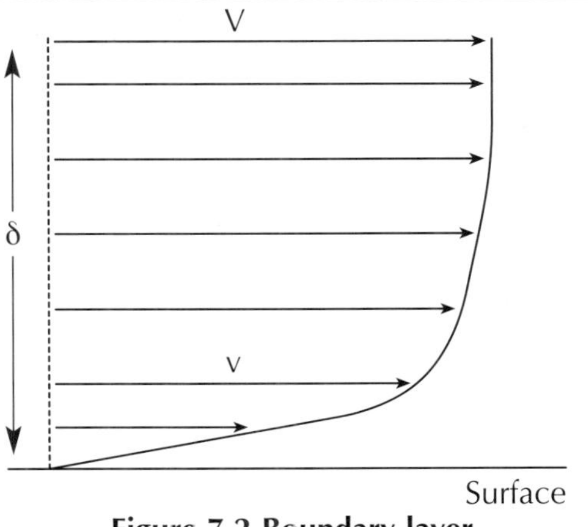

Figure 7.2 Boundary layer

7.2 is obtained. The speed v depends on how far the air is from the surface, but it gradually attains the free-stream speed V at the edge of the layer. In theory, the speed never reaches V but, in practice, the boundary layer thickness δ (Greek delta) is defined when v = 0.99V. This layer is very thin near the nose of any object but spreads with downstream passage. At the trailing edge of a wing, δ might have grown to a few cm while at the end of a very long object like a fuselage it may attain a value of tens of cm.

Engineers love dimensionless numbers and it's no surprise therefore that Fig. 7.2 is normally plotted in terms of v/V versus y/δ, where y is the vertical distance from the surface. Fig. 7.3 shows such a plot and also points to an important difference between the two types of boundary layer that aircraft encounter. When a boundary layer is in its initial stages close to the nose of an object, it demonstrates the properties of a "laminar" case, with each air layer sliding smoothly over the ones next to it. However, with downstream travel, the layers become unstable and mix violently with each other; this is known as turbulence. Because of this active mixing, the velocity profile is "fuller" than the laminar case, as shown in Fig. 7.3. In the laminar case, the slope of the graph in terms of speed against distance from the surface is less than for the turbulent one, so the shearing action at the surface is less severe and the frictional forces are therefore lower. The skin drag of an aircraft could therefore be minimised by maintaining a laminar layer for as long as possible and some aircraft exploit this with so-called laminar flow wings. This is as usual, however, a swings and roundabouts situation and there are some cons as well as pros. Most aircraft are lucky if they can maintain laminar flow for more than about 10% of the wing chord and the vast majority of boundary layers in aeronautics are turbulent ones.

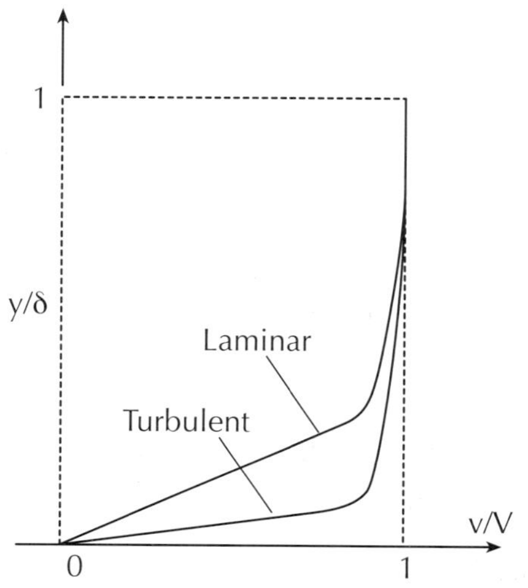

Figure 7.3 Laminar and turbulent boundary layer profiles (Non-dimensional plot)

Whether the cast off boundary layers at the rear of an aircraft are laminar or turbulent, they still give a low-energy wake, as with a bluff body's form drag, so any moves which can minimise shearing stresses or maintain laminar flow are welcome.

Calculation of skin drag

In assessing skin drag, we must for the moment ditch any ideas on frontal area and concentrate on surface or "wetted" area since even a wing with no thickness whatever (a structural disaster!) would exhibit skin drag to a marked degree. For a wing, with two wetted sides, a figure of twice the plan area would seem logical to use but because the wing must also have some thickness it would be more realistic to use:

$$\text{Wetted area} = 2.05 \times \text{Plan area}$$

and this rule would serve also for tailplane and fin. In the case of a long slender body like a fuselage, we must resort to a different rule. Most fuselages resemble a circular cylinder, with some sharpening at the nose and tail end, so we could use the surface area of a cylinder (ignoring its ends) as a starting point. The surface area of a cylinder of diameter D and length L is πDL, so an average fuselage would have a value slightly less than that. A review of many fuselages would probably produce an average figure of:

$$\text{Surface area of fuselage} = 0.8\pi DL$$

that is, 20% less than the surrounding cylinder. A well designed (or Darwinian evolved) shape like a shark might get the figure down to as low as 0.65.

We need now to express this in non-dimensional terms, as we did with lift and form drag. The defining equation is roughly the same, but the coefficient C_F is rather more difficult to put a number to. Therefore

$$\textit{Skin drag coefficient } C_F = \frac{\textit{Skin drag}}{\frac{1}{2}\rho\, V^2 S} \qquad \textit{Eqn. 7.2}$$

where S is now the wetted area. In the case of pressure drag, we could usually put a figure on C_D for any given shape, but C_F also depends on airspeed and size; in particular, on the ratio of inertia to viscous forces acting on the aircraft. This ratio is known as Reynolds number and is one of the most important parameters in aerodynamics. It is denoted by "Re" and defined by $Re = VL/\nu$ where V is the speed of the object, L its length and ν the (kinematic) viscosity of air. ν is a very small number, about 1.5×10^{-5} m²/s for air at 20°C at sea level and about 4.35×10^{-5} at 36000 ft. Therefore VL/ν represents about 67000VL at sea level and about 23000VL at 36000 ft.

The point of introducing Reynolds number is that C_F depends on it. In fact, the equation is:

$$\mathbf{C_F = 0.059 - 0.012[\log Re] + 0.00063[\log Re]^2} \qquad \textbf{Eqn. 7.3}$$

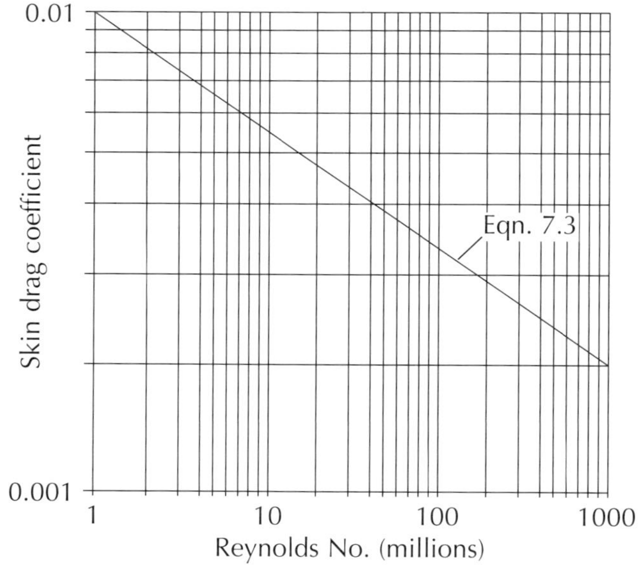

Figure 7.4 Skin friction coefficient for typical aircraft surfaces

where [log Re] means the logarithm to base 10 of Reynolds number. This equation is plotted in Fig. 7.4 and applies to surfaces which one would encounter on an aircraft. A very highly polished surface would produce a lower value of C_F; an average aircraft skin will clearly suffer from a few bad joins and more than a few dead flies.

Using Eqn. 7.3 to determine C_F, the skin drag caused by a flat plate is found from

$$\text{Skin drag} = C_F.\tfrac{1}{2}\rho V^2 S$$

where S is the total wetted area.

Form factors

Clearly, no wings or bodies could ever be regarded as plates of zero thickness and real ones will always have a "form factor" greater than 1.0; that is, they need a further multiplier to allow for their thickness causing some element, however small, of form drag. This factor is usually denoted by λ (Greek lambda) and obviously depends on how thick the object is compared to its length. For wings, tails and fins, λ is based on thickness/chord ratio (t/c) whereas for

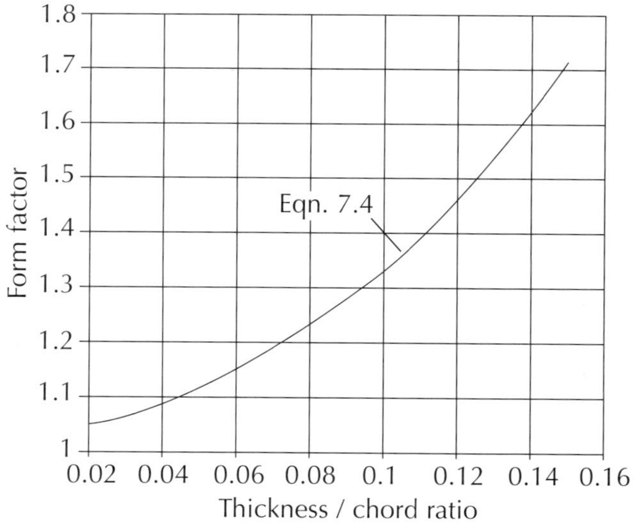

Figure 7.5 Form factors for wings, tails and fins

fuselages, it is based on length to diameter ratio L/D. The following equations are accurate enough for use here and are plotted out in Figs. 7.5 and 7.6:

Wings, tails, fins, etc: $\lambda = 1.028 + 0.11(t/c) + 29.7(t/c)^2$ **Eqn. 7.4**

Fuselages, etc: $\lambda = 1.78 - 0.118(L/D) + 0.0048(L/D)^2$ **Eqn. 7.5**

Example: Let's calculate the drag of the fuselage of a modern jet airliner at 200 knots (103 m/s). Its length is 37.5 m and its diameter 3.95 m, so L/D = 9.5. At sea level, air density is 1.225 kg/m^3. We can do this in two ways:

(i) Use the skin drag coefficient, the surface area and a form factor, or

(ii) Use the pressure drag coefficient and frontal area.

Case (i): $\frac{1}{2}\rho V^2 = 6498$ Pa $0.8\pi DL = 372.3$ m^2 $Re = VL/\nu = 259 \times 10^6$ so [log Re] = 8.413

C_F can be found from Eqn. 7.3 and is 0.00263
λ for the fuselage can be found from Eqn. 7.5 and is 1.092

so **drag** = $C_F\lambda 1/2\rho V^2 S = 0.00263 \times 1.092 \times 6498 \times 372.3 =$ **6948 N**

Case (ii) Frontal area = $\pi D^2/4 = 12.25$ m^2 Assume $C_D = 0.09$

then **drag** = $C_D\frac{1}{2}\rho V^2 S = 0.09 \times 6498 \times 12.25 =$ **7166 N**

Case (ii) gives a drag figure about 3% above Case (i); this is quite a close agreement since the assumed C_D for Case (ii) is only an approximate value.

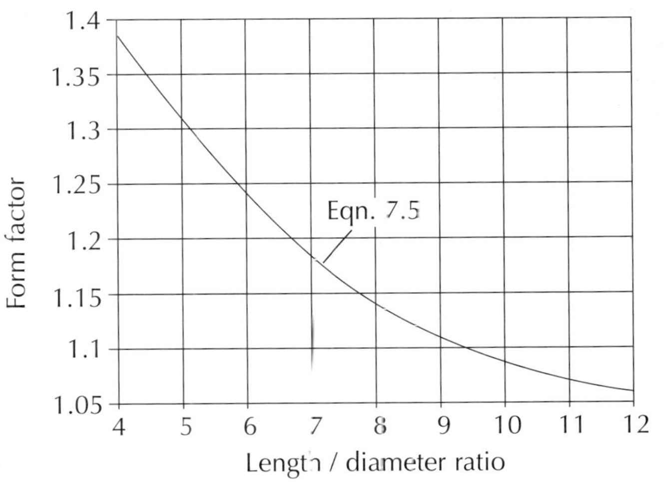

Figure 7.6 Form factors for fuselages

Profile Drag

We have seen that any object travelling in a fluid is subject to a drag force and that this is composed of two elements: pressure (or form) drag is caused by the asymmetry of pressures around the object and skin drag by the viscous shearing action along the surfaces. The sum of these two contributions is called profile drag.

Profile drag = Pressure drag + Skin drag

For bluff bodies, most of the drag will be pressure drag; for streamlined objects, most will be skin drag. Sometimes, this total will be called **parasite drag**, however, this term will be avoided here as it is not precisely defined and agreed. Two or three decades ago, the term parasite drag was applied as an addition to allow for "parasites"; that is, anything not allowed for in the straightforward calculation of profile drag, such as rivet heads, minor protuberances, aerials, etc. There is, however, an additional term called **"interference"** which must also be added on to give a realistic total for profile drag. This arises from the secondary flows which can be encountered from (for example) adding a wing to a fuselage. The wing and fuselage each has its own boundary layer and these will encounter each other at the wing/fuselage junction. The result will be an even thicker boundary layer and this can sometimes precipitate a premature separation of the flow over the rear end of the fuselage. The total drag is then found to be greater than the sum of the two individual parts and, for a whole aircraft, this term can amount to as much as 10 or 15% of the uncorrected profile drag. Adverse effects can sometimes be minimised by incorporating a fillet at the wing's trailing edge.

Induced Drag

We now come to the part of the total drag of an aircraft which is entirely due to lift. Profile drag is sometimes referred to as lift-independent drag to distinguish it from the lift-dependent **induced drag.** To understand this component, we must look in more detail at how an object produces lift in the first place. Even a symmetrical object like a golf ball can produce lift (in the sense of a sideways force) simply by having spin imparted to it. A good golfer can use this result deliberately to give the ball a curved flight for avoiding inconveniently placed trees etc, while a rotten golfer can also experience this phenomenon involuntarily by producing a massive slice.

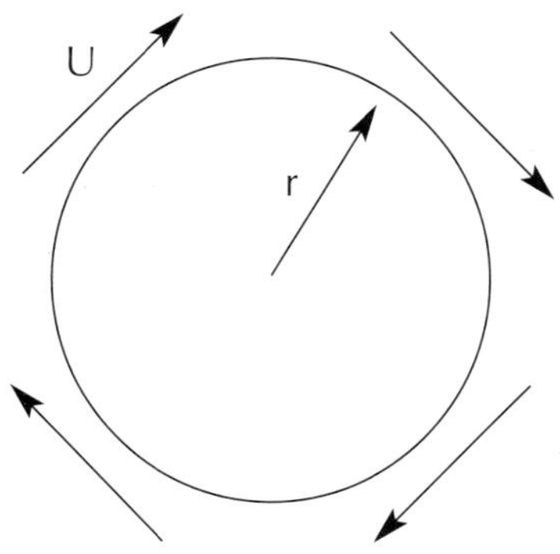

Figure 7.7 Circulation around an object

The secret is in a parameter called "circulation". This has an exact mathematical definition but for our purposes it is the sum of all the contributions of (velocity) x (distance) around a closed path. Referring to Fig. 7.7, if a circular object of radius r has fluid

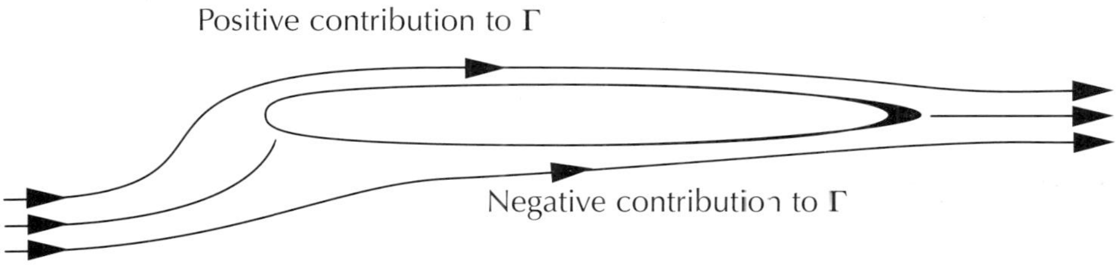

Figure 7.8 Contributions to circulation around a wing section

surrounding it with tangential speed U, then the circulation Γ (Greek gamma) is given by

$$\Gamma = \text{sum of all } [(\text{velocity}) \times (\text{distance})] \text{ contributions} = 2\pi rU$$

Moreover, it can be shown that a sideways force equal to ρVΓ (per metre into the page) is developed if the body moves at speed V in a fluid of density ρ. This is called "Magnus effect" and is familiar also to spin bowlers in cricket who can produce a swerving motion by spinning the ball. Swing can also be imparted by using the seam and by shining up one side of the ball to produce an asymmetry of pressures by having laminar and turbulent boundary layers on opposite sides of the ball.

If we now look at flow around a wing section at positive angle of attack (Fig. 7.8), we can see that, looking at the problem in circulation terms, lift is being produced by the circulation over the upper surface (clockwise = positive) being greater than that over the lower surface (anti-clockwise = negative). Looked at another way, if the aircraft is flying at 300 kn TAS and producing an air velocity of 340 kn over the upper wing surface but only 260 kn over the lower one, then we have the equivalent of the cylinder of Fig. 7.7 with a rotational speed of 40 kn around it, in the positive (clockwise) direction. That is, if we subtract the TAS of 300 from both figures, we are left with a speed of 40 m/s over the wing's upper surface and -40 m/s over the lower one.

In practice, then, a value of Γ can be assigned to any wing and the lift developed will be closely linked to ρVΓb, where b is the wingspan and V the TAS. For a given aircraft, therefore, flying at constant speed and altitude, the lift developed is directly proportional to the circulation Γ, or vice versa. One can therefore conceive of a massive vortex being superimposed on the wing with strength Γ and rotating about the lateral axis. However, one problem with this idea is that it can be shown in theory and in practice that vortices cannot come to an end in mid-air; they must either terminate at a solid surface or form a closed ring, of the type produced by skilful but otherwise ill-advised smokers.

In the case of a wing, the massive vortices turn through a right angle (conceptually speaking) and are shed from the wing as wingtip vortices. These become visible when an aircraft pulls tight turns in a damp atmosphere because the pressures at the vortex cores are very low and the water vapour condenses out as droplets. They are also visible behind any aircraft which has just landed with sufficient lack of poise to generate blue smoke behind its tyres. This raises the question of what vortex completes the ring for an aircraft in flight and the answer is that it was the starting vortex shed by the aircraft when starting its take-off roll. That vortex will of course dissipate after a short time due to air friction, but it was there to start with.

We now therefore have the concept of two giant vortices being shed, one from each tip, and the quite alarming possibility (Fig. 7.9) for anyone following an aircraft of quite severe velocity components, upwards, downwards and sideways, to be dealt with. In straight level flight, lift = weight so W is proportional to $\rho V\Gamma b$ and therefore the strength of the vortices Γ is proportional to $W/\rho Vb$. For aircraft on approach, ρ and V will be more or less fixed so Γ depends on W/b. Since weight is proportional to the cube of size (i.e. twice the size means eight times the weight) but wing span to only the first power of size, large aircraft are going to be particularly dangerous to follow and air traffic controllers need to ensure that even medium sized aircraft follow large ones at a safe distance of several nautical miles. To "put some numbers in", the following chart shows exactly why the pilot of even a medium weight aircraft should get nowhere near the back end of a "heavy".

Aircraft	**Value of weight/span (kg/m)**
Piper Cherokee	119
Airbus A320	1980
Airbus A340	4740
Boeing 747	5860

The view along the longitudinal axis in Fig. 7.9 shows that the two wingtip vortices will induce vertical velocity components, downwards inboard of the tips and upwards outboard of them. Even birds flying in formation know this; those not leading fly in the upwash of those ahead of them, leading to the well known "V" formation. They also have the decency to take their fair share of being the leader! However, reverting to aircraft, each large vortex core is in the flow field of the other and will be induced to move downwards by the other as it leaves the rear end of the aircraft. It is therefore a good rule to stay slightly high on approach if one is following a larger aircraft down a 3° approach path. The vortices are subject to friction, like everything else in aerodynamics, so they will gradually die away with time. However, that process can last for several minutes, which equates to several nautical miles.

The table above shows the comparative values of W/b, although the earlier calculations show that the vortex strength is more correctly proportional to W/Vb; that is, the problem gets even worse at low speeds, since V is in the denominator!

The most dangerous time of all is therefore when the aircraft is at lift = weight but at minimum speed; that is, the moments of touching or leaving the runway at landing and take-off. In the case of landing, the generated vortex strength will rapidly fall off as the aircraft's nose settles on its wheel and angle of attack is lost. However, the vortices which were present at touchdown will still be there, even though they are gradually dissipating. A crosswind will help to move them off the runway centreline and the prevailing wind will move them towards the downwind end of the runway, but care is still needed. If sufficient runway is available, light aircraft are well advised to try to land beyond the touchdown point or well before the liftoff point of a heavier aircraft, even if a few minutes have elapsed.

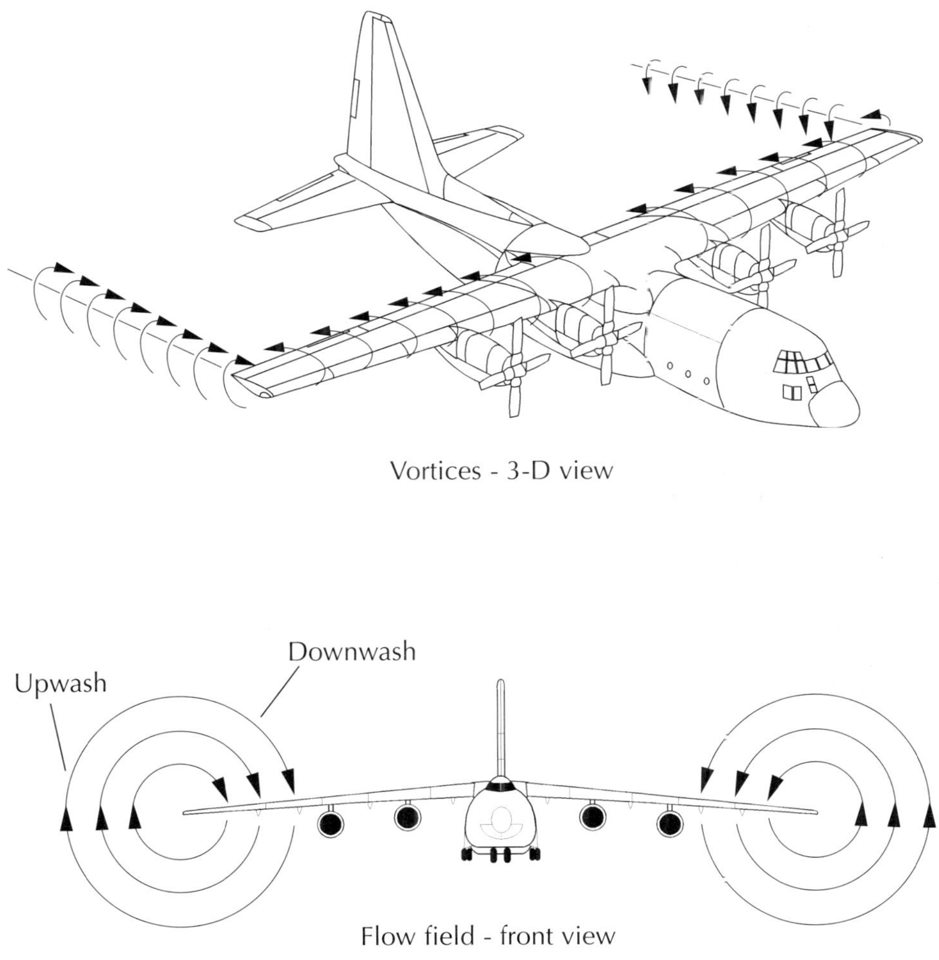

Figure 7.9 Wingtip vortices and bound vorticity over the wing

From the same figure (7.9), we can see that the whole of the wing is subject to a "downwash" which, when added to the free-stream flow, will cause a local reduction in angle of attack for the wing. This downwash will be more severe near the tips, although still marked at the roots and a mean value ε (Greek epsilon) across the span can be calculated. However, remembering that lift is by definition always perpendicular to the local stream direction, Fig. 7.10 shows that the lift vector L is going to be swung backwards (in the graphical sense) by an angle equal to the downwash ε. Relative to the direction of flight, therefore, an additional drag term Di has appeared and this is the so-called induced drag. The geometry of Fig. 7.10 shows that $D_i/L = \tan \varepsilon$ and, since ε is always a small angle, we can use the approximation $\tan \varepsilon = \varepsilon$ for ε in radians. A few seconds with a calculator shows that this approximation holds good within 1% accuracy up to $\varepsilon = 12°$.

To good approximation, therefore, $D_i = L\varepsilon$ or, dividing both sides by $\frac{1}{2}\rho V^2 S$, $C_{Di} = C_L\varepsilon$. For most aircraft, ε has a value of about 0.4 times the angle of attack α, but α is itself linked to C_L, as shown in the previous chapter. In referring to Fig. 6.8, it was stated that C_L increased by about 0.1 for every degree increase in α, so α is directly proportional to C_L and ε is also proportional to C_L. That means that C_{Di} will be proportional to C_L^2. In practice, ε is also inversely proportional to aspect ratio, since a high value of this parameter (span/mean chord) means that the wing tips are relatively further apart and the average downwash over the span is therefore lower. Combining all these links, we can write down an equation for induced drag coefficient which is found to be remarkably useful in practice:

Induced drag coefficient $C_{Di} = kC_L^2/\pi A$ **Eqn. 7.6**

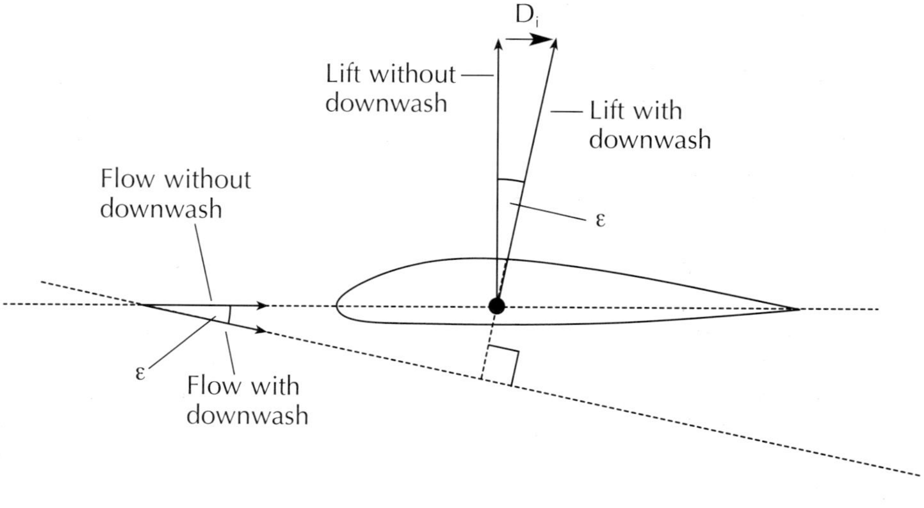

Figure 7.10 Concept of induced drag from downwash

where A is the wing's aspect ratio (span^2/area) and k is a pure number, normally between about 1.2 and 1.4, depending on the lift distribution across the span.

Induced drag can be minimised by careful design and the ideal planform for a wing would be an ellipse. However, induced drag is lowest at high speed (low C_L, see Eqn. 7.6) so a compromise is normally made in the design process to achieve minimal induced drag, although not at the expense of needing a complicated structure to achieve it. A rectangular wing is basically rather poor in this respect because most of the strength of the vortices is close to the tip but such a wing is very easy to analyse and build in the structural sense. A tapered wing with the tip chord being less than the root value has the advantage that some of the lifting power of the vortices is shed more inboard and therefore the bending moment on the wing at the root is also less.

Various methods other than wing planform have been tried to minimise induced drag and these generally centre on changing conditions at the tip. Less lift at the tip can be generated by reducing the angle of attack there, by twisting the tip in the nose-down sense. This is known as "washout" and is in common use. Its disadvantage is that at low angles of attack the tip sections may actually be at a negative value of α and therefore contributing negative lift. Another method, known as "Spillman sails" after the professor at Cranfield who developed them, uses small winglets mounted on the tip (see Fig. 7.11) which draw lift from the vicious upcurrents just outboard of the tips (Fig. 7.9). Remembering that the downwash *inboard* of the tips causes induced drag by effectively slanting the lift vector *backwards*, it's easy to see that winglets placed just *outboard* of the tips will have their lift vectors slanted *forwards*, thus generating a thrust instead of a drag. These have one disadvantage in that the extra lift developed is at the maximum distance from the wing root so the bending moment at the root is increased quite a lot. Observant birdwatchers will know that nature got there first (again!) in the form of the shape and position of primary feathers on the wingtips of soaring birds such as vultures and eagles. Under high C_L conditions, these five or so primaries spread out to resemble the Spillman sails; not surprising, since the birds' feathers have evolved in that way over millions of years to give the best soaring performance.

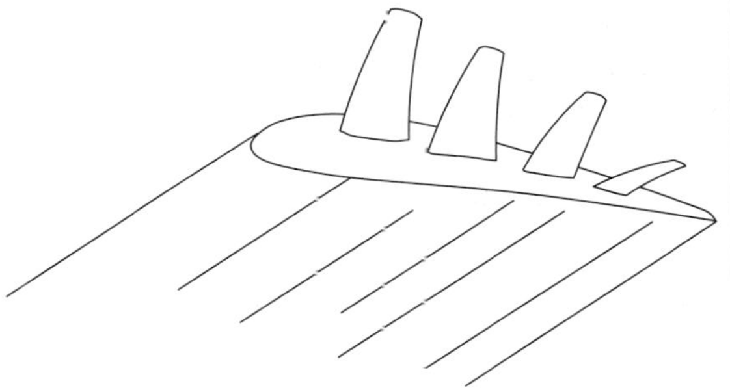

Figure 7.11 "Spillman sails" on a wing - resembling a bird's primary feathers

A variant of this is the winglets visible now on the Boeing 747-400 and various other airliners and business jets. These have the advantage that their lift vector, whilst still giving a useful forward component, is closer to horizontal than Spillman sails and therefore the moment arm about the wing root is far smaller (see Fig. 7.12).

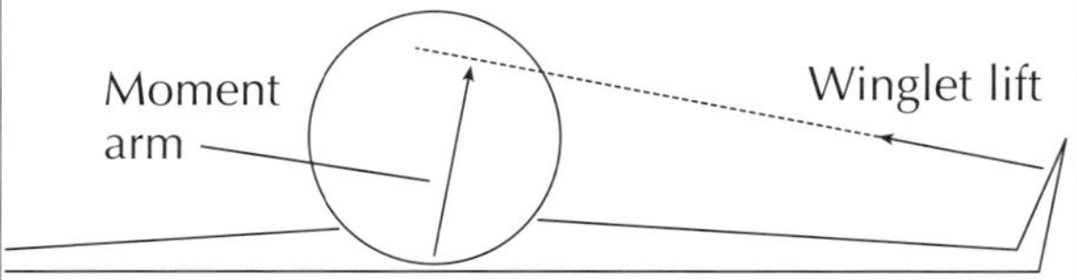

Figure 7.12 Winglet lift has a smaller bending moment arm

Ground effect

Everything said so far about wing vortices has assumed that they are unhindered in their rotation but a quite different situation occurs when an aircraft approaches the ground. The inability of vortex flow fields to penetrate solid objects means that the downwash is severely reduced by the physical proximity of the runway (or water) which means that the angle of attack of the wing is no longer being reduced by downwash and the lift vector swings forward again towards its zero-downwash position. Under these circumstances, the pilot will notice a reduced (induced) drag and an increased lift, both of which contribute to a floating tendency. This is known as "ground effect" and, although the magnitude of it varies to some extent between aircraft, it is marked enough to be felt even by inexperienced pilots during the final stages of landing.

The same logic applies to an aircraft on take-off but here the danger could be of a different type. An aircraft which is heavily loaded and close to its limits may have enough power to just lift off the runway whilst benefiting from ground effect of increased lift and reduced drag. However, when it attains a height of perhaps half a wing span above the surface, ground effect is almost lost and it could be in a situation where it has insufficient power to climb further. This has become less of a problem with more powerful engines and longer runways but was certainly not to be ignored a few decades ago.

The benefits of ground effect can be assessed using both aerodynamic theory and wind tunnel testing. It's true to say that, for many aircraft, the value of C_L when the wheels are on the runway is about 10% higher than the free air value, although this drops to only about 1.5% when the wing is one span above the tarmac. The induced drag benefit is even more marked; on the runway, the value of C_{Di} is only about a half its free air value. The magnitude of these benefits obviously depends on aspect ratio, but the above figures refer to a typical value of about A = 8.

Total Drag

All the main sources of drag have now been dealt with and the total drag force on an aircraft will obviously be the sum of all the lift-independent items and the lift-dependent contribution. The former is normally called C_{D0} so we therefore have:

Total drag $C_D = C_{Do} + kC_L^2/\pi A$ **Eqn. 7.7**

It is interesting to look at how C_{D0} is made up for a typical aircraft and we can do that by dividing the drag of individual components of the aircraft by a common denominator, normally $\frac{1}{2}\rho V^2 S$, where S is the **gross** wing plan area, as with lift coefficient in the previous chapter. The table below is based on information from McCormick's book (see Bibliography) and shows the percentage contributions to C_{D0} from the main parts of a Learjet.

Profile drag breakdown for a Learjet

Item	C_{D0}	%
Wings	0.0053	23.45
Fuselage	0.0063	27.88
Tailplane	0.0016	7.08
Fin	0.0011	4.86
Nacelles	0.0012	5.31
Pylons, tip tanks, etc.	0.0025	11.06
Interference	0.0031	13.72
Roughness and gaps	0.0015	6.64
Total	0.0226	100.00

One interesting point from the table is that the wings and fuselage combined account for about half the profile drag. Another is that interference, gaps, etc. account for about a fifth of the total, quite surprisingly high.

Engineers generally dislike dealing with very small numbers such as in the centre column of the above table so they tend to multiply everything by 10000 and talk about "drag counts". The wings therefore contribute 53 drag counts and the whole aircraft accounts for 226 of them.

An Interesting Aside

We've spent the last two chapters looking at how the forces on an aircraft can always be considered in dimensionless terms - independent of the size of the aircraft or of the units in use. It's interesting to note (as an aside and nothing to do with lift or drag) that there is at least one other quantity which can be expressed independently of size and that is (civilian) jet aircraft price per seat when new! This seems to be (at 1999 prices) about $300000 per seat, and this applies all the way from the six-seat (incl. crew) VisionAire Vantage at about $M1.75 and Century Jet CJ-1 at about $M1.85, up to 400-seat monsters at about $M120.

Conclusion

Drag may well be something we'd prefer to be without but the fact is that we can't avoid it. Over a century of improvements, form drag has been reduced by streamlining and skin drag by better surface finishing, but we cannot escape the effects of air viscosity and must simply try to minimise them. Induced drag, caused by lift, can be minimised by careful wing design, although it will always be with us so long as we need lift. Trailing vortices, the result of generating lift, are dangerous and pilots should avoid at all cost the area extending a few miles behind aircraft larger than themselves. Such vortices, after shedding, generally descend with time. If enough runway is available, light aircraft should aim to use an approach path slightly higher than a preceding larger aircraft and touch down further down the runway.

Exercises - Chapter 7

Use may be made of charts or equations but accuracy will clearly be greater in the latter case.

Reminder: 1 knot = 0.5144 m/s

1. A water tank on the edge of an airfield at sea level is spherical and has a diameter of 10.3 m. If the drag coefficient for this shape is 0.2, calculate the drag force on the tank in a 20 knot wind.

2. The drag coefficient for a parachute is 1.4. Calculate the chute diameter required to allow a person weighing 75 kg to descend at 2 m/s in air at sea level.

3. Calculate the new descent speed if the diameter of the parachute in Question 2 is limited to 14 m.

4. The four cups of a wind speed gauge (anemometer) have C_D values of 1.4 if the open cup is pointing upwind and 0.4 if downwind. Each cup has a diameter of 100 mm and its centre is at 300 mm from the rotation axis. For the two cups pointing directly into- or down-wind, calculate the turning moment (torque) generated in a 24 knot wind.

5. An airliner has a fuselage 40.3 m long and 4.2 m in diameter, and is travelling at 350 kn.TAS. If the fuselage surface area is 78% of that of its containing cylinder (ignoring the ends), calculate the drag force due to the fuselage at:
(a) sea level [ρ = 1.2256 kg/m^3, υ = 1.5 x 10^{-5} m^2/s]
(b) 36000 ft. [ρ = 0.3605 kg/m^3, υ = 4.35 x 10^{-5} m^2/s]

6. Repeat Question 6, ignoring surface area but assuming C_D (based on frontal area) = 0.08.

7. An aircraft has a wing which, in plan view, is a rectangle of wetted semi-span 4.5 m and chord 1.125 m and has a thickness/chord ratio of 14%. Calculate the skin drag force on this wing when flying at 130 kn at sea level.

8. An aircraft has a gross wing area of 11 m^2 and a total C_D (from all sources) of 0.029 when flying at 300 kn at sea level. By what percentage will the C_D increase if two drop tanks are fitted, each of diameter 450 mm and having a drag coefficient based on frontal area of 0.085?

9. An aircraft weighs 13 t, has a gross wing area of 43 m^2 and an aspect ratio of 7.8. If the k value for this aircraft is 1.28, calculate the induced drag at sea level at: (a) 220 kn (b) 170 kn.

8

Performance

How do we get the best out of our aircraft?

THERE IS A TENDENCY to forget that even an apparently simple aircraft in flight is a complex system for transporting humans and freight as safely and economically as possible. It should be obvious from the previous chapters that the actual flying condition of an aircraft is the result of balancing a set of forces and moments and that this balancing act involves throttles, elevator and aileron positions, etc. However, although the cruising speed for any particular aircraft will be quoted in the operating handbook, a pilot over the sea who is clearly running low on fuel would be far more interested in what speed to fly at for maximising the chances of reaching a coastline known to be ahead. He or she would be quite wrong to assume that flying as slowly or as fast as possible was the answer. This chapter is going to look at that sort of problem, starting by referring back to the drag and power relationships developed in the last chapter. We shall be concerned with the relationship between power available (through engine and propeller) and power required, because of drag and flying condition.

Speed for Minimum Drag V_{md}

In Chapter 7, we saw that total drag could be represented by $D = C_D \frac{1}{2}\rho V^2 S$, where C_D was composed of a profile drag term C_{D0} and an induced drag term $kC_L^2/\pi A$. Since $k/\pi A$ is more or less fixed for any particular aircraft, C_D could be written as

$$C_D = a + bC_L^2 \qquad Eqn.\ 8.1$$

where a and b are two constants, with a being equal to C_{D0}.

Total drag will therefore be $D = a\frac{1}{2}\rho V^2 S + bC_L^2\ \frac{1}{2}\rho V^2 S$. However, C_L is itself proportional to $1/V^2$ (for constant weight) so that C_L^2 will be dependent on $1/V^4$. Therefore, gathering all the constants into two "super-constants" C_1 and C_2, we can write

$$Drag = C_1 V^2 + C_2/V^2 \qquad Eqn.\ 8.2$$

If we now plot a graph of drag against speed, we shall have a combination of one curve which is increasing like a graph of $y = x^2$ and another which is falling as $y = 1/x^2$. Fig. 8.1 shows that their total is a U shaped curve, which is quite alarming since, although one might have expected total drag to increase with speed, there is clearly a range below a minimum drag trough where **drag is actually increasing as speed drops off.** At high speed, most of the drag is of the profile variety, whereas at low speed, most of it is induced. The speed at the bottom of the trough is called the minimum drag speed V_{md} and, at that speed, the two contributing curves clearly have the same value (Ind or Pr on the graph) so the total drag at V_{md} must be double the profile drag (or double the induced drag).

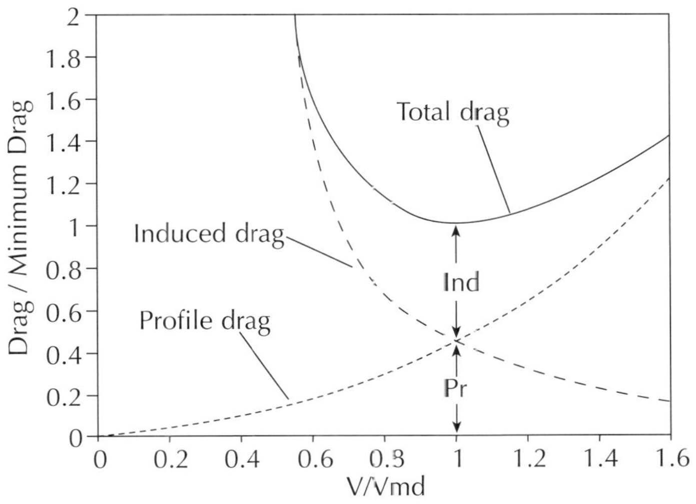

Figure 8.1 Contributions to total drag

V_{md} is above stalling speed so there is a speed range where the pilot needs to keep a close eye on his ASI because, if a speed reduction takes place (because of a gust, for example), a rapid adjustment of throttle will be needed since the speed is otherwise going to drop still more towards a stall. During basic flying training, pilots are taught to fly in this region "on the back of the drag curve" and a constant juggling of throttle and stick is needed to maintain constant speed just above the stall buzzer condition.

It's interesting to note that, for an aircraft in straight level flight, the lift is constant and equal to the weight, so **minimum drag** also represents **maximum lift/drag ratio,** a useful marker for glider pilots (and those who have just suffered an engine failure!) since this also means the best gliding angle has been reached.

Speed for Minimum Power V_{mp}

We saw in Chapter 2 that power is defined as rate of doing work and is measured in bhp or kW. In the present context, power is equal to (force x speed) so the engine power required to overcome drag would be (drag x speed) and Eqn. 8.2 becomes:

$$Power = D.\ V = C_1V^3 + C_2/V \qquad Eqn.\ 8.3$$

This equation produces a graph (see Fig. 8.2) which is of the same form as the drag graph but has its minimum at a lower speed and becomes steeper than the drag graph at speeds to the right of the trough. We'll return to this graph later when considering the power available to us, rather than the power required, but for the moment we'll relate it to two speeds which are of great interest: for maximum range and maximum endurance.

For **maximum range**, we need to consider the **distance covered** for a given fuel burn. In a propeller-driven aircraft, the power is usually proportional to the fuel flow rate while the distance covered is obviously proportional to the speed so we really need the speed which gives us the minimum value of power/speed. In Fig. 8.2, P/V would be the slope of the line joining any point on the curve to the origin so the **minimum** value is represented by the tangent to the curve, close to the trough, as shown. However, since power = D.V, then the minimum value of P/V is also the minimum of D.V/V which is therefore the minimum drag. So, quite simply,

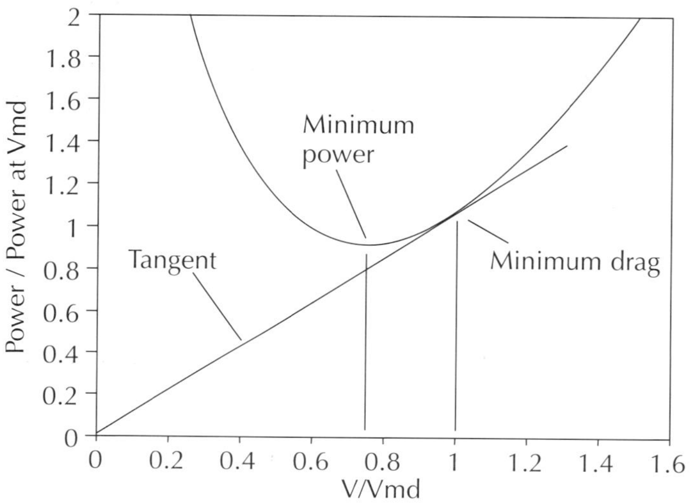

Figure 8.2 The power curve

Speed for maximum range = speed for minimum drag = V_{md}

For **maximum endurance**, we need the maximum **time in the air**; in other words, the minimum rate of fuel consumption commensurate with staying in the air. As stated above, for propeller-driven aircraft the rate of fuel consumption is usually proportional to power output so:

Speed for maximum endurance = speed for minimum power = V_{mp}

Pilots do not, of course, consult these graphs in the air; the speeds recommended for maximum range or endurance are quoted in the operating handbook. There are, however, some interesting relationships between the various "best speeds" quoted for aircraft and these relationships are often independent of which aircraft is being considered.

If Eqn. 8.1 is plotted as a graph (or, indeed for the more mathematically inclined, calculus is used), it is easy to show that the lift coefficient at minimum drag speed is given by:

$$C_{Lmd} = \sqrt{(a/b)} \qquad \textbf{Eqn. 8.4}$$

Eqn. 8.1 can be written as $C_D/C_L = a/C_L + bC_L$ so if we now insert the value of C_L for minimum drag from Eqn. 8.4 we have:

$$C_D/C_L = \sqrt{(ab)} + \sqrt{(ab)} = 2\sqrt{(ab)}$$

or $$(L/D)_{max} = (C_L/C_D)_{max} = 1/\{2\sqrt{(ab)}\} \qquad \textbf{Eqn. 8.5}$$

With suitable values of a and b inserted, Eqn. 8.5 would give a max L/D ratio of perhaps 10 for a light aircraft, about 12 to 15 for a business jet, about 17 to 20 for a large modern airliner and well over 30 for a really good glider.

If a similar analysis is carried out using the power equations, C_L for minimum power is found to be

$$C_{Lmp} = \sqrt{(3a/b)} \qquad \textbf{Eqn. 8.6}$$

If we compare eqns. 8.4 and 8.6, we see that $C_{Lmp}/C_{Lmd} = \sqrt{3} = 1.732$. However, C_L is proportional to $1/V^2$ (keeping everything else constant) so

$$V_{mp}/V_{md} = \sqrt{(1/1.732)} = 0.76 \qquad \textbf{Eqn. 8.7}$$

For all propeller-driven aircraft, therefore, **minimum power speed is 76% of minimum drag speed.**

Variation for Jet Aircraft

For jet aircraft, the **thrust** (rather than power) is proportional to fuel flow so the above figures are changed. A similar analysis gives

$$\textbf{Max. endurance speed} = V_{md}$$

$$\textbf{Max. range speed} = V_{md}/0.76 = 1.3V_{md}$$

Fixed-Pitch Versus Variable-Pitch Propellers

Just as the above ratios depend on whether one is dealing with a jet or a prop-driven aircraft, so a lot of other factors contribute to performance and not the least of these is propeller pitch. If you look at a propeller along one of its blades (from tip to root) you'll notice two things: its cross-section resembles that of an aerofoil and that there is a twist. The cross-section is like it is because the propeller acts like a wing at useful angles of attack and must have the same type of cross-section. Thrust is produced by rotation, with the lift obviously being perpendicular to the plane of rotation and parallel to the flight direction. Unfortunately, the speed of any given section depends on its distance from the prop shaft so, for any given rpm and forward speed, the pitch (angle of attack) of the propeller should depend on radius from the shaft, so that the local angle of attack will always be near the best value for producing lift. The sections near the tip are therefore at a finer pitch (i.e. closer to the plane of rotation) than those at the root. With a fixed-pitch propeller, we run into a problem here since the designer has to make a compromise regarding pitch. In deciding what pitch to give the propeller at any radius, an assumption has to be made about forward speed, since a design which is correct at one forward speed will be wrong at any other speed. Engineers use a dimensionless number called "advance ratio" J to analyse this problem; J is proportional to the ratio of forward speed V to the tip speed N.R, where N is the propeller speed and R the tip radius. Since propeller sizes are normally quoted in terms of diameter, J is usually defined as

Advance ratio $J = V/N.D$

We must be careful about units here; for J to be a pure number, independent of the unit system used, we must be consistent. If V is in m/s, D must be in metres and N in rad/s. Imperial units (ft and s) may be used but N must always be in rad/s (= rpm[$2\pi/60$]). On this basis, we can plot a graph of propeller efficiency η (power out/power in) against J and Fig. 8.3 shows that η is at a maximum value of around 80% for only a limited range of forward speeds. For a fixed-pitch propeller (solid line), the designer will normally aim to have the blade angles correct near the cruise condition. However, that means that the propeller is far less efficient at zero speed and pilots will have noticed how the thrust and general sound level improves

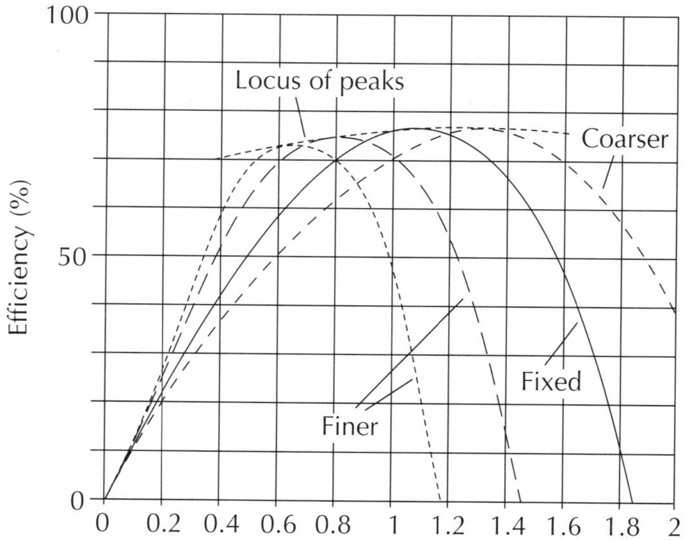

Figure 8.3 Effect of variable pitch

as one accelerates along a runway from zero to unstick speed, simply because the blade angles are all approaching design values.

A change of overall blade pitch would give a different curve on Fig. 8.3 (shown dashed) so having a variable-pitch propeller would enable the pilot always to sit somewhere near the peak η value, simply by adjusting the pitch lever to remain on the locus shown in the figure. At take-off, therefore, fine pitch would be selected and this would change to coarser values as speed increased, being markedly coarser at cruise speed.

Engine RPM and BHP

As with any other case, the performance of an aero engine depends on the speed at which it's operating. The design or "rated" value is specified by the manufacturer and this will be the speed at which all variables have been optimised. In a car engine, the fuel consumption **per second** will obviously increase with speed, but the fuel used **per mile** of progress will be at its maximum at only one speed. For a car in top gear, this might be at about 40 mile/h so that, although one would cover twice the distance per second at 80, the fuel used **per mile** would be greater and the miles per gallon figure would be lower.

With aero engines, it is customary to divide the fuel consumption per hour by the bhp (or thrust in the case of jets) and this enables engines to be compared, irrespective of their size. The units in the Imperial system would be lbm/bhp.h ("pounds per horsepower hour") and, on this basis, all piston engines produce a rated figure around 0.5 to 0.6. This quantity is known as specific fuel consumption (sfc) and Fig. 8.4 shows how its value typically increases (i.e. becomes worse) as engine speed drops away from the rated value. At least as interesting is the way in which it behaves relative to the maximum power setting. Fig. 8.5

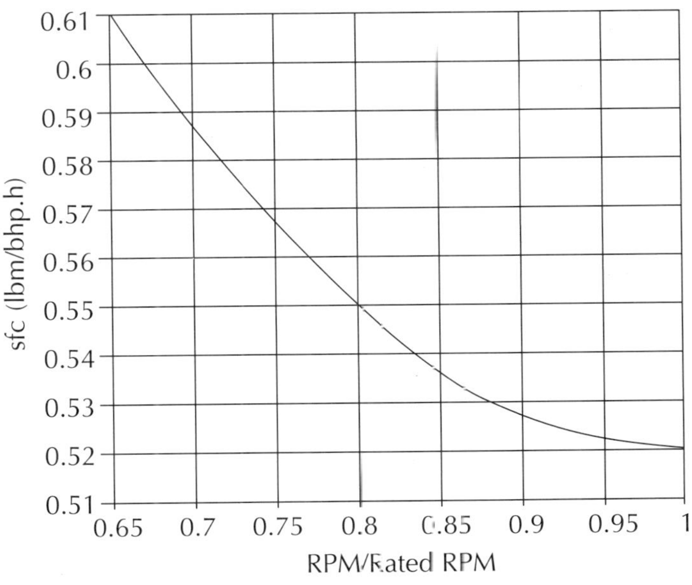

Figure 8.4 sfc is best at rated engine speed

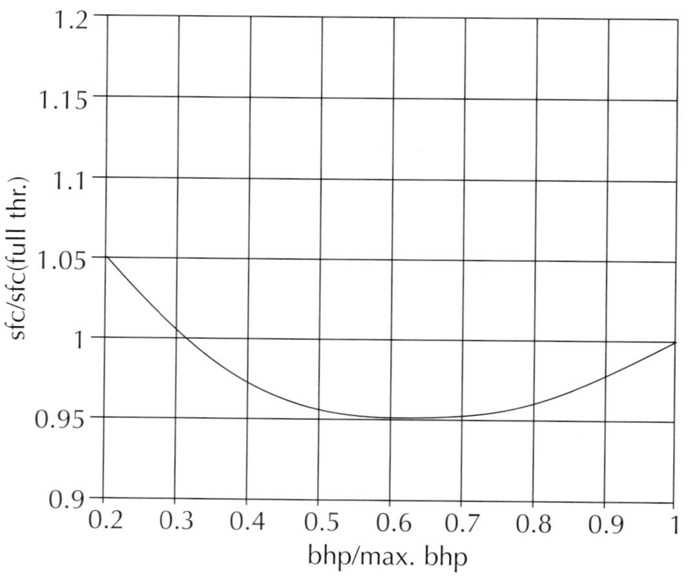

Figure 8.5 Variation of sfc with engine power

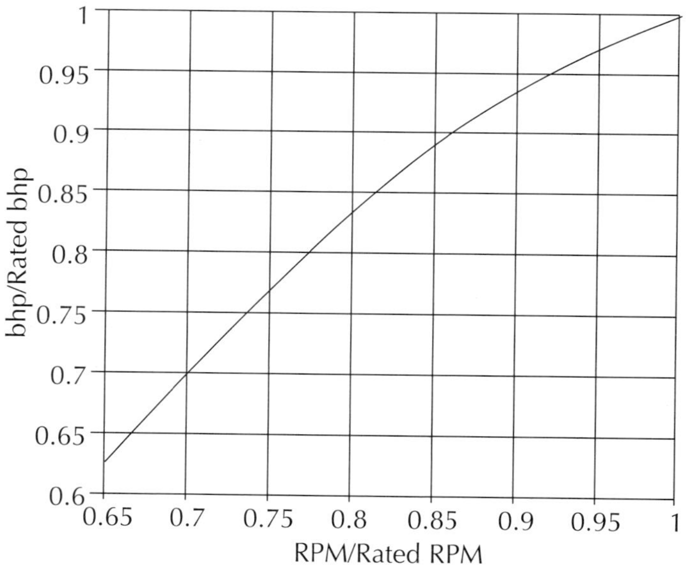

Figure 8.6 Variation of power with engine speed

shows that typically its value optimises at about 95% of the max power value in a band from about 55 to 70% full power. Graphs such as Fig. 8.6 can be used to show that this ideal condition occurs at about 65 to 70% of rated rpm.

Effect of Altitude

A typical car owner will not be too aware of the relationship between engine power and altitude because the vast majority of vehicles are operated within the first 2000 ft of the Earth's atmosphere; however, a pilot cannot afford to ignore this link. The key of course is air density and, even at 2000 ft on a hot day, air density is reduced enough to give noticeably longer take-off runs, not just because the propeller has "thinner" air to grab at but also because the engine itself is producing less power. The effect of hot air on rpm can be seen every time one carries out power checks prior to take-off; the selection of "carb air hot" at 2000 rpm gives a visible drop in engine speed. The reduced density of the hot air means that the cylinders are pulling in less **mass** of air for the same volume so the air:fuel ratio will be wrong, the number of air and fuel molecules in each cylinder will be reduced, the explosion will be less impressive and the engine will produce less power.

Air density decreases with altitude so an air-breathing engine will produce less power at altitude, even if the air entering is very cold. Fig. 8.7 shows the effect on power produced at the prop shaft as altitude increases, the drop being as high as 30% even if one climbs only to 10000 ft. Above that altitude, one begins to think in terms of providing pilots and passengers with extra oxygen and the engine will similarly benefit from such a provision. Piston engined aircraft designed to spend most of their flying time above 10000 ft would be fitted with a "blower" or supercharger, a device which takes energy from the exhaust gases or the shaft and uses it to compress the air before it enters the engine.

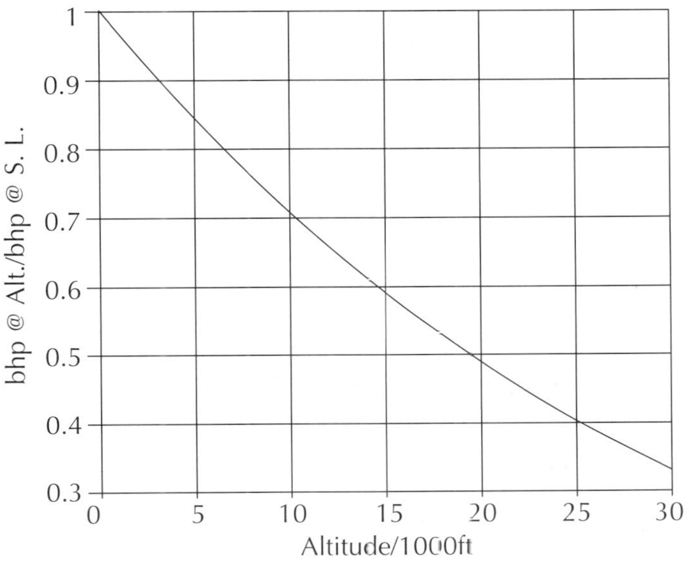

Figure 8.7 Effect of altitude on engine power

The situation is not quite as gloomy as it might appear at first sight since the same reduction of air density giving less power will also lead to lower drag forces, since these are proportional to the dynamic pressure term $\frac{1}{2}\rho V^2$ and this will clearly decrease in proportion to density ρ.

Gas Turbines

The text and graphs referred to above have been essentially about piston engines, but a few comments should be added here about gas turbines. They also suffer from the effects of altitude and at a Mach no. of 0.8, for example, their thrust at 36000 ft might fall to only about 40% of its sea level value, although the sfc will fall (i.e. improve) by perhaps 15%. Speed also has an effect, with thrust at cruising speed falling to perhaps only about 80% of its "static" (bench) value and the sfc will be perhaps 50% higher (worse).

Various Types of Airspeed

The airspeed as shown on the ASI is also altitude-dependent and the indicated figure is theoretically equal to the true figure only at sea level. The word "theoretically" is used because there are all manner of reasons why the two are not the same, even at sea level. The ASI is accurate at sea level **if** it is being fed with the correct values for total and static pressure (assuming there's nothing wrong with the instrument). The former is normally sensed by a Pitot tube pointing forwards and it can be shown that this is usually very accurate, even if it is pointed away from the true air direction by up to about 12°. However, the latter is normally sensed by a "static hole" somewhere along the fuselage where the local static pressure is reckoned to be equal to the atmospheric pressure well away from the aircraft and this is not always as easy to position. These and any other systematic errors will always mean that there is a difference of perhaps a few knots between the instrument value (indicated airspeed, IAS) and the "calibrated airspeed" (CAS).

CAS = IAS + (position and instrument errors)

The difference between these two is normally shown on a small chart in the operating handbook and can be found only by flying the aircraft against some standard, such as an already calibrated aircraft with, for example, a static pressure drogue, towed a long way behind it. In theory, there is another correction to be applied, for the change in air density as airspeed increases, but this will always be small for aircraft travelling at less than about 200 kn. The result is then known as "equivalent airspeed" (EAS):

EAS = CAS corrected for compressibility

From now on in this chapter, EAS and IAS will be assumed to be the same and both are equal to TAS at sea level, **but not at altitude.**

As an aircraft climbs, the ASI is still registering the difference $1/2\rho V^2$ between total and static pressures but is quite unaware that ρ is decreasing with altitude. The instrument was calibrated for sea level air density so it will give an artificially low indication of speed when the local air density decreases. If we represent sea level and local densities as ρ_{SL} and ρ_{ALT}, we could therefore relate these to TAS and IAS with:

$$\tfrac{1}{2}\rho_{SL}(\mathrm{IAS})^2 = \tfrac{1}{2}\rho_{ALT}(\mathrm{TAS})^2$$

$$\text{so} \quad \mathbf{IAS} = \mathrm{TAS}[\sqrt{(\rho_{ALT}/\rho_{SL})}] = \mathbf{TAS}\sqrt{\sigma}$$

Since σ is always less than one, **TAS is always greater than IAS.** Using the previous example of 10000 ft, $\sigma = 0.7384$ and therefore $\sqrt{\sigma} = 0.8593$ so at 200 kn IAS the true airspeed will be 233 kn. (= 200/0.8593)

Effect on Performance

We saw earlier in the chapter that power, being equal to drag times speed, was given by Eqn. 8.3 but, now that a variable density is involved, we should rewrite this equation, keeping the density outside the constants:

$$Power = D.\ V = C_3\rho V^3 + C_4/\rho V \qquad Eqn. 8.8$$

where ρ is the local density and V the true airspeed. However, we now know that $V = V_{EAS}/\surd\sigma$ so we could once again rewrite the equation as

$$P = C_3\rho(V_{EAS}/\surd\sigma)^3 + C_4/\{\rho V_{EAS}/\surd\sigma)\}$$

We have switched to using EAS here instead of calling it IAS because the type of graphs we are going to be looking at now are usually plotted with EAS as the horizontal axis. However, please note that for our purposes there is no difference between the two. If we multiply both sides of the equation by √σ and remember that $\sigma = \rho/\rho_{SL}$, the equation becomes

$$P\surd\sigma = C_3\rho_{SL}V_{EAS}^{\ 3} + C_4/\{\rho_{SL}V_{EAS}\}$$

Since C_3, C_4 and ρ_{SL} are all constants, we now have a power curve P√σ which is uniquely a function of equivalent (or indicated) airspeed only and this is shown in Fig. 8.8. Not surprisingly, this curve looks very much like the curve of drag versus speed but the trough is skewed slightly to the left. If we now superimpose the curve for power available (i.e. engine output power times propeller efficiency), we see two crossing points. The right hand one is where the power required exactly equals the power available at higher speeds and so represents the maximum speed at which the aircraft can fly. The left hand crossing point is usually at such a low

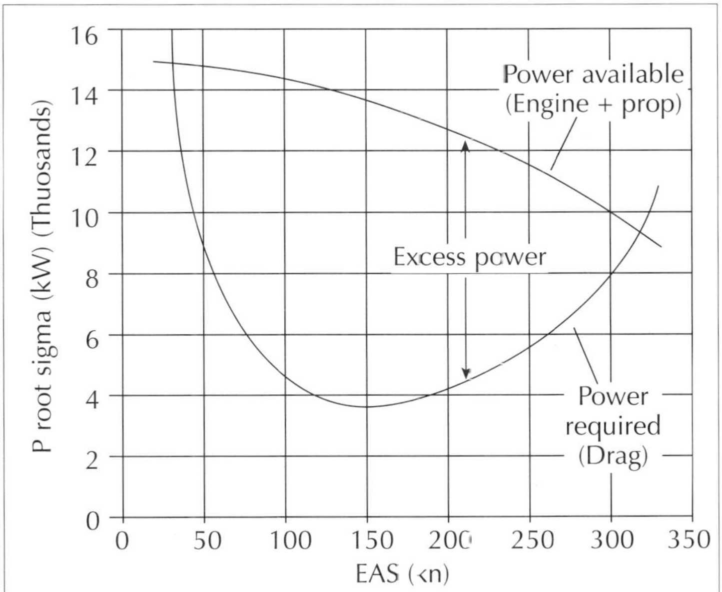

Figure 8.8 Excess power varies with airspeed

speed that the aircraft will have stalled before being able to get there. Everywhere between these two points, the power available exceeds the power required so the aircraft will start to climb. If we plot that difference against speed, we have the graph of Fig. 8.9, which shows that at one particular speed, the excess power is a maximum.

Power is rate of doing work and the work being done is to raise the weight of the aircraft to a greater height so, if the rate of climb is v_C, the rate of doing work is Wv_C and therefore

$$\textbf{Rate of climb } v_C = (P_{available} - P_{required})/W \qquad \textbf{Eqn. 8.9}$$

The speed for best v_C will always be quoted in the operating handbook but a good rule of thumb for light aircraft is that it is usually at **about 1.4 times the stalling speed.** This will give the aircraft the best performance in terms of highest needle setting in ft/min on the rate of climb gauge, but it should not be confused with the speed for **best angle of climb.** This is of far more interest to a pilot who has a short field to cope with and, horror of horrors, a line of rather intimidating trees to clear shortly after take-off. Here, the best **angle** of climb might get the pilot over the trees whereas the best **rate** of climb might send the aircraft majestically into them.

Referring once again to Fig. 8.9, the best rate of climb is obtained at the speed where the graph is horizontal (i.e. slope is zero) whereas the best angle of climb corresponds to the point where the slope of the graph is steepest. This is clearly at a lower speed and, for some aircraft, will be much closer to the stalling speed. The aircraft therefore climbs at a greater angle but it will show a lower value of ft/min on the rate of climb dial because it is actually travelling more slowly along its flight path. The speed for best angle of climb is often denoted in the operating handbook as V_x and for rate of climb as V_y, and the following figures for a Boeing 767-300 demonstrate

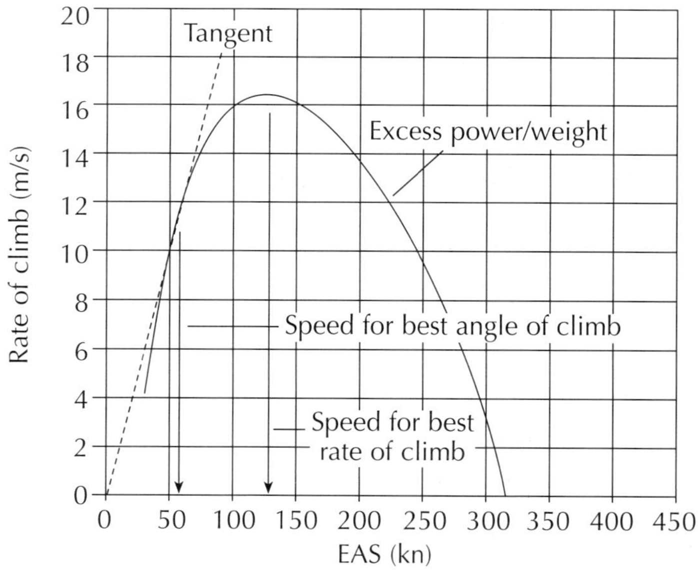

Figure 8.9 Speeds for best climbing performance

the point quite well. At sea level, V_x is 220 kn and the climb rate is 2700 ft/min whereas v_y is 340 kn and the rate of climb 3400 ft/min.

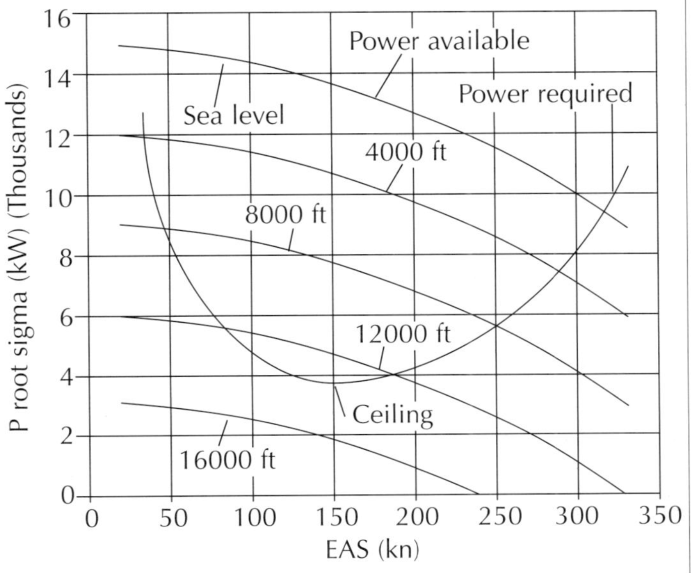

Figure 8.10 Excess power decreases with altitude

It has already been stated that power available drops off with increasing altitude because of decreasing air density and the effect of this on rate of climb can be shown by superimposing the altitude curves on the same graph as Fig. 8.8 to give Fig. 8.10. As altitude increases, the excess power available falls off and an altitude will eventually be reached where there is no excess; this will therefore be the absolute ceiling for this aircraft since it cannot gain any more height without losing speed. For the aircraft of Fig. 8.10, the ceiling seems to be at just under 14000 ft. An aircraft, particularly a military one, which had no more climb potential left would be in a dangerous position so a (lower) "service ceiling" is normally quoted where the aircraft can still climb at 100 ft/min if need be.

Variation for Jet Aircraft

As with the specification of best range speed etc., we need to look at jets separately because their performance variations with speed and altitude are not the same. Thrust is usually at its maximum when the engine is at a standstill because there is then the greatest difference between the speed of the jet exhaust and the aircraft. As the speed increases, there is some falloff in thrust although not as much as for a prop-driven aircraft at high speed, so the power available curve (which is thrust times speed) will tend to climb to the right on a plot of power versus speed, whereas the prop curve will tend to fall to the right. Fig. 8.11 shows an idealised comparison. The essential point is that the speed at which the ($P_{available}$ - $P_{required}$) difference occurs is higher for the jet than for the prop-driven aircraft.

A further advantage for the jet shows up if we look at where the crossing points in Fig. 8.10 for maximum speed occur for each altitude and Fig. 8.12 shows this quite clearly. If maximum indicated airspeed (or EAS) is plotted against altitude, it will clearly decrease, whereas if true airspeed is plotted (i.e. EAS/√σ) a quite different picture emerges. As σ is less than one, TAS is always greater than EAS. But as altitude increases beyond a certain point, the rate at which σ is falling is not as great as the rate at which EAS is decreasing, so even the TAS curve starts to curl over the top. However, the point of maximum possible TAS (the highest point on the graph) occurs at an altitude of about 30000 ft so it's not surprising that jets cruise most successfully at those rarified levels.

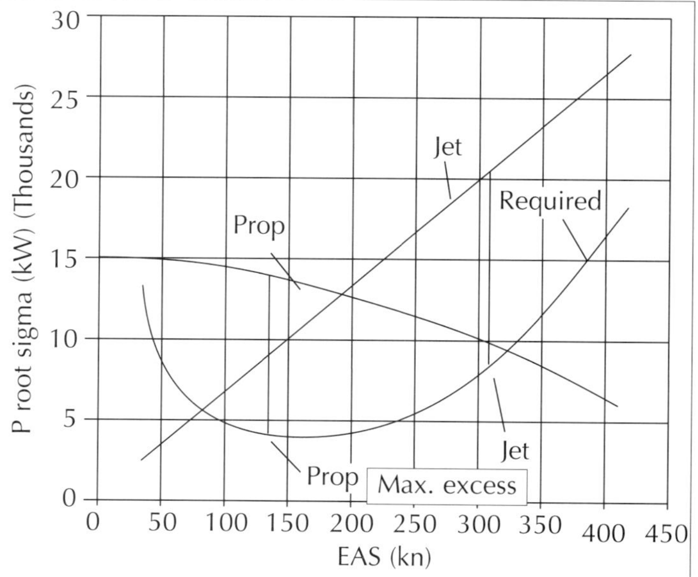

Figure 8.11 Comparison of jets with prop-driven aircraft

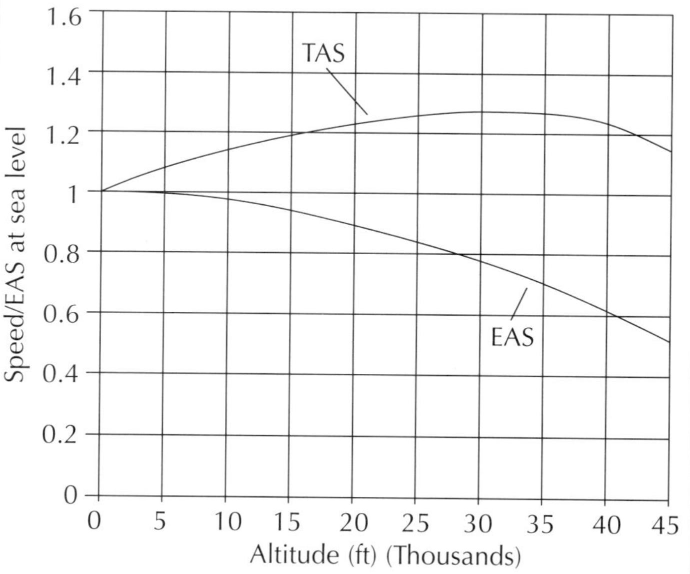

Figure 8.12 Effect of altitude on airspeeds

Descending and Gliding

At the other end of the power curves we have a similar problem. If we are forced into a gliding situation by engine failure, we would like to know the best speeds for either staying in the air longest (minimum sink rate) or reaching the furthest possible point for a forced landing (best glide speed) and, once again, these are not the same condition. An aircraft may be sinking at a minimal rate but, at the same time, not really going anywhere!

The furthest point can be reached by flying at the optimum lift/drag ratio, as for any glider, and since lift is effectively not going to vary much on the way down, this amounts to flying at minimum drag speed to get the maximum L/D value. Then, for a L/D ratio of, for example 10, the aircraft will glide a horizontal distance approximately ten times its height above the ground (assuming still air). On the other hand, it can be shown that minimum sink rate occurs at the same speed as for minimum power, so:

Best glide speed (max. distance) = V_{md}

Speed for minimum sink rate = V_{mp}

A good rule of thumb for light aircraft is that V_{mp} is about three quarters of V_{md}. In the case of a propeller driven aircraft, it's important to remember that a failed engine means either a stationary or a windmilling propeller; the former involves a higher drag than the latter, although both will involve a higher drag than when the engine was operating normally so the L/D ratio under these circumstances will be inferior to its power-on value.

Aircraft Noise

A chapter on performance, dealing as it does with maximum climb rates and angles, is the obvious place to deal with the sensitive subject of aircraft noise. Even gliders make a very audible noise as they pass, albeit this is not the noise generated by clouting something with a hammer; it's noise created by a shearing action of severe velocity gradients. This causes vortices of various sizes and associated pressure changes so the "tones" emitted are at many different frequencies. The human ear is sensitive to the frequencies from about 20 Hz to 20 kHz, but most sensitive of all between about 2 and 4 kHz. The "mains hum" from defective electrical equipment is at mains frequency (50 Hz) and middle C on a musical instrument is at 256 Hz, so the most sensitive areas are well above those. With increasing age, humans generally lose the higher frequencies first, but the tones emitted by engines are in the range of interest of everyone.

The tremendous speed of a jet exhaust causes severe shearing with the surrounding atmosphere and the older, small radius jet exhausts were the worst of all. Nowadays, greater thrust is produced not only by having larger engines but also by diverting a large fraction of the airflow along the outside sections of the engine (the so-called bypass type) so that a larger mass of slower moving air is produced. The beneficial effect on engine noise has been very marked, even allowing for the much greater thrusts now available, and some older jets have needed to be fitted with "hush kits" to change the form of their jet effluxes to conform to modern noise requirements.

Two points act in an engine's favour. One is the so-called inverse square law which says that at **twice** the distance the noise will reduce to only a **quarter** of its value. This is because the surface area of a sphere depends on the square of its radius so the noise effect is spread out that much more. The second point is that the human ear is sensitive not in proportion to the sound level (or pressure) but to its logarithm. This has the effect of stretching out quieter noise levels and compressing louder ones. The minimum pressure change the human ear can detect is generally considered to be about 20 μPa (micropascals) or about $1/10^{11}$ atmospheres, a very low difference indeed. An increase of noise level by a factor of ten is called 1 Bel, but this is quite a coarse unit to use so one tenth of it, a deciBel (1 dB), is the normal unit quoted. The logarithm to base 10 of 2 is 0.301, so a doubling of noise represents 0.3 Bel or 3 dB; for example, from 90 to 93 dB.

This is not the end of the story as the human ear responds differently to different parts of the jet noise spectrum, so the "perceived noise deciBel" (PNdB) and the "effective perceived noise dB" (EPNdB) have been defined to allow for this. However, the fine points of these differences are outside the scope of this book.

Because the effects of jet noise can be so damaging, strict rules are applied to aircraft when landing and taking off so that local residents are spared some of the more extreme tortures resulting. Noise monitors are positioned at the points specified below and fines are imposed for contraventions.

Take-off noise

For aircraft taking off, a monitor is placed on the extended runway centreline 6.5 km from the start of the take-off run. Aircraft with four or more engines must not exceed 106 EPNdB at this point if their MTOW is greater than about 385 t or 89 EPNdB for 20 t, with a linear variation between the two. Twins must not exceed 104 EPNdB at 385 t, reducing to 89 EPNdB at or below 48 t.

Approach noise

On the approach glidepath, noise is measured at a point 2 km from the threshold; this would correspond to an aircraft on a standard 3° glidepath being at about 350 ft. Here they must not exceed 105 EPNdB for MTOW greater than about 280 t, reducing linearly to 98 EPNdB for 35 t or less.

Sideline noise

Noise levels are also measured to the side of the aircraft on take-off and the measuring point can be located anywhere along a line running parallel to the runway and 450 m away from its centreline. Here the noise must not exceed 103 EPNdB for MTOW greater than 400 t, reducing to 94 EPNdB for 35 t or lower.

Noise abatement procedures

Clearly there is a balance to be struck on take-off between the extremes of using all the engine power to reach as high an altitude as possible by the time one passes over the sensing point, with the concomitant danger of triggering a fine, and the use of minimal power (and therefore noise) to clear the end of the runway, which would be dangerous. Noise abatement procedures have therefore been established for each aircraft, which usually involve reducing thrust at a specified point on the climbout. This is designed to give an acceptable noise level at the measuring point without compromising safety standards. There are associated with this some specified minimum heights **below which the power must not be reduced.** These reduce from 1000 ft for prop-driven aircraft to 689 ft for four-engined aircraft.

Summary

We can summarise all the foregoing points regarding best speeds in one graph and this is shown as Fig. 8.13. The vertical axis shows drag and power, relative to their values at V_{md}, and the horizontal axis shows speed divided by V_{md}. Both curves therefore pass through the point (1,1) but although this is obviously the minimum point for the drag curve, the power curve has its lowest point at only about three quarters of V_{md}. The tangent to the drag curve touches it at about $1.3V_{md}$ so everything of note here seems to happen at just three speeds: $0.76V_{md}$, V_{md} itself and $1.3V_{md}$.

It's worth remembering a few rules from this figure. The speed for maximum range is always 30% higher than that for maximum endurance; for a piston/prop arrangement, these are at V_{md} and $0.76V_{md}$, while for a jet these would be $1.3V_{md}$ and V_{md}. For a glider, mimimum sink rate corresponds to maximum endurance for

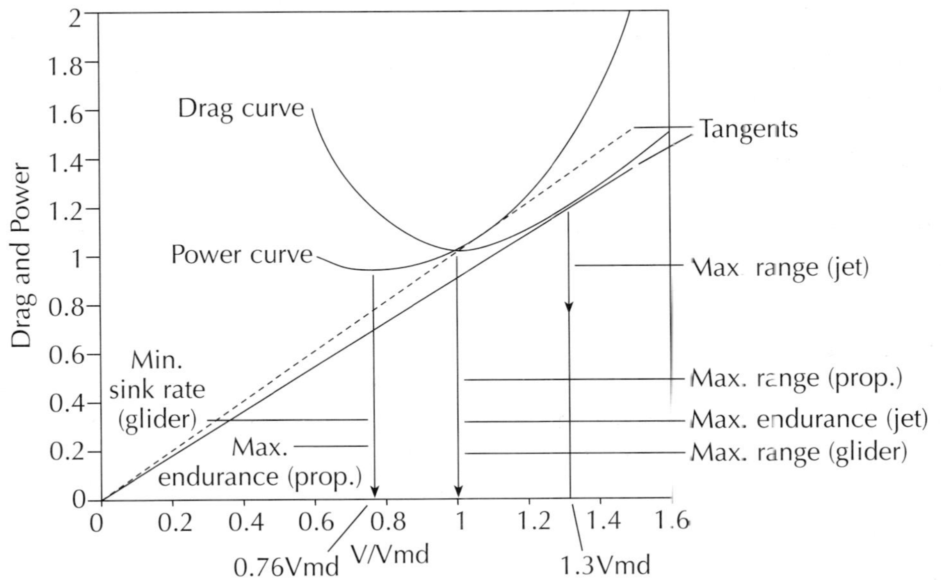

Figure 8.13 Important speed markers

a piston/prop aircraft ($0.76V_{md}$), and maximum range is obtained at V_{md}, as for the piston/prop. However, in the latter case it should always be remembered that a windmilling or stationary propeller can increase the aircraft's drag coefficient to the detriment of gliding range.

Exercises - Chapter 8

Reminder: 1 knot = 0.5144 m/s Sea level air density = 1.2256 kg/m^3

[Note: The following exercises are most easily completed using a spreadsheet but the time taken using a pocket calculator and graph paper is probably not very much greater]

The following data refer to a light aircraft, powered by a piston engine and propeller:

Gross wing area = 15 m^2 Wing span = 9.2 m Weight = 1100 kg
C_{DO} = 0.035 Propeller efficiency = 80% k = 1.4 (Eqn. 7.6)
Engine power = 120 kW @ sea level (assume constant with airspeed).

1. Using the above data, calculate the aircraft's aspect ratio and the value of 1/2ρS at sea level.
2. Derive expressions for profile and induced drags in the form of constant*V^2 or constant/V^2 respectively.
3. Draw a graph showing profile, induced and total drag versus EAS in knots by plotting the results from Q2 above at 20 knot intervals from 40 to 140 kn.
4. Draw a graph of power required and power available for the same speeds as in Q3.
5. From the first graph, determine the maximum speed of the aircraft at sea level and the speeds for minimum drag and minimum power.
6. From the second graph, determine the maximum rate of climb and the speed at which this occurs.
7. Check the graphical V_{md} and V_{mp} figures against calculation of C_L from Eqns. 8.4 and 8.6 (Reminder: a = C_{DO}; b = k/πA)

9

The Control of Flight

Putting it all into practice

SO FAR, we've looked at the flying surfaces and controls of an aircraft (Chapter 1 and Fig. 1.1), the various forces and equations involved (Chapters 5, 6 and 7) and the equations for performance (Chapter 8). We must now therefore put all this material together and look at how an aircraft is flown by the pilot. Any flying instructor will tell you that a mere knowledge of the physics and mathematics involved will not prevent you killing yourself when it comes to the nitty-gritty of flying a controlled low speed approach in turbulent conditions with a crosswind component close to the aircraft's limits, but it is still essential to know what is going on under these conditions.

Trimmed Flight

In straight level flight lift and weight must be equal otherwise the aircraft would climb or descend. However, these two forces may not act through the same point;

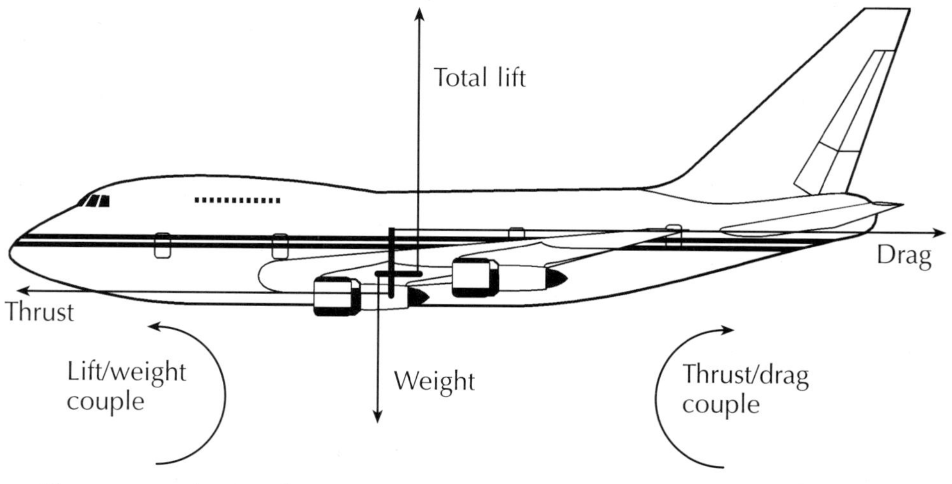

Figure 9.1 Balance of an aircraft. The lift/weight and thrust/drag couples

in fact, they hardly ever do. This means that a lift/weight "couple" is formed, two forces parallel but in opposite directions and at a finite distance apart, causing a nose-down pitching action if the lift is aft of the weight (Fig. 9.1). This must be balanced by another couple, acting in the opposite rotational sense and formed by the thrust and drag forces. The separation between the parallel forces has been exaggerated in the figure to make the point more clearly, but the thrust will obviously act along the engine centreline, the weight through the CG, the lift through the centre of lift of the whole aircraft and the drag through its own centre. This balance must be maintained during flight, although the forces or their point of action can change. In the most obvious case of engine failure in a single-engined aircraft, one whole contribution (thrust) is suddenly lost and the balance of the two couples is lost also. In the case of the setup in Fig. 9.1, the lift/weight couple will now dominate and the nose will pitch down. This would be more or less essential in a training aircraft since a nose-up action would send the aircraft towards a stall but the nose-down result would not be achieved, for example, in an aircraft with high-set engines, such as a seaplane or many modern business jets (see Fig. 3.6), where the two couples will need to be in directions opposite to those shown in Fig. 9.1. Here a lower power setting will cause a nose-up result.

Lift and drag depend on speed, thrust on throttle setting and speed, and weight on fuel usage or the release of bombs, so adjustments are often needed. Even if these parameters were constant, the pilot still needs to make major adjustments to the aircraft's flying condition, sometimes very quickly. The tailplane and its associated elevator controls the aircraft's attitude in pitch and a sharp forward movement of the control column will result in an equally rapid movement of the elevator downwards to give an increase in tailplane lift and resultant nose-down action. The elevator therefore acts like a flap deflecting up or down. Some tailplanes are of the "slab" type (all-moving) and produce the same result. Small adjustments in pitch during cruise are effected by deflecting (using the trim wheel) a small tab at the elevator's trailing edge in a direction opposite to that in which the elevator ought to move; in other words, it acts as a tiny elevator for the elevator and relieves the pilot of the need constantly to hold the control column in the required non-neutral position.

If change is needed about the vertical axis, the pilot's rudder pedals deflect the hinged flap at the fin's trailing edge to give a sideways force at the fin and a resultant yawing action to the whole aircraft. A rolling motion about the longitudinal axis is produced by ailerons on the outboard sections of the wings, deflecting in opposite directions to produce an increased lift on one wing and a decrease on the other.

In most light aircraft, a trim wheel is provided only for the elevator because most changes of balance in flight are longitudinal ones. However, it should be remembered that even an aircraft which looks symmetrical in the lateral sense can have asymmetric forces acting on it in flight. In particular, a single engine and propeller will generate a helical flow in the same direction of rotation as the propeller and this will have a marked effect on the fin, producing a sideforce and consequent yawing action. A fixed trim tab is sometimes present on the trailing edge of the rudder, at an angle set by the manufacturer, to offset this yawing action under cruise conditions. However, this means that at any other power setting (and particularly at take-off) a marked rudder pedal force will be needed to keep the nose straight. Sometimes the centreline of the engine is offset slightly to give the same balance in cruise.

Harmonisation

The pilot's actions in controlling an aircraft are therefore likely to be a combination of all the above but the forces required to effect some change in one sense may not need to be the same as in another. For example, a pilot can exert a much greater force with the legs than with the arms and therefore rudder pedal sensitivity need not be the same as for the elevators. In practice, a rule-of-thumb has been established, more or less from the early days of flying, that the ratio of forces required to move ailerons:elevators:rudder should be approximately in the order of 1:2:4 and the controls are then said to be "harmonised".

Banked Flight in a Turn

The use of only the rudder pedals for producing a turn results in a type of sideways skidding action which is at least as uncomfortable as driving a car too fast around an unbanked corner. In both cases the remedy is the same, a bank angle. In a correctly banked turn, the lift force has not only one (vertical) component opposing the weight of the aircraft but also another (horizontal) one "pulling it round the corner". Fig. 9.2 shows that the vertical component is L.cosθ, where θ is the bank angle, so if the aircraft is maintaining altitude this must equal the weight W. Lift is therefore equal to W/cosθ and clearly increases as the bank angle steepens and cosθ decreases. At 30°, cosθ = 0.866 so lift must increase to 115% (=1/0.866) of its normal value; at 60°, cosθ = 0.5 and the lift must double! The pilot is also subject to this marked increase in turning force and will feel as if he weighs double his normal weight ("pulling 2g") but, more alarmingly, because the wing is being required to produce double the lift, the stalling speed of the aircraft will increase to √2 times its normal value (see Chapter 6), a 41% increase!

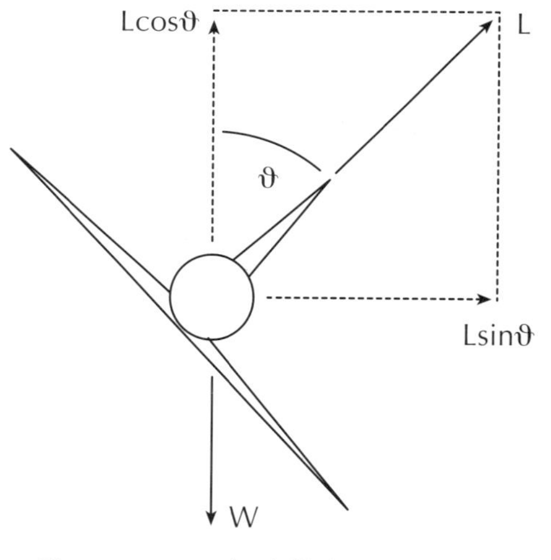

Figure 9.2 Banked flight in a turn

The last point demonstrates very well that **steep turns should never be attempted close to the ground** in case there is insufficient height left to recover from a stall.

Application of Newton's laws to motion in a circle shows that a force mV^2/R is required to pull a body of mass m in a circular path of radius R at a peripheral speed V and that force will always be towards the centre of the circle. In our banked aircraft that force will be $L.\sin\theta$ so $L.\sin\theta = mV^2/R$. We now therefore have:

$$\frac{L.\sin\theta}{L.\cos\theta} = \tan\theta = \frac{mV^2/R}{mg} = \frac{V^2}{gR} \qquad \text{Eqn. 9.1}$$

Eqn. 9.1 is a relationship between bank angle, airspeed (TAS) and radius of turn. The same type of analysis would give us an indication of bank angle required for a so-called "rate one turn", by definition a turn of 3°/s or a complete turn through 360° in two minutes. For light aircraft, there is a rule-of-thumb that suggests that, for a rate one turn:

Bank angle in degrees ≈ 15% of the TAS in knots.

In a turn, an aircraft will often start to sideslip towards the lower wing. This will cause a side force on the fin, tending to turn the nose towards the lower wing, so the maintenance of a correctly banked turn will often require some rudder action. If a turn co-ordinator is fitted, a push will be needed on the pedal on the side to which the little black ball has moved. A secondary effect of bank, if uncorrected, is therefore to yaw and, since a yawing action on its own will cause the outboard wing to have a higher airspeed and lift, a secondary effect of yaw is a banking or rolling motion. The two are clearly linked. If the turn co-ordinator is used to produce zero sideslip then the aircraft will be at exactly the correct bank angle for its speed and radius of turn.

Another interesting point is that if an aircraft is turning about its own vertical axis, as it is in a banked turn, the tailplane is subject to a slight increase in angle of attack because of its distance from the CG. There is therefore a slight increase in tail lift and an elevator up/stick back movement is needed to stop the nose dropping below the horizon. Ab initio pilots have this drummed into them as they perform their first practice turns. By the time they are performing their first 60° banked turns, they realise how much force is needed to hold the nose on the horizon under these conditions and since this represents a 2g turn, the concept of "stick force per g" is introduced. An aircraft in which the stick force per g is small would obviously be far less sluggish than one with a high value, but it would also be easier for less experienced pilots to get into trouble with this increased manoeuvrability. A typical figure for a docile aircraft would be about 15 lbf/g (i.e. 30 lbf rearwards pull in a 60° turn). Most trainers are probably in the 5 to 12 lbf/g range and a good aerobatic aircraft would be as low as 2 lbf/g.

Asymmetric Flight

In a sense, asymmetric flight is any mode of flight in which symmetry has been lost and occurs most often when a multi-engined aircraft loses power from an engine not on the centreline of the fuselage. This involves the pilot in taking rapid action to balance the aircraft again, since there is now a moment trying to yaw the nose towards the dead engine. He or she must now apply rudder by pushing the pedal on the side of the good engine. As if this were not bad enough, the pilot has also lost a fraction of total power, most damaging of all in a twin-engined case.

Minimum control speed

If an engine failure occurs in a twin during take-off, the consequences can be dire and this is why so much time is devoted to simulating this when converting pilots to twins. If the aircraft is at cruising speed, application of rudder will certainly straighten the nose and maintain constant heading. However, at lower airspeeds more rudder deflection will be needed since $\frac{1}{2}\rho V^2$ is less as will therefore be the correcting moment from the rudder. It is easy to see that there is going to be a lower limit speed at which full rudder application (i.e. on the stops or a "bootfull") will only just hold the aircraft straight and this is known as minimum control speed V_{mc}. Below this, the aircraft will continue to yaw towards the dead engine. Clearly, the most dangerous time is therefore when the aircraft has only just left the runway, with its speed still building and V_{mc} must not be so high that the pilot cannot keep it straight. It is normal to require V_{mc} to be no greater than 1.2 times stalling speed (JAR 25). If this condition is not satisfied, the rudder is simply not big enough for the aircraft. This concept of V_{mc} is still further split into two sub-values, depending upon whether one is close to the ground (V_{mcg}) or in the air (V_{mca}). In the former case, the lateral displacement of the aircraft must not exceed 30 ft; in the latter, V_{mca} is the lowest speed at which it is possible to trim the aircraft with zero yaw and no more than 5° of bank angle.

In an aircraft with hydraulic power, the need to apply opposite rudder may not cause too much of a problem, but in a light aircraft the question of pilot leg power comes into play. For constant application, probably not more than about 60 lbf (270 N) is acceptable, although the maximum that can be produced by human leg is probably nearer 200 lbf (890 N). A maximum of 150 lbf (670 N) is normally stipulated, but even at lower values there is always the danger of cramp setting in.

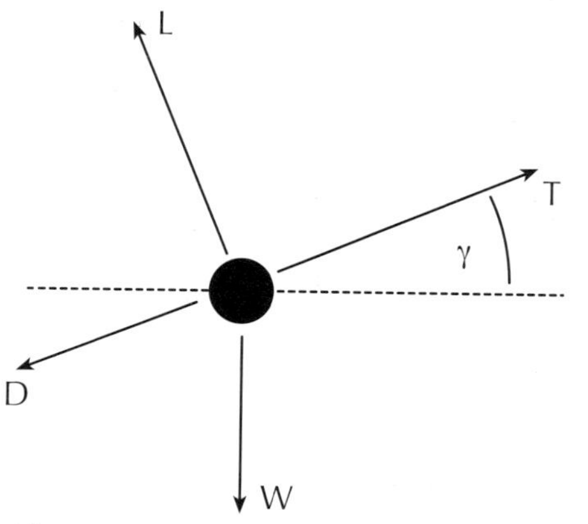

Figure 9.3 Forces in a shallow climb

In large transport aircraft, the requirement is still that they shall be able to continue to haul themselves into the air with one dead engine, so modern twin jets are, in a sense, considerably overpowered when taking off with two good engines. Fig. 9.3 shows the forces on an aircraft in a shallow climb. The net force along the direction of flight is (T - D) and opposing this is the component of weight along the same line Wsinγ, where γ is the angle of climb which, for a twin, is required to be at least 2.4% (1.37°). Lift is perpendicular to this line and therefore plays no part in this force equation. The thrust to weight ratio T/W is usually about 0.25 and D/W about 0.1, so if one engine fails, T/W falls to 0.125 and (T - D)/W (= sinγ) is only 0.025. This gives γ = 1.43° (2.5%), only just sufficient! The development of very powerful engines has enabled very heavy twins to take to the sky and a look at the following table shows that T/W for them is more like 0.3, although it does decrease with size.

Aircraft	Max. T.O. Weight (t)	Total Thrust (t)	T/W
A310	164	52.6	0.32
A330	217	67.7	0.31
777-300	299	86	0.29

Changes with altitude

We saw in Chapter 8 that an aircraft's ability to climb depended on the excess of power available over power required and that this difference became less with increasing altitude. If we draw a similar plot for an aircraft with one engine out, the situation is seen to be even worse than before because the aircraft is now slued round with the nose not pointing in the same direction as the path of the CG through the air. This means that a fraction of the benefits of streamlining have been lost since the aircraft now has rudder deployed and presents a "dirtier", yawed shape to the oncoming air. The power required curve therefore rises at the same time as the power available curve drops by the amount of lost engine power.

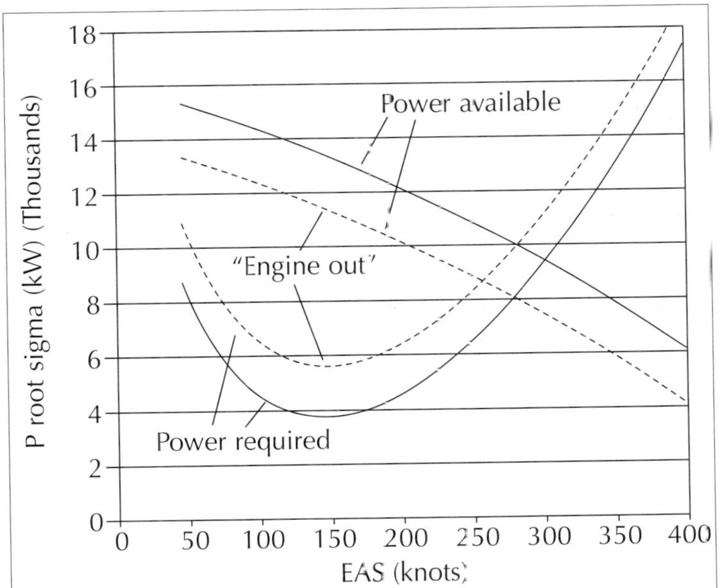

Figure 9.4 "Engine out" performance

The operational ceiling of the aircraft is therefore reduced, as well as its cruising speed. Fig. 9.4 shows this is graphical form, with the full power curves shown as solid lines and the engine out ones as dashed.

Stalling

We saw in Chapter 6 how lift is generated by a wing section and what happens when the angle of attack becomes too large. References above to the ever present danger of stalling when pulling hard in tight turns simply remind us that stalling is a phenomenon to be avoided if we can and that although a wing always stalls at the same angle of attack, dependent on its shape, it certainly does not always stall at the same speed, since this depends on the aircraft's actual weight or its apparent weight (g-loading) in a turn.

Since breakaway of the boundary layer from the top surface of the wing in a stall results in a noticeable loss of suction from the upper front half, there is a useful tendency for it to pitch nose down. This is obviously in the safe direction since speed can then build again although not all wing sections exhibit this useful result, especially swept ones where the tips stall before the root. The loss of lift also results in a marked rate of descent, even if the nose is still pointing above the horizon, so a drop rate of several hundred feet per minute can be seen on the vertical speed gauge. The changed airflow pattern following breakaway also often produces a buffeting effect on the tailplane, if the latter is anywhere near the wing wake, and this can act as a useful stall warning device.

"Power on" stalls

Stalling speeds are often quoted "power on" or "power off" and Fig. 9.3 enables us to see why. In climbing flight, the difference of thrust and drag (T-D) enables the aircraft to overcome gravity and increase its altitude. However, the vertical component of (T-D) is added to lift L to oppose weight W so, under these conditions, lift can actually be less than weight, leading to a lower stalling speed. V_{stall} power on is therefore lower than the power off figure. Indeed, modern jet fighters sometimes have such enormous thrust available that they can fly at angles of attack well beyond the stalling angles for their wings, simply because the jet thrust is providing a large lift component. This is known as "high alpha" flight and intense research is being conducted in this area, mainly in the USA, because this gives fighters increased manoeuvrability in air combat which they would otherwise not have.

With propeller driven aircraft there is an additional consideration leading to lower stalling speeds in that, with power on, there is a considerable propwash flow over the wing's surfaces immediately behind the prop so the flow over that part of the wing is less likely to stall.

Stall recovery

Recovery from the stall is usually straightforward. The nose should be pushed downwards, if it hasn't already adopted this position, power should be applied, flaps should be reduced to take-off setting if they were at their landing value and a gentle pull-up towards the horizon should follow the acquisition of higher airspeed again. Flaps can be reset to zero when a positive rate of climb is established. An over-zealous pull-up could result in simply returning to a stalled condition since the aircraft will be pulling out of a dive at a g-loading well above one, with the concomitant increase in stalling speed.

When an aircraft is close to stalling, directional and lateral control should be effected entirely by rudder action and the reason for this leads us neatly into the next section: spinning.

Spinning

When an aircraft approaches a stall, the chances of both wings stalling at exactly the same time are minimal; this would require that they were geometrically identical and had identical airflows over them. In practice, one will appear to dip first and, under these conditions, applying opposite aileron is just about the worst thing one can do. If the wing has dipped, it is already close to losing a major fraction of its lift and applying down-aileron will cause it to stall even sooner. The aircraft will then enter a manoeuvre exhibiting just about every mode of motion one can imagine - a spin. The aircraft starts to sideslip towards the dropped wing, causing it also to turn in that direction because of fin action. The unstalled wing is now travelling faster than the stalled one so its lift will therefore increase, pushing the aircraft even further into the spin. The aircraft now rotates about a vertical axis fixed in the ground, with its nose pointing severely downhill and with whatever lift it has left holding it in its circular (helical) path against the centrifugal effects trying to dislodge it from the helix.

After one or two turns, it will enter a stable (!) state, constituting a superb example of stall, roll, yaw, pitch (down), sideslip and rapid height loss, a pilot's and aerodynamicist's nightmare! Figs. 9.5(a) and (b) show the two identifiably different modes of spinning and most aircraft will fit one of these two models, although those resembling Fig. 9.5(b) will probably have gone through that of Fig. 9.5(a) to get there. The aircraft is basically sinking at speed V m/s whilst rotating about the vertical axis at speed Ω rad/s. The angle of attack α between the chord line and the vertical wind direction is likely to be about 35 to 40° in case (a) and 60 to 70° in case (b), the latter being referred to often as a "flat spin". It is found in practice that the resultant aerodynamic force F on the aircraft is usually perpendicular to the wing chord and the lift (L) and drag (D) components of it will, by definition, be perpendicular and parallel respectively to the velocity V.

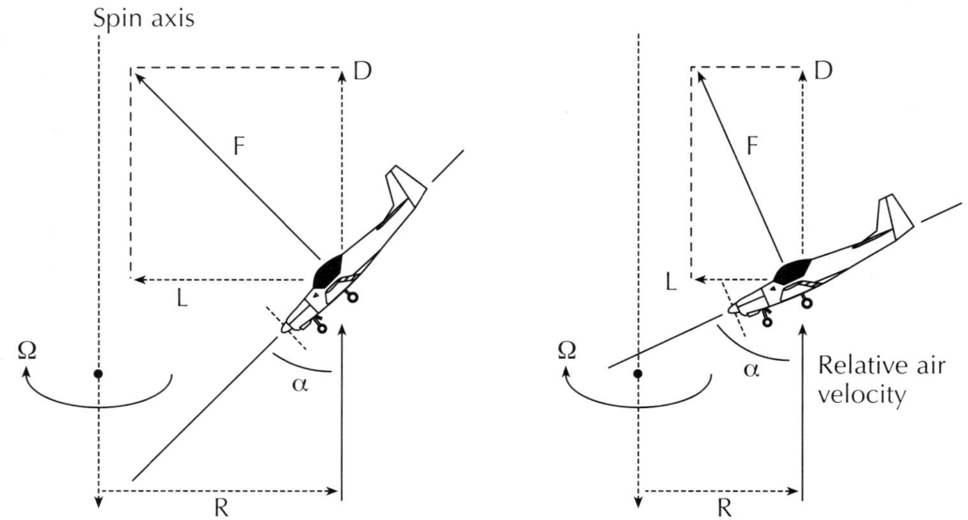

Figure 9.5 Spinning modes

If a detailed analysis of the mechanics of this situation is carried out, it can be shown that:

Radius about vertical axis $R = \dfrac{g.\cot\alpha}{\Omega^2}$ *Eqn.9.2*

The cotangent of an angle (= 1/tan) decreases as the angle increases so the above equation gives us some valuable clues about the two distinct states. If the spin rate Ω is constant, a large angle of attack α means a small rotation radius R and *vice versa*. On the other hand, if the angle of attack is constant, R decreases with increasing Ω. A flat spin would therefore be a fast one at a small distance from the axis whereas a steep spin would be a slower one at a greater radius from the axis. In scientific terminology, this is in accord with the idea that the angular momentum for the two cases should be roughly the same, a low moment of inertia spinning at a greater rate than a high one. Moment of inertia in this case would be the aircraft mass times R^2. The value of R is hardly ever more than about half the wingspan and the "fast" case is usually about twice the rotational speed of the "slow" one. The values of all these parameters depend to a large extent on the shape of the aircraft and its mass distribution, but Ω can vary from about one revolution every three seconds to more than one rev/s.

The flatter, faster spin is generally considered to be the more dangerous because it tends to be more stable and difficult to escape from. A light aircraft may lose 350 ft for every turn and might need five turns to recover, so this is an important consideration. Recovery from the spin varies to some extent between aircraft, some being vicious in their capabilities and some being virtually unspinnable. One very important indicator is the relative positions of tailplane and fin. At the extreme values of α evident in Fig. 9.5, the wake from the tailplane could well engulf the fin and rudder, or at least a major fraction of them. Under these circumstances, the pilot would have little chance of generating a yawing action in the direction opposite to the spin and may well have to consider leaving the aircraft. The Aerospatiale TB10 is a good example of design to avoid this problem; the tail is actually aft of the fin so no "shadowing" can occur. However, the TB10 also has two ventral strakes on its underbelly, which indicate the solution to another problem here. At such high angles of attack, the fuselage becomes more of a cylinder with flow perpendicular to its axis rather than parallel to it, as in normal flight. The flow around a cylinder breaks away from the thickest part (see Fig. 5.2), in the same way that a wing stalls at high α, and this results in the fin and rudder being in this separated, low-energy flow. The strakes have the job of tripping the airflow to form vortices rotating in a direction which will send air towards the fin. In some cases, for example the Bulldog and Chipmunk, the strakes have been taken to the part of the fuselage just ahead of (and adjoining) the tailplane leading edge, although the purpose is the same - they are all anti-spin strakes.

Methods for recovery from the spin vary from aircraft to aircraft and are indicated in the operating handbook, based on recommendations from company and CAA or FAA test pilots, but they generally do not vary much from the basic need to stop the rotation and *then* pull out of the ensuing dive. The recommendation will normally be to apply opposite rudder to stop the spin and then to push the stick forward to gather speed in a dive. Premature use of the stick can be counter-productive since the deployment of down-elevator could result in a flow which shields the fin and rudder even more, so a distinct pause is needed. If spinning is to be practised, it is advisable to have a forward CG position (aft is decidedly dangerous), power off and zero flap setting, the last two causing secondary flows near the tail and fin which could make it more difficult to recover. Recommendations for spin recovery are published in operating handbooks but Stinton, in his 1996 book (see Bibliography), makes the very good point that most pilots under stress will revert to basic recovery techniques learned under training, so publication of more exotic methods is unnecessary if the basic method (above) works for a given aircraft.

Flight Envelopes - The V-n Diagram

So far in this chapter, we have looked at the control and manoeuvring of aircraft and have seen how flight can be continued up to the point where, for example, the wings may not be able to provide any more lift or the rudder is unable to prevent the nose from yawing; flight, in fact, up to the limits. But limits there certainly are. An aircraft put into a power-on dive will accelerate to a speed much higher than its cruising speed and that "terminal" speed may be so high that parts of the aircraft start to break off. A "never exceed" speed V_{ne} is therefore always quoted in the operating handbook. In the same way, a pilot undertaking a very tight turn or aerobatics may have sufficient physical strength to be able to pull 3 or 4g, but it is an entirely different matter whether the wings have been stressed to take that sort of load without buckling.

All aircraft are designed with safety margins built in but extremes of flight can sometimes take the aircraft very close to its limits. Obviously, those limits will differ with the intended use of the aircraft. A large airliner would not be expected to subject its passengers to more than about 1.15g, the value in a rate one turn, but it must be stressed to survive a good shaking in clear air turbulence. The pilot of an aerobatic aircraft, on the other hand, will subject his or her machine to negative g loadings, as well as high positive ones. Pushing the stick hard forward at high speed will cause the pilot to rise into the safety straps and a championship standard aircraft might well be stressed for +9g to -6g, a truly horrendous range.

These various limits can be expressed on a graph, with speed as the x axis and g loading as the y axis, and this is known as a V-n (or n-V) diagram (The "-" stands for versus, not minus). The V represents speed and "n" the number of gs so n = 3 for 3g. Fig. 9.6 shows a V-n diagram for a typical light aircraft and the limits alluded to above can be seen to be the outer markers of the diagram. "g limits" of +3.8/-1 have been assumed. At the extreme right hand end of allowable speed is V_{ne} and this must never be exceeded under any g loading. Left of this, but inside the envelope, is V_{no}, the normal operating maximum. Flight within the range between V_{no} and V_{ne} is allowable but would be very unwise in conditions of turbulence. Severe g loadings can be experienced by an aircraft under gust conditions and these get worse as flight speed increases. The subject of gusts is dealt with in Chapter 10.

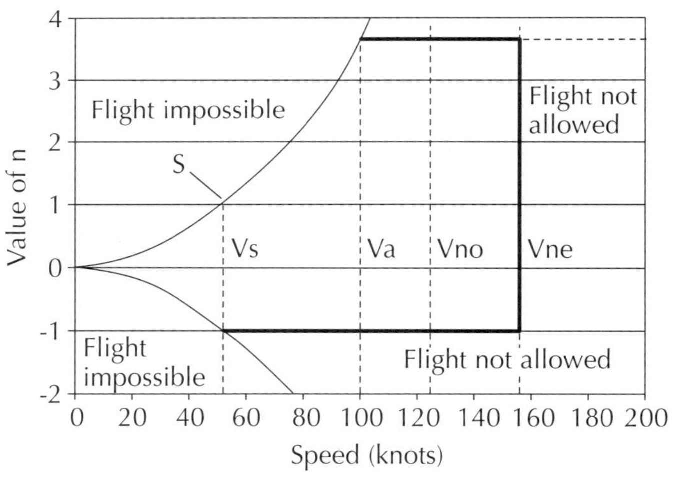

Figure 9.6 A typical V-n diagram

To the left of the graph are two parabolas, each representing the minimum speed at which the aircraft could be flown at the plus or minus g loadings indicated. At n = +1 (point S), lift exactly equals weight so the speed corresponding to this is the usual 1g stalling speed of the aircraft, V_S. At n = 2, as we saw in the section on banked turns, $V\sqrt{2}$ (= 1.414V) is needed to keep the aircraft aloft so the curve climbs as a $y = x^2$ graph would. A similar, but mirror-image, curve accounts for the negative g flight conditions. This would be an acceleration propelling the pilot out of his or her seat and zero g would correspond to just about rising out of the seat, as in a space shuttle in correct orbit. Flight to the left of these parabolas is therefore impossible; the wings simply could not generate enough lift at the speeds shown.

The upper and lower limits of the V-n diagram are set by the design maximum positive and negative g loadings. Flight above or below these limits is theoretically possible but with the risk that the wings, or some other part of the structure, might break up. The speed at which the +3.8 horizontal line cuts the rising parabola is called V_A. This is an important corner point because at speeds greater than this, the pilot can pull g loadings higher than +3.8 without stalling the aircraft, so flight at $V > V_A$ involves this added caution.

We see therefore that all flight should be within the envelope bounded by the upper and lower g limits, V_{ne} and the two parabolas (solid lines in Fig. 9.6). Most flights, of course, will be somewhere near the n = 1 horizontal line passing to the right from point S to the V_{no} limit.

Conclusion

This chapter has attempted to show that any deviation from trimmed, straight, level flight is worthy of study and that some deviations are positively dangerous. Under the latter heading we can include steeply banked turns shortly after take-off, stalling and spinning at low altitude and any flight condition outside the published V-n diagram limits for the aircraft in question, whether this be excessive speed, unjustifiable g loadings or flight beyond V_{no} in very turbulent atmospheric conditions. For trainee pilots, it is essential to have an adequately qualified instructor on board when trying anything close to the limits. That apart, most conventional aircraft are fairly stable in normal flight and we look at the question of stability next.

10

Stability

Will it fall out of the sky?

AIRCRAFT STABILITY is an immensely important subject and it is as well that designers have developed the subject to such a fine art that the stability characteristics of a new aircraft on first flight are usually accurately predicted before it even takes to the air. For the average pilot, the stability of an aircraft will have been tested by company and CAA or FAA test pilots during the development phase so that knowledge of the pilot's handbook and the adherence to certain basic rules should ensure they never approach any danger points in the performance envelope.

In basic terms, the stability of an aircraft can be assessed in the same way as for any other system. For example, a pendulum has so-called positive stability because, following a small disturbance, gravity will ensure that it returns to its original position. It will also overshoot, but this will be gradually damped down by air resistance. A pencil standing on its end, however, has negative stability because a slight sideways disturbance will not only cause it to begin to topple but the rate of toppling will continually increase as gravity acts on the pencil's CG. The stability of an aircraft is far more complicated than that and must generally be looked at under two different headings: static and dynamic. We also need to differentiate between stability about the lateral axis, confusingly called *longitudinal* stability, and that about the remaining two axes (longitudinal and vertical), called *lateral* stability.

Static Stability

When an aircraft is subject to a sudden vertical or sideways gust, the pilot is entitled to expect that it will respond in such a way that, following the above reasoning, it will tend to return to its original state rather than continue to diverge from it. This is termed **static** stability to differentiate it from the **dynamic** version, which is concerned with the long-term response to a disturbance. We shall look at the latter in the next section.

Lateral Static Stability

A pilot experiencing a gust which causes the aircraft to yaw suddenly hopes the aircraft will right itself equally rapidly without too much effort on his part and this facility is provided by the fin. As shown in Fig. 10.1, the sudden yawing motion gives the fin an angle of attack to the oncoming airsteam which it didn't have before. It therefore develops a sideways lift force, thus giving a restoring moment about the vertical axis and a return to zero yaw angle. The size of the fin and the distance l_F of its aerodynamic centre from the CG are clearly the important parameters here. There will be an overshoot but the opposite will then happen and the process is repeated in the reverse direction. This whole action subsides quickly and is said to be "heavily damped". Damping is a term used by control engineers to describe the rate at which such a disturbance drops to zero and the phenomenon is familiar to all drivers of cars whose "dampers" (shock absorbers) have the job of deadening as quickly as possible the vibrations in the suspension system after passing over a road bump.

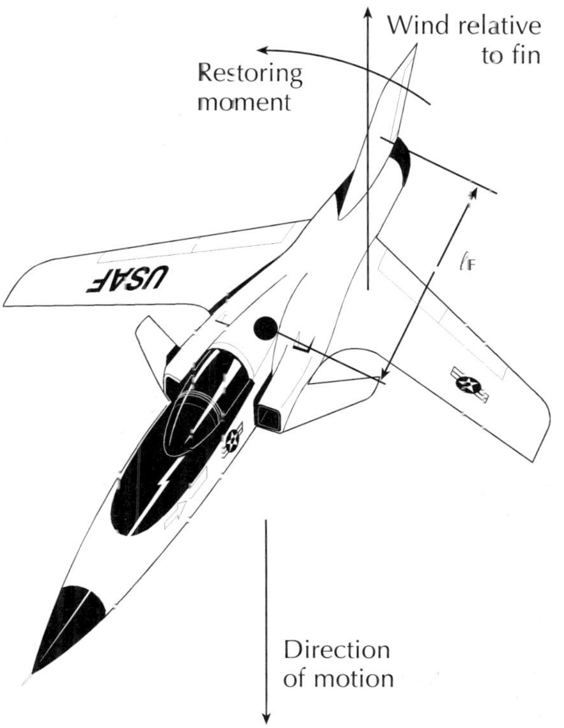

Figure 10.1 Weathercock stability

This ability of an aircraft to always keep its nose pointing straight ahead is called, not surprisingly, weathercock stability and is one of the most basic flying characteristics determining the acceptability of an aircraft. Since, in scientific terms, a moment is a force times an arm (radius), lack of weathercock stability would be evident in aircraft having a fin too small or too near to the CG, or both. Where this lack of stability has been evident, either for the above reasons or because a change of design or task has rendered it so, the designer has had to add fins to the tailplane tips or increase the fin area. An obvious case was the Boeing 747 mother ship which carried the space shuttle on its back; the presence of the latter, even though it was itself stable, led to the need for extra fins on the 747 so that the weathercock stability of the combination of two aircraft did not suffer.

There will also be a contribution, but much smaller, from the wings, especially if they are swept. The forward going wing will develop more lift and drag because of its greater airspeed and this increase will be in the direction of opposing the yawing motion.

Longitudinal Static Stability

Just as a pilot is entitled to expect an aircraft to return to normal after a sideways disturbance, a similar confidence in its ability to respond to a vertical one is essential; the alternative is rapid progress to either a stall or a terminal dive. This version of static stability is provided by the action of the tailplane. If a nose-up disturbance develops, the tailplane is thrust down into the airstream below the fuselage and rapidly develops more lift, returning the nose to the horizontal. As with the fin, its ability to do so depends on its size and its distance from the CG. We thus see that CG position is important here and a slight diversion into theory will help in seeing just how important.

Pitching moments are considered positive, by convention, when they are nose-up. If we consider a wing on its own, Fig. 10.2 shows that if moments are taken about the wing leading edge, the lift force produces a negative pitching moment and this would become even more negative at increased angles of attack, as the lift increases. If moments are taken about the wing's trailing edge, however, the reverse is true; a positive pitching moment is obtained and this will increase with α. There is therefore a point somewhere on the wing section where the **change of pitching moment with α will be zero**; this is called the **aerodynamic centre (a.c.)**. For a tailless aircraft, the CG must be forward of the a.c. so that any increase in lift caused by a nose-up disturbance immediately results in a nose-down pitching moment, as required for static stability. At first sight this situation seems crazy because in undisturbed flight the weight acting ahead of the lift force would seem to cause a permanent nose-down moment. But remember that there are two other forces acting on the aircraft as a whole - the engine thrust and the drag. These could be used to produce a moment in the opposite direction, in addition to the reflexing of the trailing edge referred to in Chapter 3.

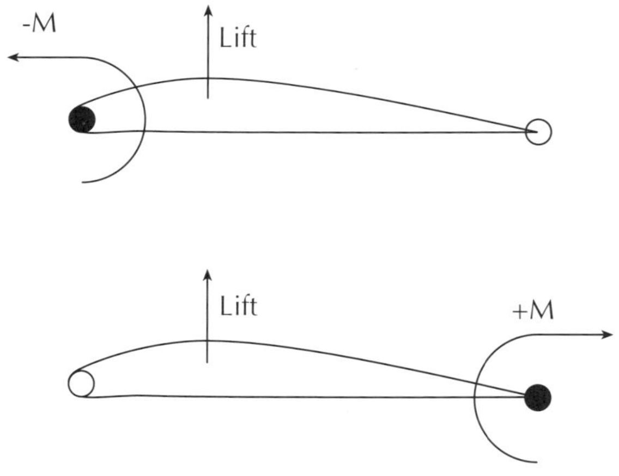

Figure 10.2 Pitching moment due to wing lift

With a conventional aircraft, the tailplane will have its own aerodynamic centre, as will the fin, and the distance from the tail's a.c. to the CG is referred to as the tail arm l_T (see Fig. 10.3). In a nose-up disturbance, as α increases, both the wing and tailplane lift forces increase, although the latter is on a much longer arm so the overall effect is a nose-down restoring moment; that is, away from a stall condition.

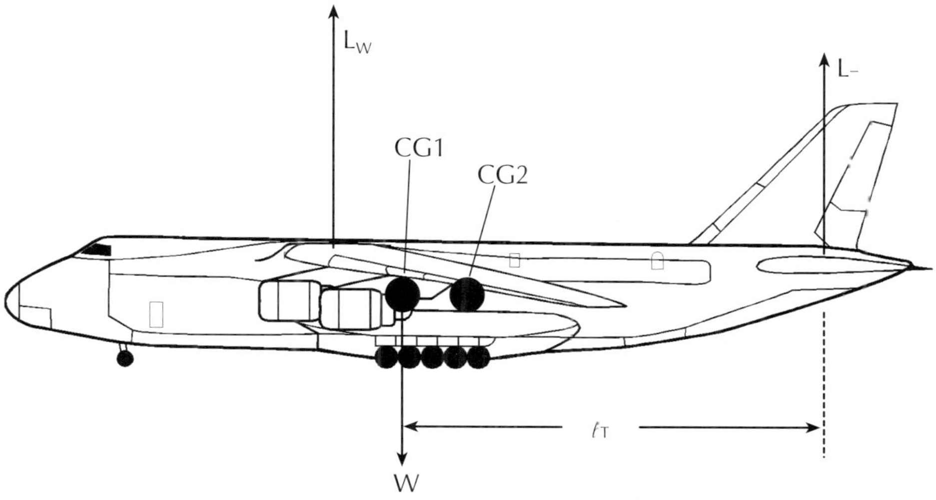

Figure 10.3 Tail arm – longitudinal stability

If the CG is moved aft to position CG2, the tail arm will be shorter and the nose-down moment due to tailplane action will thus be smaller (i.e. less negative). If one therefore plots a graph (see Fig. 10.4) of the pitching moment coefficient C_M against α (or against C_L since this is proportional to α), two lines would be obtained, one for each CG position, with CG2 corresponding to the more aft position. The lines slope downwards to the right because as α increases, the tail lift also increases, giving an increased (i.e. more negative) nose-down pitching moment. It can be seen that not only does the CG2 line lie above that for CG1 but it has a lesser slope, so that a CG position could be reached, sufficiently aft, where the slope becomes zero. In practical terms, this means that the tailplane would lose all its ability to produce automatically a restoring moment and the pilot would need to make constant elevator adjustments to keep the aircraft on an even keel. This would in fact be a quite unacceptable state of affairs, but fortunately this CG position can

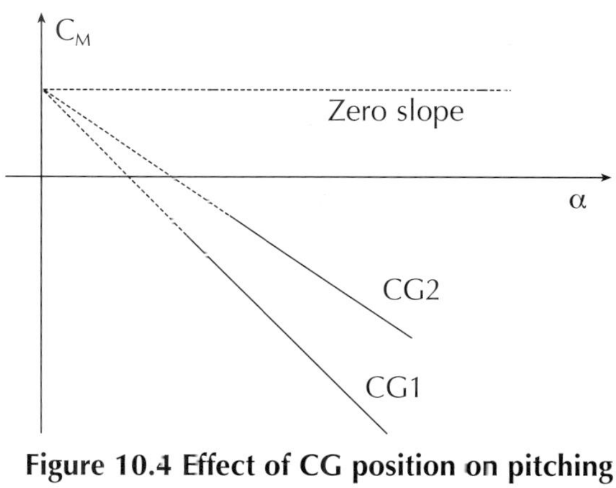

Figure 10.4 Effect of CG position on pitching moment

be found by indirect means. If the slopes in Fig. 10.4 are plotted against CG position, the point at which they cut the horizontal axis can be calculated and the so-called "neutral point" position h_n defined (Fig. 10.5). Well before this point was reached, the pilot would complain that the aircraft was uncontrollable!

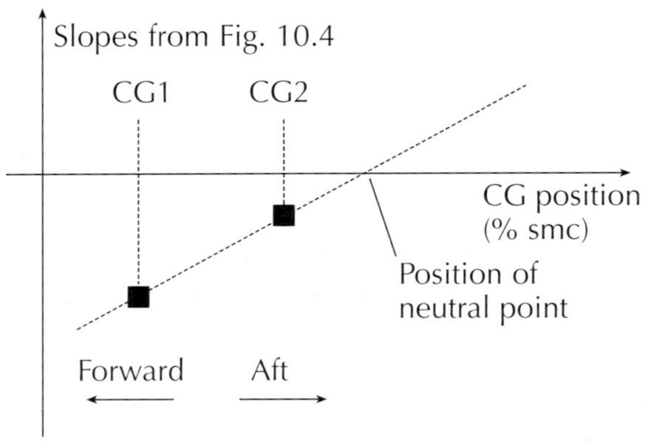

Figure 10.5 Determination of the neutral point

Engineers like to work in dimensionless terms if they can and quoting a CG position is no exception. Distance is often measured from the wing's leading edge or the aircraft's nose, but some datum point **must** be specified. This distance is then divided by the "standard mean chord" (smc) of the wing (= wing area/span) and CG locations quoted in "%smc" terms. A typical case might be that the CG position could lie between 15 and 43 %smc from the leading edge, with the neutral point being at 53%smc. A pilot operating at the forward CG limit (15%) would therefore have a very stable aircraft, albeit with a need to exert increased elevator stick forces. Operation at the aft limit (43%) would be easier in terms of stick forces, but the pilot would be very much busier trying to keep his aircraft at a fixed altitude.

The actual distances involved (as opposed to %smc) are not very great and pilots must take great care not to operate with a CG too far aft. For larger aircraft like the Airbus A340 and A320, the values of smc are about 7.3 and 4.2 m (24 and 14 ft) respectively so that the range 15 to 43%smc represents about 2 and 1.2 m (6.6 and 4 ft). However, in small aircraft like the Piper Warrior and Tomahawk the ranges are respectively 25.4 cm (10 in.) and 15 cm (6 in.)! The sudden addition of two heavy passengers and four sets of golf clubs in the back of a fully fuelled, single-engined light aircraft could have a disastrous effect on CG position and total weight!

Load and balance calculations

Since this is so important, let's have a look at a few typical numbers. As an example, we'll consider a four-seat light aircraft for which the manufacturer's handbook states that the maximum take-off weight (MTOW) must not exceed 2400 lb (1088 kg) and the CG limits measured aft from the nose are 83 and 93 in. The leading edge is known to be 74 in (1.88 m) aft of the nose and the standard mean chord (smc) is 64 in (1.625 m). The forward limit is therefore at (83-74)/64 = 14% smc from the leading edge and the aft limit is at 30% (some rounding off has taken place here). The following table shows the weights of the various components making up the MTOW and also the distance from the datum point (the "arm"). These are usually quoted in inches but the SI equivalents are shown alongside.

Item	Weight (lbf)	Arm (in)	Moment (lbf.in)	Weight (kgf)	Arm (m)	Moment (kgf.m)
Empty aircraft	1500	87	130500	680	2.210	1503.27
Pilot	160	80	12800	73	2.032	147.45
Front passenger	160	80	12800	73	2.032	147.45
Rear passengers	320	120	38400	145	3.048	442.34
Fuel	330	95	31350	150	2.413	361.13
Baggage	30	150	4500	14	3.810	51.84
Totals	2500		230350	1134		2653.47
CG posn.		92.14 in			2.340 m	
%smc		28.34%			28.34%	

The empty weight of the aircraft is as supplied by the manufacturer and remains a constant in the above table unless we replace, for example, some of the navaids by heavier or lighter versions. The weights of crew and passengers vary considerably so those shown in the table are typical values. The fuel weight will obviously depend on how much is loaded on before take-off and how quickly the engine burns it in flight and baggage weights are rather variable too.

Each weight is multiplied by the distance of its centre of gravity from the datum point (the nose in this case) to give a pitching moment contribution in the fourth column. The total moment divided by the total weight will then indicate the CG position of the whole aircraft now and that figure can be converted into a %smc figure, knowing the position of the leading edge of the wing. An interesting point to note here is that the CG of the pilot and front passenger is forward of that of the empty aircraft whereas the CGs of everything else are aft of it.

With all seats occupied, a full fuel load and 30 lb of baggage, the above aircraft exceeds the certified MTOW and should not therefore take to the air; amongst other problems, its stalling speed will be artificially high and its take-off distance will be increased. It is, however, within the CG limits set by the manufacturer (i.e. between 14 and 30%) so it will be statically stable. The pilot will need to offload some fuel and if only half the maximum is carried (165 lb), the total weight comes down to 2335 lb, which is now acceptable. Moreover, mass has been removed aft of the "empty" CG so the new CG will be slightly further forward, in fact at 28.03 %smc. The aircraft is now stable and at a weight lower than MTOW. The danger in the opposite direction would be to load up with full fuel, two passengers only (and insisting on sitting in the back!) and 90 lb of baggage. If these figures are inserted in the above table, the total weight now becomes 2400 lb but the CG moves aft to 31.9%; the former is just acceptable, the latter is certainly not.

The essential point to be emphasised here is that even if a pilot's calculations show his aircraft to be within limits for **maximum take-off weight**, there may still be danger lurking in a **CG position** which is too far aft. The opposite problem of a dangerously forward CG position is not often addressed but would manifest itself as an inability of the pilot either to flare just before landing or to rotate on take-off; there would simply be insufficient elevator power at the low speeds involved.

Speed Stability

The above reasoning applies essentially to the ability of an aircraft to remain stable following a change in angle of attack, although another interesting facet of this problem is concerned with its stability when changing speed. Many conventional aircraft are designed to have a slight download on the tailplane when in the cruise condition. If the aircraft is then, for example, subject to a speed decrease for any reason, the tail's **negative** lift (being proportional to the square of speed) will decrease; this means that the tail force previously helping to keep the nose up is now lower, giving the aircraft a nose-down pitching moment and a concomitant speed increase. Since this is in the safe direction, the aircraft is then said to be "speed stable". However, if the aircraft is flying with an aft CG position, the negative tail lift required for balance in cruising flight will be less (because the aft CG is "helping to push the tail down") and therefore the wing lift will itself need to be less, being equal to the sum of the weight and tail download. If the lifting forces (up or down) are lower, then the induced drag is lower and the aircraft's total drag is lower. It's true to say, therefore, that flying with an aft CG position will use less fuel per mile but at the expense of some static stability.

CG margins

From the previous paragraphs, we can see that not only can a designer specify the fore and aft limits for a CG position for any given aircraft but that the static stability of that aircraft is directly related to the distance of the actual CG position from the neutral point and this is called the "static margin". If h_{cg} and h_n are respectively the distances from the datum point of the CG and of the neutral point, then

$$\textbf{Static margin} = K_n = h_n - h_{cg} \quad (\%\text{smc})$$

On this basis, a designer would normally quote an aft CG limit to give a static margin of at least 5%smc but, as usual, this does not represent the whole picture and we need two more terms here because the value of the static margin will depend on whether the aircraft is being flown hands on or hands off. In the former case, the elevator is in a fixed position, controlled by the pilot, so a sudden change in flight condition caused by a gust, for example, will be carried out at constant elevator angle. The result will not be the same if the elevator is allowed to flap or "trail" and the motion of the aircraft will depend on whether the forces on the elevator tend to make it rise or fall. In the case of a droop, increased tail lift is obtained and the aircraft will tend to pitch nose down, which is stable, so the CG could be moved further aft before the neutral point stick free is reached. We therefore have two different neutral points and two static margins, one called "stick fixed", the other "stick free".

Manoeuvre margins

As if that weren't bad enough, there are also two other "fixed" and "free" critical points to consider - the so-called "manoeuvre points". If an aircraft is pulling out of a dive, its nose is rising so, by definition, it is rotating about its pitch axis and in a direction which will cause an increased angle of attack for the tailplane because of that rotation. This means that the tailplane is developing more lift and, as with the drooping elevator case above, the manoeuvre point can therefore be aft of the neutral point. The manoeuvre margins are always therefore greater than the static ones.

$$\textbf{Manoeuvre margin} = H_m = h_n - h_{cg}$$

Since the pilot is having to "pull g" to maintain the aircraft in its roughly circular flight path, the manoeuvre margins can clearly be related to the movement of, and forces on, the stick. By analogy with the terminology for static margins, the stick fixed condition becomes the **stick travel per g** and the stick free one the **stick force per g**. The latter was mentioned in the previous chapter when discussing manoeuvrability.

Because the manoeuvre margins are always greater than the static ones and the stick free margin is greater than the stick fixed one, we can see that the four critical points named above can be placed in order of progress aft along the longitudinal axis:

Furthest forward:	neutral point, stick fixed
⇓	neutral point, stick free
⇓	manoeuvre point, stick fixed
Furthest aft:	manoeuvre point, stick free

Dynamic Stability

In the section above, we have looked at the ability of an aircraft to return towards its trimmed state immediately after a disturbance and the importance of CG position, tailplane, fin size and positioning were obvious. We are at least as much concerned, however, with what happens in the longer term. An aircraft may well respond by starting to return in the direction of its trimmed state, but if there is insufficient damping for the mode concerned, the longer term behaviour may become quite unacceptable in terms of passenger comfort or, in extreme cases, the pilot may simply not be able to control the aircraft over a long period. We shall now therefore look at this aspect of stability, which carries the handle "dynamic", and we shall find that there are two modes to consider in the longitudinal sense and three in the lateral.

It will be useful first to look at a graph of how an aircraft might respond to a sudden disturbance and this is shown in Fig. 10.6. If the shape of the aircraft is such that the disturbance can be damped out, it will start an oscillation in which the peak values will decrease with time. The time between successive troughs B and C (or peaks) is called the periodic time t_p and a "time to half amplitude" $t_{1/2}$ can be identified as the time needed for the amplitude A to fall to half its initial value. If the damping is large enough, oscillations may not occur at all and the curve will return to the horizontal axis (i.e. its value before disturbance) without overshoot. If the response is **unstable**, the oscillations will grow with time and $t_{1/2}$ will be replaced by t_D, the time to **double** amplitude. This terminology will be used in what follows.

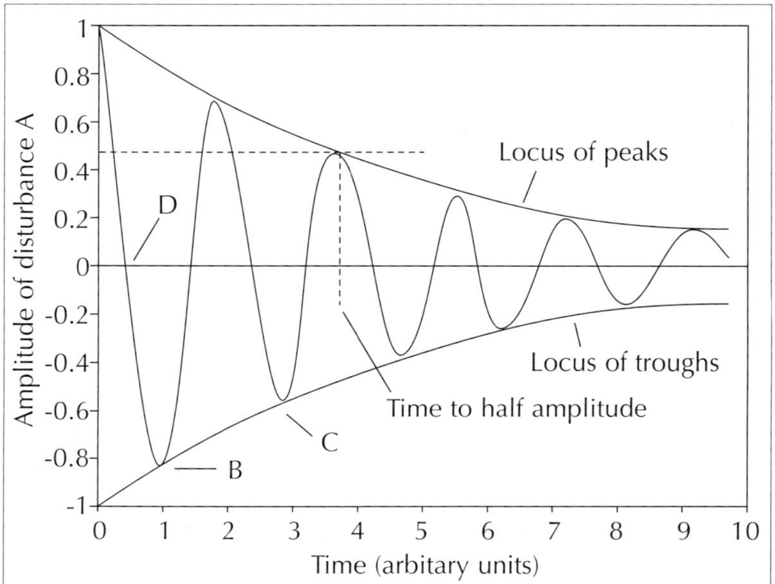

Figure 10.6 A damped oscillation

Longitudinal - Short Period Pitching Oscillation

In considering the longitudinal dynamic stability, we are concerned with forward motion, vertical motion and rotation about the lateral axis. For brevity, designers call these speed, heave and pitch, terms largely borrowed from nautical parlance and evoking all the usual memories of vomit bags. If an aircraft is suddenly disturbed in pitch, we need to be sure that not only will it respond by producing an opposite restoring moment (tailplane effect, as above) but that it will do so quickly. There will be rapid changes in pitch rate and α but no major change in forward speed and the tailplane must be of such a size that the subsequent motion must be heavily damped. This mode is called the **short period pitching oscillation (SPPO)** and can be demonstrated by a sharp stick movement and return, producing an elevator motion either up or down. The whole movement should be completed in under a second and the corresponding aircraft response will be similarly rapid. If the tailplane is doing its job properly, the mode will be so highly damped that the whole incident will be over in under a second for a light aircraft and in only a few seconds for a large airliner. However, the sudden changes may have caused a longer-term mode to show itself - the so-called phugoid.

Longitudinal - The Phugoid Motion

Although the SPPO is thought of as almost a constant speed mode, the activation of elevator will induce an almost immediate climb or dive, however short-lived, and the aircraft will suffer a small speed change to accompany the gain or loss of altitude. This brings us into the area of constant energy concepts. When any body loses height and gains speed under the action of gravity, it is exchanging potential energy (due to altitude) for kinetic energy (due to motion) and the sum of the two must remain constant, except for losses due to drag (for example) which can never be recovered. An aircraft, on the other hand, has the property that as its speed increases so does its lift, so there is a tendency for it to start to climb again from what was a very shallow dive. As height is gained, the speed will gradually decrease and so therefore will lift, giving an aircraft an inherent ability to produce a roller coaster ride once an initial disturbance (the SPPO) has died away. The roller coaster effect is gradually damped out by drag, but this is a very low order of damping and the mode lasts for a long time with a periodic time vastly longer than the SPPO. Instead of two seconds, we are looking here at anything between about 40 and 100 s.

This phenomenon was first analysed by the great engineer Lanchester who assumed that slow changes in pitch and speed were involved but virtually no change in α. He called it the phugoid, but this is almost certainly a pun on the Latin verb *fugere* (to fly). He presumably substituted the Greek "ph" instead of "f" to confuse people even more! His very elegant analysis showed that the periodic time is independent of aircraft type or size and is approximately equal to a quarter of the aircraft's speed in knots (or half the speed in m/s), something that has been found to be a remarkably good rule of thumb.

The phugoid can most easily be demonstrated by placing the aircraft in a gentle dive (perhaps 15°) and letting go of the controls completely when the speed has built up to about 110% of cruise speed (point D in Fig. 10.6). The periodic time is so long that an ordinary watch can be used to time the successive troughs (points B and C, with nose exactly on the horizon). Some aircraft are more prone than others to produce a recognisable phugoid, although modern autopilot systems are sensitive enough to damp out this mode almost completely. Because the damping by drag is so low, it is sometimes the case that an aircraft can have an unstable phugoid motion and, whereas one normally hopes for a stable one with a time to half amplitude $t_{1/2}$ of less than about 40 s, pilots can cope with an **unstable** one with a t_D as low as 25 s but they don't like it and would not usually tolerate it for very long.

Lateral - Roll Subsidence

In considering **lateral** stability, we need to deal with three modes, not two, and we are concerned with motion along and about the vertical and roll axes. The easiest of these to understand is the so-called roll subsidence (or pure roll) mode. If an aircraft is subject to a sudden wing up or down disturbance, caused for example by encountering an upgust or thermal, the descending wing is heading towards the air underneath it so that its angle of attack is suddenly increased; vice versa for the upgoing wing. There is therefore an increase of lift on the downgoing wing and a concomitant decrease for the other one, giving a restoring rolling moment in the opposite direction. This effect is so strong that aircraft of high aspect ratio are positively sluggish in this mode; that is, it is very heavily damped indeed. Even on high performance gliders, however, the effect is noticeable and a good pilot will react by turning towards the wing which has risen to move into the thermal which is obviously on that side. The roll damping is obviously going to be far less for a military or aerobatic aircraft needing agility and the ability of an aircraft like the BAe Hawk to perform rapid flick rolls is well known.

Time to half amplitude is typically about 0.3 s for an airliner and 0.13 s for a Cherokee.

Lateral - Spiral Mode

However well damped the roll mode may be, a disturbance causing a slight bank angle will produce also a so-called spiral mode. Because the overall lift vector is now inclined away from the vertical and no longer exactly opposes the weight (Fig. 10.7[a]), a sideways motion will develop (sideslip) in the direction of the lower wing. The sideways airflow thus induced will cause a side force on the fin L_F, resulting in a yaw developing towards the lower wing. This will obviously make the situation even worse and an increasing bank angle and yawing action will result in a spiral dive, progressively. However, a restoring moment could be produced by giving the wings a dihedral angle of a few degrees (Fig.

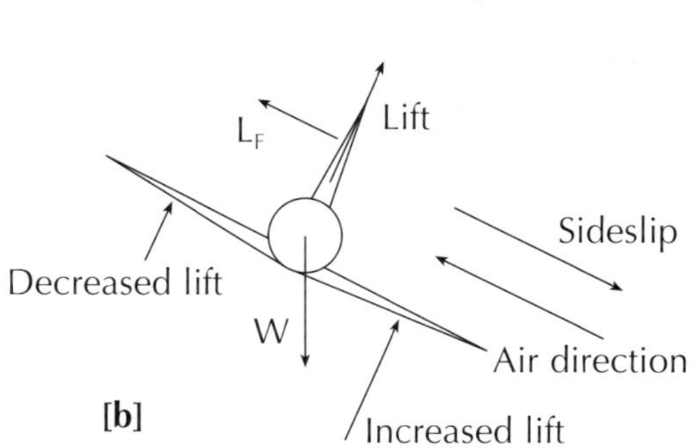

Figure 10.7 An aircraft in sideslip [a] No dihedral [b] With dihedral

10.7[b]). The lower wing will now have an increased angle of attack, giving a restoring moment due to increased lift, whereas the other wing will experience almost no benefit at all, being in the "shadow" of the fuselage. Any sideslip air velocity on that side, however, would give a beneficial decreased angle of attack because of dihedral.

A designer can give an aircraft more or less stability in this mode by the quite different facility of mounting the wings high or low on the fuselage. In a state of sideslip, a fuselage acts as a large cylinder with its axis perpendicular to the sideslip direction so the lateral flow of air about it resembles the streamlines shown in Fig. 10.8. The high-winged aircraft [a] has an increased angle of attack for the wing pointing towards the ground and a reduced value for the other wing, both giving a restoring moment in roll and adding to any dihedral effect. The low-winged aircraft [b] has a reduced angle of attack for the wing pointing towards the ground and so on, which **reduces** the benefits derived from dihedral. It is clear, therefore, that high-winged aircraft need lower dihedral angles than low-winged ones, in practice about half the value.

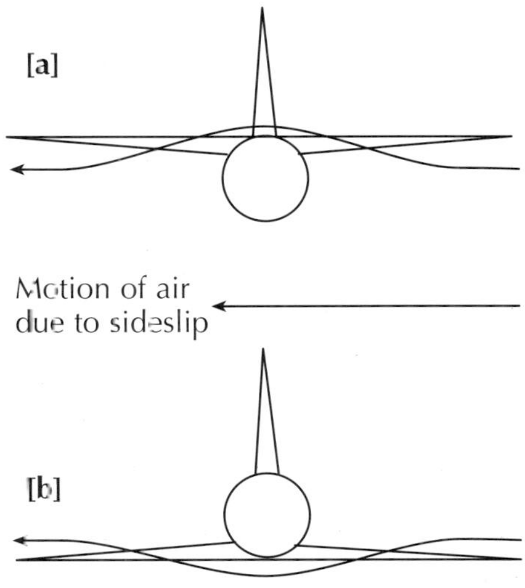

Figure 10.8 Effect of wing mounting position on angle of attack in sideslip [a] High wing [b] Low wing

If the fin is too large or the dihedral angle too small, the trajectory of the aircraft will worsen towards a spiral dive even more rapidly than described above. This should not be confused with a spin, described in the previous chapter, which is essentially a stalled condition, the aircraft executing a very uncomfortable manoeuvre with its CG following a helical path a short distance away from a vertical spin axis. The spiral dive, by contrast, is a manoeuvre of gradually increasing speed with the aircraft being at no time anywhere near a stalled condition.

In general, the spiral mode is a sufficiently slow development for the average pilot to be able to correct for it with no haste and autopilots would certainly have no trouble in dealing with it. At cruising speed, a light aircraft should have a spiral mode t_D value of more than 20 s and a Cherokee, for example, easily satisfies this requirement with a value of about 30 s. In fact, after about a minute, a typical response would be to have rolled about 5°. and yawed about 50°. With some aircraft, there is a complication in that their spiral stability is speed-dependent. In slowing down from cruise speed to approach speed, a **stable** value of $t_{1/2}$ of 50 s could well have turned into an **unstable** t_D of 50 s, having gone through neutral stability on the way. However, this does not usually represent much of a threat because of the slow response rates involved.

Lateral - Dutch Roll

The final stability mode to look at is the oddly-named Dutch roll and aircraft exhibiting this response are usually uncomfortable rather than dangerous. In order to see what is happening aerodynamically, it is best to think of an aircraft hanging on a torsional spring, so that it is free to swing in yaw (Fig. 10.9). At one point in the cycle, when the nose is yawing to the right, the port wing will be travelling faster than the starboard one so extra lift will be developed and therefore extra drag. The yawing movement will therefore slow down but not before the increased lift has produced a port wing up rolling action. The aircraft is then going to sideslip to starboard, although any dihedral present will cause a restoring starboard wing-up rolling moment. An uncomfortable combination of yawing and rolling is therefore set up and the pilot looking at either wing tip would see it trace out an ellipse against the horizon, with the forward motion of the tip being at the lowest point. An observer on the ground would see a rolling and yawing motion not unlike a speed skater on a frozen Dutch river - hence the name. In control engineering terminology, the rolling action "lags" on the yawing motion, not surprising since the latter is essentially causing the former.

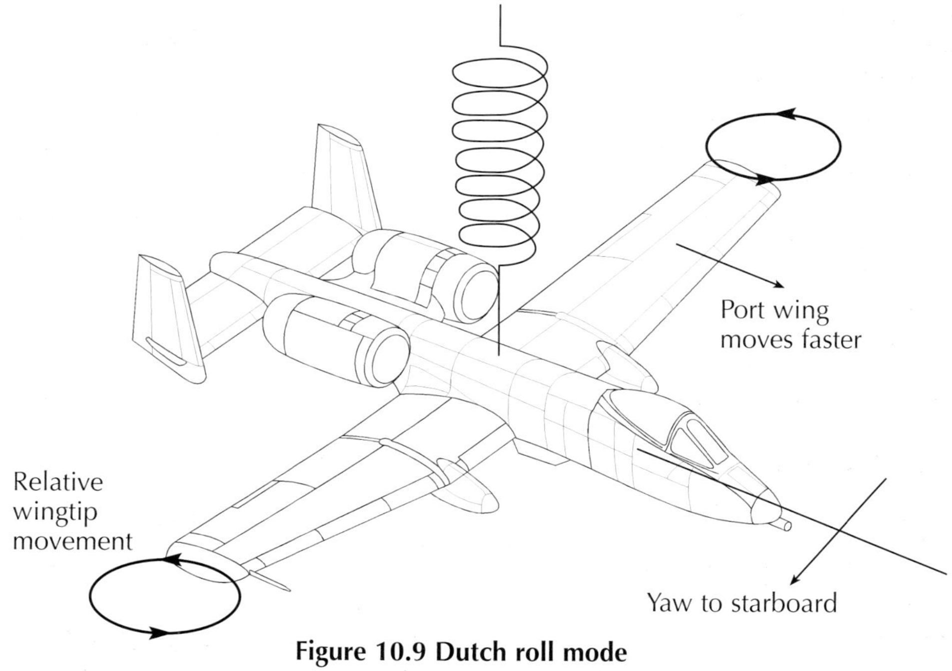

Figure 10.9 Dutch roll mode

For a Cherokee, the periodic time for this mode is about 2.5 s and the time to half amplitude about 2.7 s, so Dutch roll is not a problem. But an aircraft with too much dihedral or too small a fin or heavy engines mounted somewhere along the span and thus increasing the inertia in yaw (or all three!) could well have a problem. This represents a potential headache for the designer since he or she may well have given the aircraft those geometrical properties expressly to prevent it being spirally unstable. If this dilemma does occur, the solution is always the same: the designer will cure the Dutch roll at the expense of reducing the spiral stability, since the latter is nearly always containable by the pilot.

Those of an inquisitive disposition can induce a Dutch roll in the cruise condition by alternately "paddling" the rudder pedals. If this is carried out at exactly the right frequency, a very uncomfortable Dutch roll mode can be generated.

Gust Response

Another facet of aircraft control which ought to be looked at in this chapter is "gust response". Although this is normally considered in terms of longitudinal response, it can apply to any sudden change of local airflow, sideways, upwards or downwards. By way of illustration, it's probably best to consider what happens to an aircraft when it suddenly flies into a vertically upwards gust generated, for example, by wind rising up the face of a cliff. If the vertical speed of the air is W, we need to consider how the aircraft will respond to the sudden **but sustained** imposition of this extra wind vector (Fig. 10.10[a]). The wing is clearly going to experience an increase $\Delta\alpha$ in its angle of attack α by an angle given by tan $\Delta\alpha$ = W/V. Since W is always much less than V, W/V is usually a small enough number to put the tangent equal to the angle so $\Delta\alpha \approx$ W/V (radians).

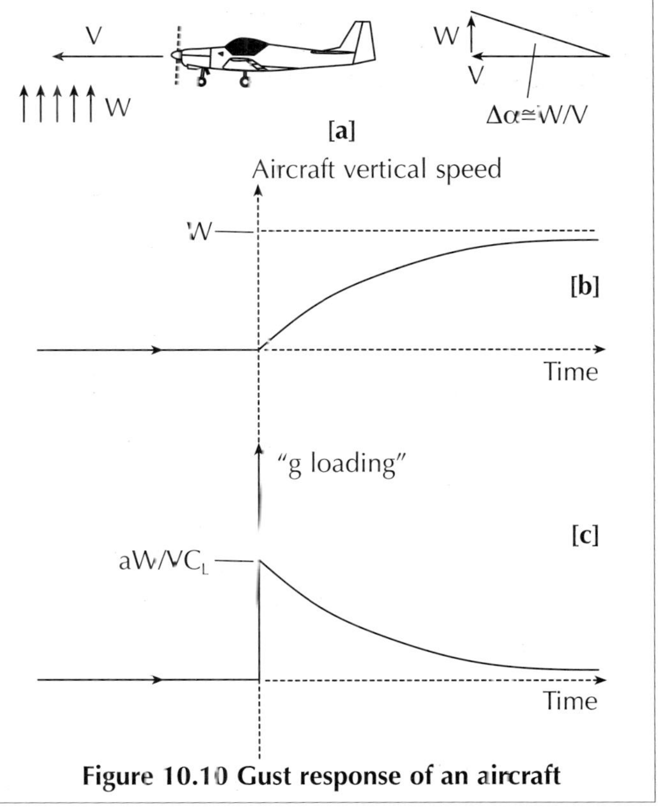

Figure 10.10 Gust response of an aircraft

The aircraft will start to climb under this increased lift but as its climb rate increases, the effect of W will decrease because the aircraft is rapidly acquiring the vertical speed W itself and $\Delta\alpha$ is becoming zero. A plot of how it would do this is shown in Fig. 10.10[b], where it can be seen that the vertical speed W is reached "asymptotically". The initial slope of this graph is important because it represents the kick in the pants that the pilot experiences on entering the gust and this can not only be calculated and measured but also converted into a "g" loading. Fig. 10.10[c] shows what this graph looks like in theory and the peak g loading is experienced straightaway. It can be shown that the value of this peak g is given by aW/VC_L, where a is the slope of the C_L versus α graph (Fig. 6.6), so we can see that a severe kick in the pants is administered if a or W (or both) are large and V or C_L (or both) are small. We can't do much about the gust speed W but a depends on wing planform and V and C_L clearly depend on how fast we are flying.

The value of the lift curve slope a is maximum for aircraft with high aspect ratio so a glider would feel worst and a delta wing would be smoothest. In military use, the latter would be very good at low level, where gusts are usually worst. V and C_L apply to any aircraft and high C_L would be obtained for low speed, low air density and high wing loading. An uncomfortable ride would therefore be obtained in a high aspect ratio, low wing loading aircraft at high speed and low altitude.

It may be the case that, for a given gust speed and EAS, the excess g load exceeds even the maximum value allowed on the V-n diagram (Fig. 9.6) and V_{no} is specified on the basis of a maximum vertical gust speed of 50 ft/s specified in JAR 25 (Joint Airworthiness Regulations) for flight at less than 20000 ft. At higher altitudes, lower maxima are specified, since severe gusts are rarer there.

Conclusion

This chapter has essentially been about what happens to an aircraft when it is disturbed from normal flight, the initial disturbance being generally outside the pilot's control. The pilot's reaction will of course be to initiate some control action to try to restore the aircraft to its original state, although a stable aircraft would, in any case, tend to do this itself. Since design is always a compromise between competing requirements, any given aircraft may have some instability inherent in its design as a trade-off against eliminating an even worse instability and, in any case, some aircraft need more stability than others, depending on their role in life. The pilot can therefore be seen as an essential part of a "control loop", making corrections when instabilities do manifest themselves. A complete control system, without the pilot, would of course be provided by an autopilot.

Exercises - Chapter 10

Reminder: 1 stone = 14 lb

Using the aircraft empty weight and all the arm dimensions shown in the table in this chapter, calculate the total weight and CG position for the following weights:

1. Pilot 14 st 3 lb Co-pilot 12 st 6 lb Fuel 300 lb
Baggage 40 lb

2. Pilot 13 st 3 lb Front pass. 10 st 2 lb Rear pass. 9 st 0 lb
Fuel 270 lb Baggage 100 lb

3. Pilot 63 kg Front pass. 59 kg Rear pass. 102 kg
Fuel 122 kg Baggage 61 kg

4. Case 3 is unstable! How many kg of (a) baggage or (b) fuel would the captain need to offload to bring the CG within the aft limit again?

5. In tests, an aircraft produces the following results for pitching moment coefficient C_M against angle of attack α for the given CG positions:

α (degrees)	CG at 20% smc	30% smc	38% smc
5	C_M = -0.14	-0.10	-0.06
10	-0.30	-0.21	-0.13
15	-0.44	-0.31	-0.20

By plotting two graphs, determine the approximate position of the neutral point h_n. [Hint: see Figs. 10.4 and 10.5]

11

High Speed Flight

What happens if we go faster?

AT VARIOUS PLACES in this book it has been necessary when describing certain flight phenomena to limit the statements to cases where the speed was not too high or where there was no chance of contravening Bernoulli's equation. However, most modern airliners cruise in conditions where these provisos are certainly not true and we must now grasp the nettle and look at what happens at these higher speeds.

The Importance of the Speed of Sound

We have seen in Chapter 5 that when any object moves in a fluid, the streamline flow which exists around that object divides into a part moving above it and a part below. The dividing line between these two halves is the streamline passing through the stagnation point S (see Fig. 5.4). The shape of the streamlines upstream of S is an indication of how the fluid is sorting itself out to divide but, in order to do that, it must have prior notice that the object is approaching and that message is always in the form of pressure waves, generated by the object and travelling at the speed of sound, usually denoted by "a".

If the surface of a pond is regularly tapped with a stick, ripples appear to flow outwards as concentric circles from the impact point and their equal spacing is clearly visible. In the same way, a tuning fork activated in air sends out regular pressure waves as concentric spheres (Fig. 11.1[a]) and, if their frequency is within the range detectable by the human ear, we can hear the musical tone produced. If that fork is stationary, the sound waves are concentric with the fork. However, if the fork is moving the picture will be distorted in the sense of the fork appearing to "catch up" on the waves moving in its own direction (11.1[b]). If the tuning fork is travelling at the same speed as the sound waves, the air ahead of it will experience the fork and the wave arriving at the same instant (11.1[c]) and, as the ultimate case, if the fork is travelling faster than the waves, it will penetrate them (11.1[d]).

In the case of Fig. 11.1[d], the lines (loci or tangents) joining the edges of the waves clearly divide the fluid which is aware of the tuning fork's presence (the "zone of

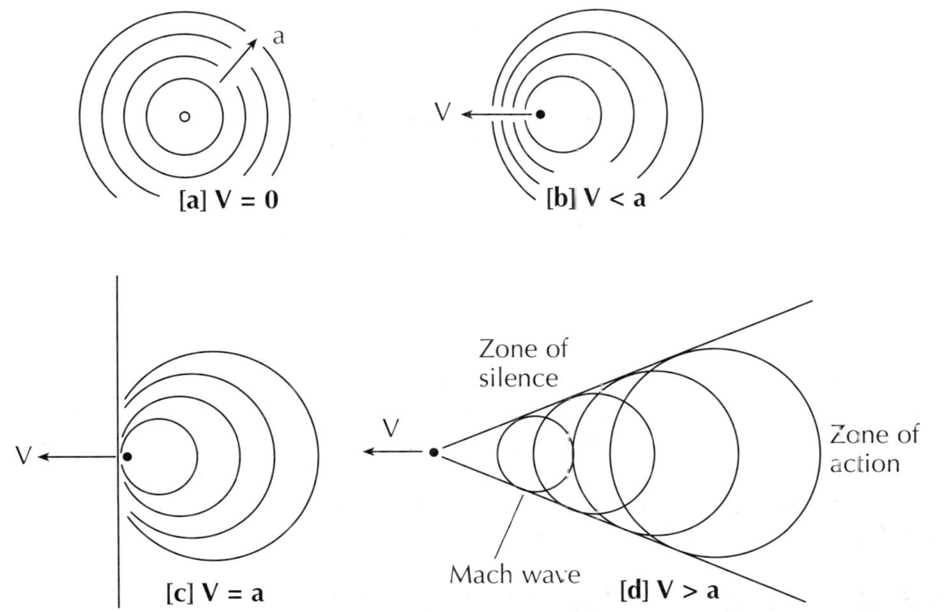

Figure 11.1 Effect of a moving object on pressure waves

action") from that which is **not** aware of it (the "zone of silence") and these tangents are known as Mach waves, after the Austrian physicist who pointed out their importance. In three dimensions, these will of course form a "Mach cone".

Mach Number and Compressibility

The same type of situation would obtain for an aircraft travelling at a major fraction of the speed of sound; the air ahead would receive increasingly unsatisfactory warning of the aircraft's approach as its TAS increased and ultimately, when it reached the speed of sound, no warning at all, as in Fig. 11.1[c]. The **shapes** of the four drawings in Fig. 11.1 are obviously dependent on the ratio of the aircraft speed V to the *local* speed of sound "a" and this ratio is also named after Ernst Mach:

Mach number M = Aircraft TAS/local speed of sound

The word "local" in the sentence above is italicised because the speed of sound varies as the square root of temperature and therefore decreases with altitude. A given TAS at sea level will therefore represent a higher Mach number if that same TAS is flown at 36000 ft, in fact by about 15%.

We can now envisage regions of flight speeds from zero upwards where the flow characteristics depend simply on the Mach number and these carry names derived from the Latin words for under, across and over and finally from the Greek word for over:

Subsonic: $M < 0.7$
Transonic: $0.7 < M < 1.2$
Supersonic: $1.2 < M < 5$
Hypersonic: $M > 5$

These regions are not exactly defined by the above limits but they give a reasonable idea of the divisions. Aircraft experiencing no high-speed effects at all would need to be flying at a Mach number below about 0.3.

The speed of sound is easily calculated from the following equation, using SI units:

Speed of sound in air = $a = \sqrt{(\gamma RT)}$ Eqn. 11.1

where γ for air is 1.4, R is 287 J/kg.K and T must be in degrees Kelvin. If T = 15°C (= 288 K) at sea level and -56.5°C (= 216.5 K) in the stratosphere, the equation gives:

At sea level, speed of sound = 340 m/s = 661 kn approx.
In the stratosphere, speed of sound = 295 m/s = 573 kn approx.

A light aircraft with a TAS of 100 kn at sea level therefore has a Mach number of only about 0.15, whereas a modern airliner doing 450 kn at 36000 ft is at about M = 0.785. Although the light aircraft will experience no real speed of sound effects, the airliner certainly will and the changes which occur at high speeds are generally lumped under the heading of "compressibility" effects. This reflects the fact that at higher speeds the air is subject to density changes (simply due to speed) whereas Bernoulli's equation was derived on the assumption of constant density.

Critical Mach Number

It should be remembered that although the aircraft's Mach number may be only 78.5% of the speed of sound, there are considerable areas around it where the local airspeed is even higher. The upper surfaces of the wings are generating lift by accelerating the air to speeds well above TAS so at some Mach number called the "critical" value M_{crit}, the speed of air just above the wing will exactly reach the speed of sound. A thin, high speed aerofoil at zero angle of attack α might typically have an M_{crit} of about 0.8, but a commercial airliner wing carrying a load at $\alpha = 4°$ might well have an M_{crit} as low as 0.6.

This is where we can cheat! If the wing is given a sweep angle Λ, it was shown in Chapter 3 that not only does the component normal to the leading edge drop to

VcosΛ (Fig. 3.4), but also that the wing chord parallel to the flow direction is lengthened, giving a lower thickness/chord ratio (a slimmer wing section). Swept wing aircraft therefore can delay the effects of compressibility somewhat and a Boeing 777, for example, with Λ = 35° has a component of Mach number normal to the leading edge of only 0.68 when flying at M = 0.83. Increasing sweep angle is not the ideal answer, however, because fast aircraft also need to fly satisfactorily at low speeds, on approach and landing, but the best of both worlds is available with variable sweep. A Panavia Tornado can sweep its wings back to 68° so that it has a component normal to the leading edge of only M = 0.82 when flying at M = 2.2.

As an aircraft accelerates beyond M_{crit} the regions containing air at sonic speed or greater will become more extensive (Fig. 11.2[a]) and eventually cover most of the wing area (Fig. 11.2[b]). In the latter case, extensive areas of the undersurface will also have supersonic regions. Unfortunately, although air can be accelerated smoothly to supersonic speed, the deceleration process is almost instantaneous and certainly violent and when the air over the wing needs to slow down, as it always does (even at subsonic speeds) after passing the suction peak, it does so through a so-called shock wave, the distinct black lines in the figures. This is a normally invisible boundary between high speed/low pressure air and low speed/higher pressure air, in that order as the air progresses downstream. In theory, it has no thickness but the effects of viscosity and other physical parameters result in its being thick enough to produce a visible line on a photographic plate when suitable optical apparatus (Schlieren mirrors) are used in a wind tunnel. The savage change of density and refractive index through the shock wave produces a deviation in the light beam.

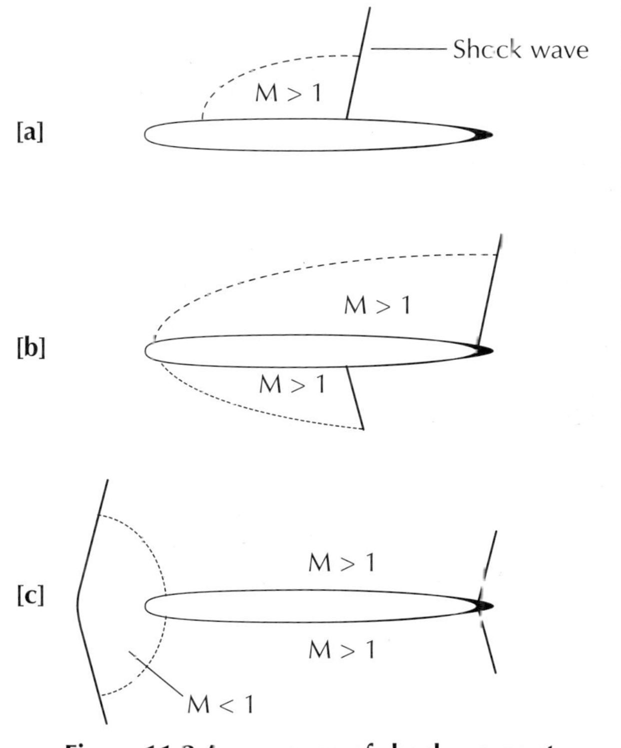

Figure 11.2 Appearance of shock waves at transonic speeds

By the time a wing is travelling at a speed well above M = 1, there is also a shock wave at the front of the wing (Fig. 11.2[c]) because the air which ultimately hits the leading edge has to be decelerated too and can do so only through a shock. The area around the leading edge is therefore characterised by subsonic flow and a large area of high pressure, giving enormously increased drag, so there is a benefit to be obtained in using sharp leading edges in supersonic aircraft. The shock waves represent very severe pressure changes and, although their effect is attenuated as they progress away from the aircraft, their ability to produce loud double bangs at ground level has led to supersonic flight over land areas being banned.

Effect on Aircraft Handling

Fig. 11.2[c] shows a flow quite unlike that at subsonic speeds and the effects on aircraft handling can be just as marked. In particular, the severely rearranged pressure distribution causes the centre of lift to move from its subsonic position at about a quarter of the chord aft of the leading edge to about the mid-chord point. Shifting the lift vector aft by this distance obviously produces a large nose-down pitching moment and a serious retrim is needed. In the case of Concorde, which had to spend a major part of each flight at supersonic speed, large quantities of fuel are pumped aft to rebalance the aircraft without sticking flying control surfaces out into the airstream to produce a counterbalancing nose-up effect.

As well as changes to lift and pitching moment, there are also major changes in drag. In subsonic flight we had to deal with form, skin and induced drag, while transonic and supersonic flight produces an additional factor, wave drag. The effect on lift-independent drag coefficient C_{D0} can be seen in Fig. 11.3. The value of C_{D0} gradually drops with increasing airspeed (or Mach No.) because the skin friction coefficient is falling with Reynolds No. (see Fig. 7.4). However, a shock wave is a very inefficient way of compressing a gas because of the losses which occur in it. At low speeds, we were able to assume that total pressure p_o was a constant so that airspeed could be measured from the difference of total and static pressures. However, this does not apply at speeds above a few hundred knots and certainly not through a shock wave. At M

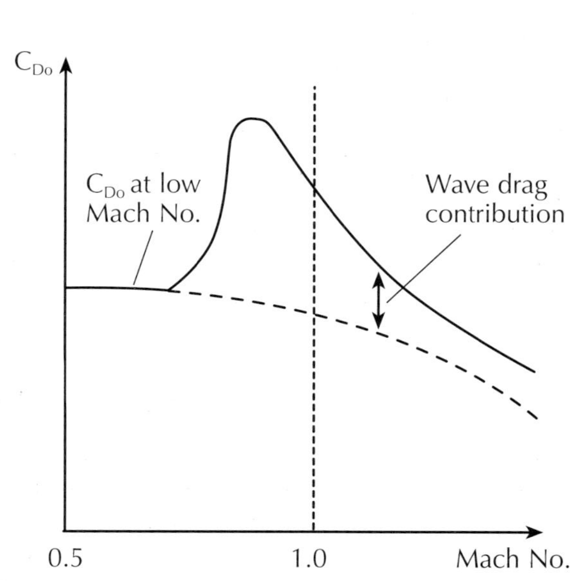

Figure 11.3 Profile drag coefficient at transonic speeds

= 2, something like 30% of the total pressure is lost in passing through a shock wave and cannot be recovered.

A shock close to the thickest part of a wing section, as in Fig. 11.2[a], will have a very adverse effect on the boundary layer there because it represents a very sudden and large pressure rise. The flow will tend to separate from the upper surface, producing a "shock stall" loss of suction there, just as a conventional stall does at low speeds. The associated increase in drag will show up as a major addition above the C_{D_0} curve, reaching a peak just below the speed of sound (Fig. 11.3). As the upper and lower surface shocks progress towards the trailing edge as Mach number increases, this effect is much reduced and the wave drag coefficient at supersonic speeds is not as high as in the transonic region. Sustained flight is therefore possible at supersonic speeds but is generally restricted to the military or to those who can afford Concorde prices. Flight in the transonic region where C_D climbs rapidly would be very uneconomical indeed.

Area Ruling

As well as using wing sweep to minimise problems in the transonic region, reductions can also be made in the extra drag due to shock waves by carefully ensuring no sudden changes in cross-sectional area of the aircraft as the air travels from nose to tail. To see how this works, we need to introduce the shock wave's opposite number - the expansion fan. Sudden changes of direction of flow (and deceleration) in the sense of an "inside corner" (Fig. 11.4[a]) cause a shock to form, whereas flow around an "outside corner" (11.4[b]) is achieved through a set of Mach waves called an expansion fan and result in an acceleration of the flow. If the two types of wave ever overlap, as they can when approaching from opposite sides of a wind tunnel, for example, they tend to cancel each other out to an extent dependent on their relative strengths, since one involves an increase of pressure and the other a decrease.

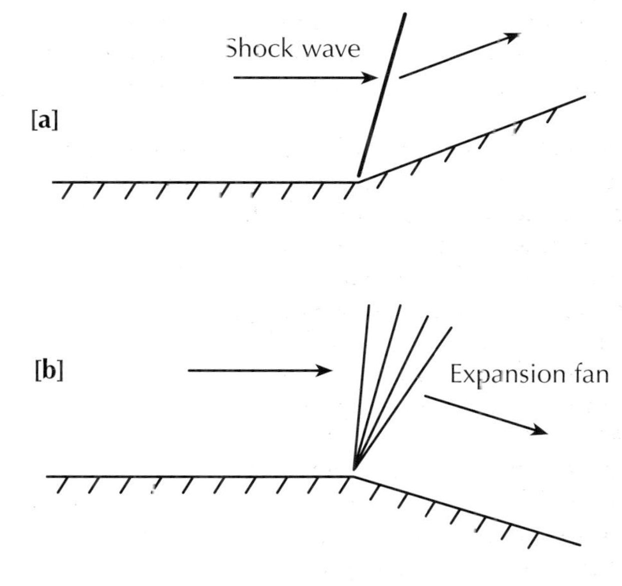

Figure 11.4 Flows in inside and outside corners

At a wing root/fuselage join, a shock will form because of the inside corner nature of the change but, looked at in three dimensions, this effect could be lessened by changing the shape of the fuselage in the sense of an outside corner to give some expansion fans at roughly the same place. This line of approach leads to the fuselage becoming slimmer wherever the addition of a wing, tailplane or fin adds to the overall cross-sectional area. We therefore have the familiar "Coke bottle" waisted fuselage (Fig. 11.5), developed by Whitcomb in the USA and Kuchemann at Farnborough, for minimising transonic drag.

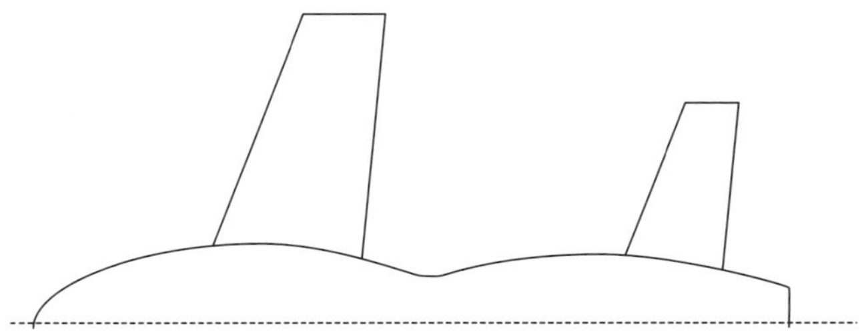

Figure 11.5 Area-ruled "Coke-bottle" fuselage

In some cases, particularly in the USA, fuselages were redesigned to enable subsonic (but supposedly supersonic) aircraft to pass through the transonic region. In others, area was added elsewhere on an aircraft to give the correct total cross-section; "Kuchemann's carrots" were a good example on the Victor bomber.

Effect on Aircraft Flying Controls

The effects of compressibility are not restricted to drag, lift and balance; they show up also in the response of an aircraft to control inputs. The shock stall which can occur in transonic flight, as mentioned above, can cause a major disturbance to the wake flow from the wing. If the tailplane is positioned in this wake, a marked buffeting will be evident and designers of high-wing configurations have sometimes needed to place the tailplane either well above the wing (BAe 146) or well below it (BAe Lightning) to avoid buffet problems. However, even then there may be further complications.

An aileron, elevator or rudder produces a side force by deflection into the surrounding airstream. This, as we saw in Chapter 6, has the effect of increasing the camber and effective angle of attack of the main flying surface. In a supersonic airflow, on the other hand, changes **cannot** be transmitted upstream because the air is travelling faster than the pressure waves resulting from the change, so the control surface effect remains entirely **local** to the surface itself. The upstream flow has no idea that the camber has been effectively increased so the force produced is only a fraction of that which might have been expected from the full surface under subsonic conditions. Considerably increased control forces are therefore needed to give the same rolling, pitching or yawing moments as in subsonic flight. One approach to resolving this problem has been the introduction of all-moving "slab" tailplanes; that is, there are no elevators and the whole tail rotates to give a different angle of attack. In some aircraft, the tail not only moves as a slab but the port and starboard halves can also rotate in opposite directions; the X-15 used this technique. There are disadvantages in this approach, however, not the least being that the radius arm (from the fuselage centreline) for a rolling manoeuvre represented by half a tail semi-span is nothing like as large as the radius at which conventional ailerons normally operate, so massive angular changes are needed to produce a roll. Also, there may be problems involved in using the slab tail to produce a rolling and pitching action at the same time.

Problems with Deformation - "Aeroelasticity"

When an aircraft is in flight, it suffers a change of shape because of the various loads on it. This process is called "aeroelasticity" and, although it is not restricted to supersonic cases, this is where it shows itself in its most extreme form. Even metal aircraft bend under load and the amount of bending is allowed for in the design process. Passengers looking out along the span of a large modern airliner are sometimes alarmed to see the tips flapping, often by a matter of feet, but the wing is stressed to take loads well beyond what might be expected, even in turbulent flying conditions.

One particular case is worth looking at here because, if not allowed for in the design stage, it can actually lead to a **reversal** of control function! If an aileron is deflected in supersonic flow then, for all the reasons given above, the force produced has to be very large to produce enough rolling moment. Once again, the force change is entirely localised and will obviously be transmitted to the wing structure through the aileron hinge (Fig. 11.6). This will usually be well behind the centre of the wing section and will therefore produce a twisting action about that centre. In the case of a roll to starboard being required, the port aileron will be depressed, giving an upward lift force aft of the wing section centre. At the extreme distance from the wing root at which this moment is imposed, the wing could twist markedly in the direction of decreasing its angle of attack, thus producing a **decrease** of lift and **roll to port!** The exact opposite of the pilot's wishes has therefore occurred and this dangerous phenomenon is, not surprisingly, called control reversal.

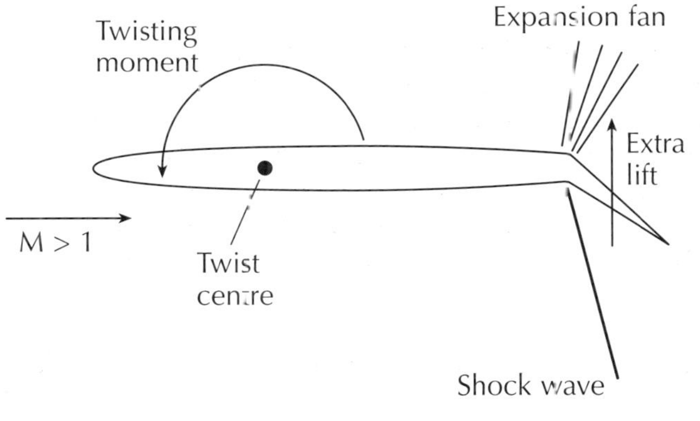

Figure 11.6 Aileron reversal

Even Faster?

Aerodynamic heating

When an airstream is brought to rest on the nose of a moving object, it not only experiences an increase in pressure to p_0, the ram or stagnation pressure, but also an increase in temperature to T_0, stagnation temperature. The difference between the static temperature T and T_0 increases as the airspeed increases and it's fairly easy to show that (for air) the ratio T_0/T is given by

$$\frac{T_0}{T} = \left[1 + \frac{M^2}{5}\right] \qquad \textit{Eqn. } 11.2$$

Since T_0/T is a ratio, we must use absolute values when calculating, so at 36000 ft, for example, T = -56°C = 217 K. This means that an aircraft cruising at M = 3 at that altitude would have a nose temperature of [1 + (9/5)]T = 2.8T or 600 K (about 330°C). This is the temperature on any front-facing surface but, because of conduction in metal and convection and friction in the boundary layers, the rest of the aircraft's surface will also be at a raised temperature, probably about 260°C. This is hot, to say the least, and the design of such aircraft would need to allow for considerable thermal expansion during flight. At a Mach number of 5, the situation is even worse with the nose being at about 1030°C and the rest of the skin at about 600°C.

The fastest air-breathing aircraft is the Lockheed SR-71 Blackbird, which can attain about M = 3.5 and cruise at 3.0, but the rocket-powered X-15 could manage M = 6.7 and the Space Shuttle attains a Mach number of about 25 on re-entry to the Earth's atmosphere, although this high value is partly because the ambient temperature there is so low, giving a lower speed of sound. The heating effect is just as severe, however, and the shuttle uses expendable tiles which protect the rest of the craft by an ablation action.

The aluminium alloys normally used in aircraft construction cannot withstand these temperatures and even at Mach numbers around one, extensive use is made of titanium alloys, although even these, in turn, are useful only up to about T = 800 K and the extension to about 1000 K is made with nickel alloys. For surface temperatures greater than that, ceramics and composites (mainly based on silicon) will have to be used.

Wave riding

For sustained flight at high Mach numbers, designers will always try to ensure that the component of Mach number normal to the wing leading edge is subsonic, thus minimising the problems associated with shock waves. In practice this would mean keeping all of the aircraft within the Mach cone introduced in Fig. 11.1[d]. If we redraw that figure to show the speeds involved (see Fig. 11.7), we see that we are dealing with a right-angled triangle having a height a and a hypotenuse of V. If we

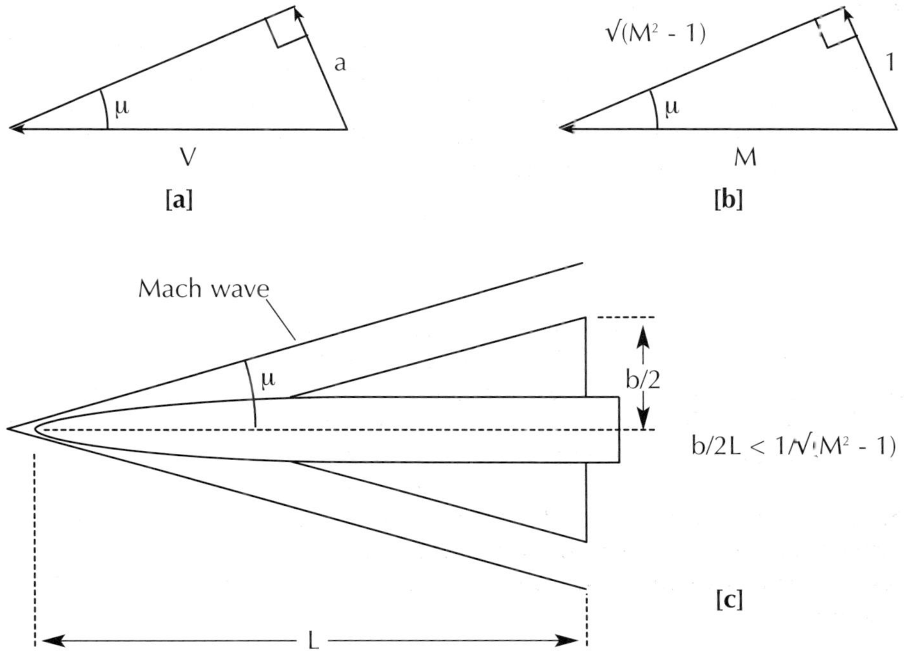

Figure 11.7 Keeping an aircraft within its own Mach cone

divide **all** the sides by the speed of sound, we shall not change the shape of the triangle, merely its size (Fig. 11.7[b]). The height is now 1 (=a/a) and the hypotenuse is M (=V/a) so the third side, by Pythagoras, must be $\sqrt{(M^2 - 1)}$. The angle between the base and the hypotenuse is called the Mach angle μ (how did you guess?) and this is obviously given by $\tan \mu = 1/\sqrt{(M^2 - 1)}$.

If we now fit an aircraft inside this triangle (Fig. 11.7[c]), we can see that to keep its whole shape within the Mach cone, its semi-span b/2 divided by its length L must not be greater than tan μ so:

$$b/2L < 1/\sqrt{(M^2 - 1)} \qquad \textbf{Eqn. 11.3}$$

If we plot a graph of b/2L versus Mach number (Fig. 11.8), Eqn. 11.3 appears as a curved line. Any aircraft to the left of this line will be entirely enclosed by its own Mach cone whereas any aircraft to the right will not. The concept of a Mach cone does not, of course, apply to the left of M = 1. Regions occupied by various types of aircraft are shown on the figure and clearly the X-15 and the Space Shuttle do not operate within their Mach cones although the bulk of supersonic aircraft do. Another type of aircraft shown in the figure as a large band are those called "wave riders"; these are designed not only to be exposed to shock waves but to make use of the enormous pressure rise across them to gain lift. They quite literally "ride" the wave, on the basis that if you are going to travel at these highly elevated Mach numbers anyway, you might as well make use of the shocks which cannot be avoided. Needless to say, none of this type can yet be seen in commercial operation.

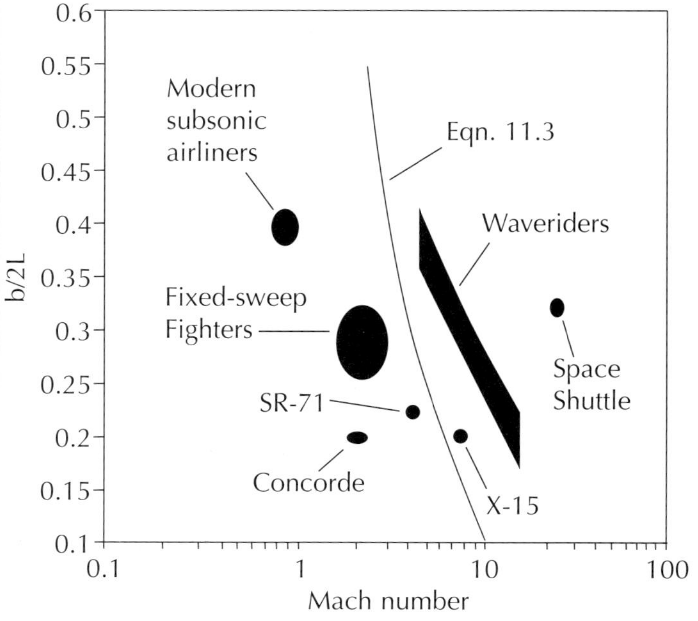

Figure 11.8 Speed regimes

Conclusion

This chapter has attempted to show the limits of what can be achieved at present and the likely direction in which aeronautics might go in the future. However, it's important to remember that, no matter how weird and wonderful the shapes may become, the physical laws controlling their flight cannot be contravened and the same equations apply to slow moving light aircraft; these equations simply become much less horrifying when all the terms involving M and M^2 (and higher powers!) become very small.

Exercises - Chapter 11

Reminder: 1 knot = 0.5144 m/s   0°C = 273 K
For air: R = 287 J/kg.K $\gamma = 1.4$
Data for the International Standard Atmosphere are given in the appendix to Chapter 4

In these exercises, assume EAS to be the same as IAS.

1. Calculate the speed of sound at 25000 ft on an ISA day.

2. Calculate the speed of sound at 35000 ft on an ISA + 20 day.

3. Calculate the speed of sound at 12000 ft on an ISA - 20 day.

4. An aircraft flies at a Mach number of 0.52 at 35000 ft on an ISA + 12 day. Calculate (a) its TAS and (b) its IAS, assuming no compressibility corrections.

5. An aircraft flies at 254 kn.IAS at 15000 ft on an ISA day. Calculate (a) its TAS and (b) its Mach number.

6. Calculate the temperature on an aircraft's nose if it is flying at 280 kn.IAS at 35000 ft on an ISA + 10 day.

7. Calculate the temperature on Concorde's nose if it is flying at M = 2.2 in the Stratosphere.

8. An aircraft is designed to fly at 1030 kn.TAS in the Stratosphere. What sweep angle will be needed to ensure that the wings always lie within the aircraft's Mach cone?

Bibliography

READERS requiring a different angle on the material of this book or simply needing more depth or detail of coverage might like to look at the following books. Comments are given at the bottom of the page.

A. C. KERMODE, *Flight without Formulae*, 5th Edn. (Updated by Bill Gunston), Longman Scientific, 1989.

C. CARPENTER, *Flightwise, Vol. 1, Principles of Aircraft Flight*, Airlife Pub. Ltd., 1996.

C. CARPENTER, *Flightwise, Vol. 2, Aircraft Stability and Control*, Airlife Pub. Ltd., 1997.

D. STINTON, *The Anatomy of the Aeroplane*, Blackwell Science, 1980.

D. STINTON, *The Design of the Aeroplane*, Blackwell Science, 1989.

D. STINTON, *Flying Qualities and Flight Testing of the Aeroplane*, Blackwell Science, 1996.

B. W. McCORMICK, *Aerodynamics, Aeronautics and Flight Dynamics*, John Wiley, 1995.

Notes:

Kermode's book has long been regarded as a classic and deals with flight in a non-numerical way, as its title suggests. Carpenter's two volumes go into much more detail and introduce some equations, although the overall approach makes them more suitable as background reading for those who are going to pursue aeronautics in a professional manner rather than as a spare-time interest. Stinton's books are also classics and go into considerable detail. They are written by someone who has qualified as a test pilot *and* engineer and represent a goldmine of information written in a very readable style, dealing particularly with small and medium size aircraft. McCormick's book is specifically for aeronautical engineering students and involves all the mathematical rigour needed in such an approach; it is, however, still very readable.

Answers to Problems

Chapter 2

1. 46297 lbm
2. 2.359 t
3. 158731 lbm/min
4. 1829 m and 2743 m
5. 60.3 m
6. (a) 494.8 mile/h
(b) 221.2 m/s
(c) 725.7 ft/s
(d) 796.4 km/h
7. 1098 ft^2
8. 9 flights
9. (a) 540.3 ft^3
(b) 9.336×10^5 in^3
(c) 15.3×10^6 cm^3
(d) 4042 USgal
(e) 3367 gal
10. 32.175 ft/s^2
11. (a) 117757 N
(b) 26472 lbf
(c) 12.01 t
(d) 11.818 ton
12. (a) 1416 kg/m^3
(b) 1.416
(c) 88.426 lbm/ft^3
13. 0.5095 lbm/s
14. 14.29 lbf/in^2

Chapter 4

1. 13°C
2. (a) 1.184 kg/m^3
(b) 1.091 kg/m^3
3. 750 ft
4. 450 ft
5. 960 ft
6. 10 ft! (and the Cessna is higher)
7. 6800 ft

Chapter 5

1. 21.24 litres/s
2. 0.0112kg/s
3. 5.19 m/s
4. 0.0873 kg/s away from the tank
5. (a) 5173 Pa
(b) 527.4 mmH_2O
6. (a) 1947 Pa
(b) 198.5 mmH_2O
7. 199 kn
8. 121.3 kn
9. 58.8 mbar
10. 977 mbar

Chapter 6

1. (a) (ii)
(b) (i)
2. 16.6%
3. 388 kn.TAS
4. (a) 0.299
(b) 0.405
5. 104.2, 93.2, 81.7 kn.TAS
6. (a) 135 kn.TAS
(b) 145 kn.TAS
7. 199.5 kn.TAS
8. 0.107°
9. Increase by 4.09°
10. 300.8 m^2

Chapter 7

1. 1081 N
2. 16.52 m
3. 2.36 m/s
4. 0.22 Nm
5. (a) 20.78 kN
(b) 7.63 kN
6. (a) 22.0 kN
(b) 6.47 kN
7. 636 N
8. 8.5%
9. (a) 2517 N
(b) 4217 N

Chapter 8

1. $A = 5.64$
   $\frac{1}{2}\rho S = 9.192$
2. Profile drag = $0.3217V^2$
   Induced drag = 10^6V^2
5. $V_{max} \approx 122$ kn
   $V_{md} \approx 81$ kn
   $V_{mp} \approx 60$ kn
6. Max. RoC ≈ 985 ft/min (5.004 m/s) @ 60 kn.
7. $a = 0.035$; $b= 0.079$ $C_{Lmd} = \sqrt{(a/b)} = 0.6656$ so $V_{md} \approx 42$ m/s ≈ 82 kn
   $C_{Lmp} = \sqrt{(3a/b)} = 1.153$ so $V_{mp} \approx 31.8$ m/s ≈ 62 kn

Chapter 10

1. 2213 lb 21.94 %smc
2. 2326 lb 27.26 %smc
3. 1088 kg 30.86 %smc
4. (a) About 11 kg of baggage
   (b) Even offloading all fuel will not bring the CG within the aft limit so the obese rear passenger will have to be asked to get out and walk!
5. The neutral point is at approx. 54% smc.

Chapter 11

1. 309.6 m/s
2. 309.75 m/s
3. 313.3 m/s
4. (a) 307.8 kn
   (b) 171.3 kn
5. (a) 320.2 kn
   (b) 0.511
6. 262 K
7. 425 K
8. 56.2^c

Index

A-10 37, 38
absolute zero 22, 39
advance ratio 92
adverse aileron yaw 11
aerodynamic centre 120
aerodynamic heating 142
aeroelasticity 141
Aerospatiale TB10 115
ailerons 11, 12, 15, 32, 107, 108, 141
air:fuel ratio 95
Airbus A320 67, 80, 122
Airbus A340 36, 80, 122
Airbus A3XX 67, 68
aircraft noise 101
airspeed 32
altimeter 41, 44 - 46, 48, 52
aneroid capsule 52
angle of attack 31, 33, 58, 60 - 63, 65, 66, 69, 70, 79, 82, 84, 92, 109, 112 - 114, 119, 124, 125, 128, 129, 131, 133, 136, 140
angle of incidence 58
anti-spin strakes 115
Antonov 124 36
Antonov 225 67, 68
area ruling 139
aspect ratio 82 - 84, 87, 105, 128, 132
asymmetric 14, 107, 110
asymmetric flight 110
atmosphere 39 - 41, 43, 44, 47, 50, 59, 70, 80, 94, 101, 102, 142, 145
axis system 13, 15
BAC 111 35
BAe 146 140
BAe Hawk 128
banked flight in a turn 108
bar 41
Beech King Air 67
Bel 102
bending stresses 11
Bernoulli 50, 51, 54, 55, 57, 59, 61, 66, 134, 136
best angle of climb 98
best glide speed 100, 101
biplane 28, 29, 51
Boeing 707 36
Boeing 727 35
Boeing 737 9, 27, 36, 65
Boeing 747 36, 50, 80, 84, 119
Boeing 777 137
boundary layer 59, 64, 73, 74, 78, 112, 139, 142
Boyle's Law 43
Bulldog 36, 115
calibrated airspeed 96
camber 10, 60, 61, 69, 70, 140
canard 12, 29, 30
centre of gravity 13, 14, 31, 123
centre of lift 61, 107, 138
Cessna 36, 48, 148
CG margins 124
Challenger 35
Charles' Law 43
Cherokee 128, 129, 131
Chipmunk 36, 115
chord 33, 36, 58, 60, 61, 63, 70, 74, 76, 82, 83, 87, 113, 122, 137, 138
circulation 78, 79
compressibility 136, 137, 140, 145
Concorde 33, 34, 138, 139, 144
control reversal 141
critical Mach number 136
Damping 119, 126, 127, 128
DC9 35, 65
deca 17
decalage 31
decanewton 21
deciBel 102
deep stall 30
density 20, 21, 27, 39, 41 - 50, 52, 55, 57, 61, 63, 66, 69, 73, 77, 79, 94 - 97, 99, 105, 132, 136, 137
density altitude 45, 48
dihedral angle 128, 129
downwash 59, 81 - 84
drag 11, 12, 15, 23, 29, 31 - 33, 45, 46, 49, 51, 53, 56, 59 - 61, 64, 71 - 78, 82 - 86, 88 - 91, 97, 101, 104, 106, 107, 112, 119, 120, 124, 127, 130, 138, 140
drag coefficient 72, 75, 77, 82, 87, 104, 138, 139
drag flap 64
Dutch roll 130, 131
dynamic pressure 51, 52, 66, 72, 95
dynamic similarity 66, 68
dynamic stability 125, 126
effective perceived noise dB 102
elevators 12, 13, 15, 32, 108, 140
energy 23, 24, 29, 33, 39, 40, 43, 50, 51, 74, 95, 115, 127
equation of state 43
equivalent airspeed 96
expansion fan 139 - 141
F117 38
F16 36
F84 32
F86 32
fin 12, 15, 28, 30, 31, 34 - 36, 75, 77, 107 - 109, 113, 115, 119, 120, 125, 129, 131, 140
fixed trim tab 108
fixed-pitch propeller 92
flaps 10 - 12, 53, 63 - 65, 69, 70, 73, 113
flight envelopes 115
flying wings 9, 31, 32
form drag 71, 73 - 76, 86
Fowler flaps 64
frise ailerons 12
fuselage 9, 10, 12, 28, 30, 32 - 36, 52 - 55, 58, 62,

66, 67, 74, 75, 77, 78, 85, 87, 96, 110, 115, 120, 129, 139, 140
Galaxy C5 36
gallons 19
gas constant 43
General Dynamics F111 34
geometric similarity 66
giga 17
gross area 62
ground effect 84
gust response 131
harmonisation 108
Harrier 11, 36, 37
heave 14, 126
hecto 17
helicopter 11
hock stall 139
horizontal stabiliser 12
Hunter 32, 37
hush kits 101
hypersonic 136
Ilyushin 62 36
imperial system of units 16
indicated airspeed 46, 47, 66, 96, 100
induced drag 71, 78, 82 - 84, 86 - 89, 105, 124, 138, 150
International Standard Atmosphere 39, 47, 145
inverse square law 101
joule 23, 24
Kelvin scale 22, 39
kilo 17
kinetic energy 23, 24, 50, 127
Kuchemann 140
laminar 74, 79
laminar flow 74
Lanchester 127
lapse rate 39, 40
lateral axis 13, 14, 36, 79, 118, 126
lateral stability 33, 118, 128
lateral static stability 118
lift 11, 12, 15, 21, 23, 28 - 31, 33, 34, 39, 43, 45, 46, 49, 50, 53, 56 - 67, 69 - 72, 75, 78 - 86, 89, 91, 92, 101, 106 - 109, 112, 113, 115, 117, 119 - 121, 124, 125, 127 - 130, 132, 136, 138, 140, 141, 144
lift coefficient 61, 62, 64, 66, 69, 70, 72, 85, 91
lift flap 64
Lightning 33, 35, 140
litre 19, 149
Lockheed SR-71 Blackbird 142
longitudinal axis 14, 15, 20, 80, 107, 125
longitudinal stability 118, 121
longitudinal static stability 120
Mach 19, 32, 38, 95, 135 - 139, 142 - 145
Mach angle 143
Mach cone 135, 142, 143, 145
Mach number 135 - 137, 139, 142 - 145
Mach waves 135, 139
Magnus effect 79
mainplanes 10, 29, 30
Manoeuvre margin 125
mass 17, 20 - 24, 31, 39, 43, 45, 49, 57, 66, 94, 101, 109, 114, 123
maximum endurance 90, 103
maximum range 90, 103, 104
McDonnell Douglas MD-11 35
mega 17
Meteors 32
micro 17
MiG15 32
milli 17
millibar 41, 44, 46
minimum control speed 110
minimum drag speed 89, 91, 101
minimum power speed 91
minimum sink rate 100, 101
moment 22, 23, 31, 32, 34, 35, 40, 65, 75, 81, 83, 84, 87, 88, 90, 114, 119 - 121, 123, 124, 126, 128, 129, 138, 140, 141
momentum 23, 114
monoplane 28, 29
Mosquito 34
nautical mile 18, 80
net area 62
neutral point 122, 124, 125, 133, 150
newton 21, 23 - 25, 41, 109
non-dimensionalising 55
Panavia Tornado 34, 137
pascal 21, 25, 41, 43, 56, 102
perceived noise deciBel 102
periodic time 126, 127, 131
Phantom 36, 37
phugoid 127
Piper Warrior 122
pitch 14, 15, 23, 30, 32, 35, 54, 60, 91 - 93, 107, 112, 120, 121, 123 - 127, 138, 140, 141
Pitot-static tube 52, 54, 55, 66
potential energy 23, 24, 127
poundal 21
power 24, 35, 36, 43, 46, 51 - 53, 64, 80, 84, 88 - 95, 97 - 103, 105, 107, 110 - 113, 115, 124
pressure 21, 22, 25, 31, 33, 39 - 48, 50 - 59, 61, 62, 65, 66, 71 - 73, 77 - 79, 95, 96, 101, 134, 135, 137 - 140, 142, 144
pressure altitude 44, 45, 48
pressure coefficients 55
pressure drag 59, 71, 73, 75, 77, 78
profile drag 78, 85, 88, 89, 138, 150
propeller efficiency 92, 97, 105
q-feel 52

QFE 44, 46, 48
QNH 44 - 46, 48
quarter-chord point 61
radian 18, 82, 131
rate of climb 98, 99, 105, 113
rate one turn 109, 116
Rockwell B-1 34
roll 14, 15, 19, 29, 37, 113, 128, 130, 131, 141
roll subsidence 128
rolling moment 11, 128, 130, 141
rotor 11
rudder 12, 15, 31, 34, 107 - 111, 113, 115, 131, 140
rudder authority 12
SAAB 340 65
separated flow 51
shearing stresses 74
shock stall 140
shock wave 137 - 139, 141, 142, 144
short period pitching oscillation 127
sideflow 30
sideslip 14, 109, 113, 128 - 130
skin drag 71, 73 - 76, 78, 86, 87
slats 64, 65, 69
slots 64
slug 21, 73
sound waves 134
Space Shuttle 142, 143, 144
specific fuel consumption 93
speed of sound 32, 33, 38, 59, 134 - 136, 139, 142, 145
speed stability 124
Spillman sails 83, 84
spin 30, 72, 78, 113 - 115, 129
spinning 113 - 115, 117
spiral mode 128, 129
Spitfire 28
stagnation temperature 142
stall 60, 62, 64 - 66, 69, 70, 89, 98, 107, 108, 110, 112, 113, 117, 120, 123, 129, 139, 140
stall recovery 113
standard mean chord 122
static margin 124, 125
static pressure 51, 52, 55, 57, 96, 138
static stability 118, 120, 124
stick force per g 109, 125
stick travel per g 125
streamline 49, 51, 53, 54, 58, 72, 73, 78, 129, 134
streamline curvature 58
streamline flow 58, 134
subsonic 32, 38, 136, 137, 138, 140, 142
supersonic 136 - 139, 143
superstall 30
swept wing 32, 33
swept wings 32, 33
Système International d'Unités 16
tail arm 23, 120, 121
tailless aircraft 31, 32
tailplane 10, 12, 13, 15, 23, 28, 30, 31, 33, 53, 75, 85, 107, 109, 112, 115, 119, 120, 121, 124 - 127, 140
temperature 39, 40, 42, 43, 45, 46, 48, 57, 135, 142, 145
thermals 10, 39
thickness/chord ratio 33, 36, 60, 61, 70, 76, 87, 137
thrust 11, 12, 16, 17, 21, 27, 45, 60, 68, 71, 83, 91 - 93, 95, 99, 101, 103, 106, 107, 111, 112, 120
thrust to weight ratio 111
time to double amplitude 126
Tomahawk 36, 122
ton 17, 27, 148
tonne 17, 27, 50
torque 22 - 24, 87
total drag 59, 78, 85, 88, 89, 105, 124
total pressure 51, 52, 58, 138, 139
transonic 136, 138, 139, 140
Trident 35
trim wheel 107
Tristar 35
turbulence 74, 116
undercarriage 11, 36, 53, 65, 73
V-n Diagram 115 - 117, 132
Vampires 32
variable pitch propeller 93
VC10 36
ventral strakes 115
vertical axis 13 - 15, 62, 103, 107, 109, 113, 114, 119
vertical stabiliser 10, 12
Victor 34
viscosity 71, 75, 86, 137
volumetric flow rate 49, 57
vortex 29, 33, 79, 80, 81, 84
Vulcan 34
wake 74, 112, 115, 140
washout 83
wave drag 138
wave riding 142
weathercock stability 119
Whitcomb 140
wing loading 28, 132
wing section 58, 61, 62, 79, 112, 120, 137, 139, 141
wings 10 - 12, 28, 30, 32 - 38, 50, 53, 55, 57, 60, 62, 63, 65, 69, 74, 76, 85, 107, 112, 113, 115 - 117, 119, 128, 129, 135 - 137, 145
wingtip vortices 30, 80, 81
work 23 - 25, 41, 42, 45, 51, 89, 98, 115, 122
Wright brothers 28, 65
X29 29, 33
yaw 14, 15, 31, 32, 34, 35, 37, 54, 107, 109, 110, 113, 115, 118, 119, 128 - 130, 140
zone of action 134
zone of silence 135